"It's all right. I'm not going to let anyone hurt you," he murmured.

He wore a black T-shirt, heated by the filtered sun and by the skin beneath it. He smelled of the woods, fresh laundry soap and some deeply masculine aftershave. For a time she was oddly content to ride the comforting rise and fall of his breaths. He held her carefully, as if he feared she might break, or as if he was afraid too tight an embrace would serve to frighten her more. And for the first time in longer than she could remember, she felt safe and protected.

Here was a man she wouldn't have thought had any soft edges, soothing her hair and quieting her hitching sobs.

Her hands opened, spreading wide and not coming close to encompassing the breadth of his shoulder. Soft edges? _____ He might well have been hewn of warm _____ pull of cotton.

Her thumbs shifted, tra _____ and in one breath, her s _____ something suspiciously like a sign....

Dear Reader,

Love is in the air, but the days will certainly be sweeter if you snuggle up with this month's Silhouette Intimate Moments offerings (and a heart-shaped box of decadent chocolates) and let yourself go on the ride of your life! First up, veteran Carla Cassidy dazzles us with *Protecting the Princess*, part of her new miniseries WILD WEST BODYGUARDS. Here, a rugged cowboy rescues a princess and whisks her off to his ranch. What a way to go…!

RITA® Award-winning author Catherine Mann sets our imaginations on fire when she throws together two unlikely lovers in *Explosive Alliance*, the latest book in her popular WINGMEN WARRIORS miniseries. In *Stolen Memory*, the fourth book in her TROUBLE IN EDEN miniseries, stellar storyteller Virginia Kantra tells the tale of a beautiful police officer who sets out to uncover the cause of a powerful man's amnesia. But this supersleuth never expects to fall in love! The second book in her LAST CHANCE HEROES miniseries, *Truly, Madly, Dangerously* by Linda Winstead Jones, plunges us into the lives of a feisty P.I. and protective deputy sheriff who find romance while solving a grisly murder.

Lorna Michaels will touch readers with *Stranger in Her Arms*, in which a caring heroine tends to a rain-battered stranger who shows up on her doorstep. And *Warrior Without a Cause* by Nancy Gideon features a special agent who takes charge when a stalking victim needs his help…and his love.

You won't want to miss this array of roller-coaster reads from Intimate Moments—the line that delivers a charge and a satisfying finish you're sure to savor.

Happy Valentine's Day!

Patience Smith
Associate Senior Editor

Please address questions and book requests to:
Silhouette Reader Service
U.S.: 3010 Walden Ave., P.O. Box 1325, Buffalo, NY 14269
Canadian: P.O. Box 609, Fort Erie, Ont. L2A 5X3

Warrior
Without a Cause
NANCY GIDEON

Silhouette®

INTIMATE MOMENTS™

Published by Silhouette Books

America's Publisher of Contemporary Romance

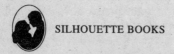 **SILHOUETTE BOOKS**

ISBN 0-373-27420-3

WARRIOR WITHOUT A CAUSE

Copyright © 2005 by Nancy Gideon

This edition published by arrangement with Harlequin Books S.A.

® and TM are trademarks of Harlequin Books S.A., used under license.
Trademarks indicated with ® are registered in the United States Patent
and Trademark Office, the Canadian Trade Marks Office and in other
countries.

Visit Silhouette Books at www.eHarlequin.com

Printed in U.S.A.

Books by Nancy Gideon

Silhouette Intimate Moments

For Mercy's Sake #648
Let Me Call You Sweetheart #851
Warrior Without a Cause #1350

NANCY GIDEON

attributes her output of over twenty-six novels to a back-ground in journalism and to the discipline of writing with two grade school-aged boys in the house. She begins her day at 5:00 a.m., when the rest of the family is still sleeping. While the writing pace is often hectic, this Southwestern Michigan author enjoys working on diverse projects. She's vice president of her local Romance Writers of America chapter and a member of a number of other groups. And somehow she always finds the time to stay active in her son's Cub Scout pack. Fans may know her under the pseudonyms Dana Ransom and Lauren Giddings.

Prologue

Glass.

Shards glittered like scattered gems upon the hardwood floor as dim light from the hallway shifted across them. Closing her apartment door behind her, a puzzled Tessa D'Angelo reached for the wall switch. When the impotent click yielded no welcome home glow, she put it together. Exasperation made a bleak addition to her already heavy mood.

"Tinker, doggone it. I'm going to line a pair of gloves with you."

Taking a cautious step into the darkness, she heard crunching beneath the low heels of her sedate black pumps. She bent to assess the damage, half hoping for the best but discovering the worst. The heirloom lamp meant to light the way into her apartment with its warm rainbow glow lay on its side, the Tiffany shade in pieces atop the littering of her mail.

Sighing wearily, she pictured the scenario: Tinker, her battle-scarred rescue cat, jumping up onto the table by the door as he heard her come down the hall, eager to greet her as he did each evening. She could envision the hefty feline losing his declawed footing on the forgotten bills Tessa had stacked there awaiting a trip to the mailbox. Tinker's scrambling leap had sent the lamp crashing to the floor. What a fitting end to her melancholy day. She closed her eyes against the sudden swell of anguish. A dark apartment with only a stray cat to miss her. Her treasured link to family in pieces just like her well planned future.

Tears that had crowded for release all afternoon burned against the backs of her eyes. For a moment she let her shoulders hunch beneath the weight of her grief as a tremor shook them. It wasn't about the lamp or the dreams now denied her. She'd just buried her father and she'd never heard him say he loved her.

A deafening silence filled her apartment. The same stillness had followed the thud of that first clod of dirt atop her father's coffin.

In that void of sound, in the part of her mind not shut down by loss, she acknowledged the stir of seemingly trivial questions. Why hadn't she heard the lamp fall as she approached her door? Why wasn't a recalcitrant Tinker here to weave through her legs in a purring demand for attention and supper.

Odd…

From the back rooms of her apartment, she heard a soft scuffling. Probably Tinker scooting under the bed in hopes of escaping her wrath. Tessa dragged in a cleansing breath. Life goes on. So she'd been told by the faceless mourners who'd squeezed her hand in sympathy even as they feasted on the tease of scandal surrounding the day's solemn circumstances. Hypocrites in friends' clothing. But they were right. Time to carry on with what still needed to be done. And the first thing was to clean up the mess on her floor. She righted the lamp and reached to check the bulb. It was gone.

Not broken. Gone.

She frowned over the puzzle, then understanding clicked on like that proverbial missing light bulb.

Someone had removed it.

Out of the corner of her eye, Tessa caught a flash of movement, too large to be the approach of her forgiveness-seeking cat. She raised her head, noting the sight of creased trousers before her world exploded in pain.

She hit the floor hard, registering only darkness and a paralyzing swell of panic. The tinny taste of blood filled her mouth as she cried out, hoping to touch some chord of mercy in her unseen assailant.

"Take whatever you want. Just don't hurt me."

Fingers fisted cruelly in her hair, twisting to wring a whimper from her.

And then she heard that voice.

"You should have thought of that before you started poking around where you don't belong. You won't like what you find. Stop now or your pretty momma will be crying over you, too."

He cracked her head against the hardwood to punctuate his point. Blackness welled but didn't take her completely under. Not then.

Not until much later.

Chapter 1

"I hear you're the man to see if you want someone killed."

That's how she introduced herself on the phone. It took him by surprise and not much did anymore. He didn't like surprises.

Ordinarily, Jack would have ended the conversation right then with a dial tone, but there was something in her voice. A soft tug of reluctant vulnerability beneath the tough fabric of her words. It made him pause when he should have relied on self-preserving instinct. A dangerous error in judgment.

But there was something about her voice.

Instead of severing the connection, he leaned back in his age-worn leather chair and shifted his feet to his cleared desktop. Maybe it was an unexpected empty calendar that had him willing to waste a few minutes baiting his uninvited caller. He only visited this shabby little office in the city about once a month to collect bills and to check the answering machine. He kept it for a mailing address and the air of permanence as a business entity. After the first thirty minutes surrounded by traffic and chaotic noise, he was always ready to head back to the proverbial hills. That she'd managed to catch him during that slim window of opportunity was reason enough to give her a few more minutes of his time. His curiosity peaked. He wanted to know how she'd found him and why she'd begun with that eye-popping statement.

"I'm flattered," he drawled, reaching out of habit to switch on the small recorder that would preserve their dialogue. "And just where did you hear that?"

"I know a lot of people in your business, Mr. Chaney."

Evasion wasn't the best way to get on his good side. His tone sharpened. "And what business is that? The killing business? If that's true, why do you need me?"

"The law and order business, Mr. Chaney." Her words picked up an interesting bite, too. Interesting enough for him to smile as he began to doodle lightning bolts and rain clouds on the blank calendar page.

"Ah, correct me if I'm wrong but law and order isn't about killing and it isn't what I do."

"That's why I need you. This isn't about law. It's about justice and your special talents. Can you help me?"

"I don't know you, Miss—"

There was silence, then she supplied, "D'Angelo." Why was that so familiar to him? Another warning he decided to ignore for the moment.

"Like I said, I don't know you, Miss D'Angelo, and I don't do business with people I don't know."

"I can pay you." How suddenly desperate she sounded as that persuasion rushed out. "The money doesn't matter."

"It doesn't matter to me, either."

"What does, Mr. Chaney? What will make you agree to meet with me? If you'd just listen to what I have to say—"

"Lady," he interrupted smoothly, "everybody's got a story to tell. I'm not a priest or a four-year-old, so why should I want to listen to your story?"

She cursed in a low aside, passionately, using words that made his brows arch and his lips purse. She continued with a rough rumble of anger that he found…well, he found it sexy as hell.

"I was told you were a professional, a man who could get things done. I see I was misled, Mr. Chaney. I'm sorry for wasting your time and mine when it's clear you're not interested."

"Did I say that?"

His quiet interjection had her hauling in her temper. He could hear it in the sudden silence and the quick pace of her breathing that followed. Finally she asked for clarification in a husky whisper.

"What are you saying? That you'll help me?"

He closed his eyes. The ripple of raw silk being drawn over the head of a bed partner in the night incited the same kind of urgent response as the whiskey-edged melody of her voice. Like soft blues music and slow, wet kisses. Exciting enough to make him linger in the exhaust-laced and crime-infested hell of Detroit. This was a woman he had to meet face-to-face.

"No promises. I'm not big on premature commitments." He wasn't big on commitments of any kind. Caution was his middle name. "We'll share a cup of coffee in some very public place and look each other over first."

"And then?"

"Then, if I like what I see, you can tell me your story. But first—" his tone toughened, getting back to the important point "—I have to know how you got my name and this number. I'm not listed in Killers-R-Us."

She hesitated, but only for a moment. "I got it from Stan Kovacs."

Of all the references she could have given, she picked the one he couldn't toss off with a shrug. And that made him all the more suspicious, and uncomfortable, as though some trap was about to be sprung now that he'd been suckered in with the right bait. But he wasn't sticking his neck out just yet.

"Ah, good old Stan. He still into fitness and jogging to work every day?"

Humor brushed like a warming breeze against the chill of her anxiety. "I don't know which Stan Kovacs you know, but this one would have a coronary going up the steps of a bus too fast."

Tension eased from his shoulders as that picture came to mind. Good old soft-on-the-outside, sharp-as-a-razor inside Stan. Jack chuckled softly. "Yeah, that's Stan. How do you know him?"

"He was a friend of my father's. And mine. He told me to mention his name if you got…difficult."

Yes, that's how Stan would describe him. She was obviously in the old P.I.'s small inner circle of friends. But she hadn't played that trump card right off the bat to smooth her way into his good graces. She'd held it back until he'd given her no choice but to lay it down. Perhaps Ms. D'Angelo preferred difficult to trading on favors.

And damned if he didn't like that about her.

On the blank desktop calendar, Jack wrote, "Call Stan/D'Angelo." To his husky-voiced wannabe client, he added, "All right, Miss D'Angelo, do you know where Cuppa Jo's is on Woodward?"

"I'll find it." The steely determination was back, fortified by his momentary lapse in sanity. He hoped his libido wasn't leading him into more trouble than he wanted but he seemed to have forgotten his middle name. Oh, yeah. Caution.

"Seven o'clock." That would give him time to do the necessary background checks so he wouldn't feel so off balance.

"How will I know you?"

He smiled into the receiver. "Well, it won't be by the violin case and red carnation. I'll find you."

By seven o'clock, he'd know everything there was to know about Miss Smoky Voice D'Angelo.

And then he'd listen to her story.

* * *

Cuppa Jo's was one of those dingy inner-city dives that served a questionable round-the-clock clientele. Jack liked it because the coffee was always hot and because he could collapse into one of the mended vinyl booths at 4:00 a.m. and not have to explain anything to anybody. Not even about the occasional contusions on his face. At Jo's, everyone kept their troubles to themselves. And Tessa D'Angelo could mean the capital-T kind.

He'd read her file. Smart mind, good family, loyal to the bone when it came to her up-and-coming D.A.-turned-hopeful politician father. The glossy photos he'd flipped through showed her at her father's right hand, smiling, poised, beautiful, an asset in any public circle, while her equally gracious and gorgeous mother stood at his left. She'd given up the promise of her own law career to support her father in his. She was supposed to have seen him on to bigger and better things. Not see his reputation go down in a blaze of rumors not even the grave could extinguish.

She sat in the rear of the hazy diner, her back to the wall leading to the rest rooms he wouldn't use on a dare. The fact that she was out of place was as glaringly apparent as the cost of her tailored business suit. Classy clothes, classy lady. The dusky-colored plum wool suit, creamy silk blouse opened in a modest vee, tasteful pearls and gravity-defying heels belonged in the business district not in the back booth of a greasy spoon. Even though the sun had all but disappeared, she still wore trendy wraparound dark glasses. But if it hadn't been for a pair of the most luscious lips this side of an adolescent boy's dreams, Jack wouldn't have recognized her from the society page photos he'd studied. This woman had none of the healthy sorority girl sparkle and confidence that had beamed out at him from the newspaper file he'd sneaked a peek at. This dangerously fragile Tessa D'Angelo looked as though she'd gone several brutal rounds with the reigning middleweight champ and lost. Badly.

The Veronica Lake spill of her sleek blond hair couldn't quite cover the stitching that ran from delicately arched eyebrow to temple. The shades couldn't conceal the telltale bruising of two spectacular shiners. Slender fingers clasped the chipped coffee mug before her in a two-fisted death grip that betrayed a near-the-edge tremor. Her shoulders hunched protectively. At first glance, she looked like a poster child for domestic battering, but Jack knew better. He'd seen her police file, too.

A robbery, they'd called it.

Unsolved.

An unfortunate coincidence in light of her recent tragedies.

"Miss D'Angelo?"

Her head jerked up and he was sure her eyes behind the opaque lenses had that deer-in-the-headlights glaze of alarm. He fought against the want to soften his tone with an apology for startling her. But she was expecting a kick-butt assassin not a Boy Scout, and he didn't want to disappoint her illusions. At least, not yet.

"I'm Jack Chaney."

She was motionless for a long moment. Not with fright, as he at first assumed, but to look him over as thoroughly as he'd done her. He fought against the impulse to stand just a little bit straighter and finger-comb the wind damage to his usually immaculate hair. He didn't care if his chin was a bit burly, if his clothing was rumpled or if the truck outside sported more rust than attitude. If he surrendered to the gods of arrogance, it was in that one small spot of vanity. He had great hair and preferred none of it out of place. But then he wasn't here to be interviewed. Tessa D'Angelo was the one on the hot seat. She nodded toward the opposite bench. "You're late." It wasn't an accusation but rather a relieved observation, as if she'd feared he wouldn't show.

"Traffic," was his casual excuse. He couldn't very well tell her that it had taken some time and some big promises to get a look into the official records, not until he'd at least had a cup of coffee for his trouble. "You need a refill there?" He gestured toward the half-full cup. She took a sip from it and grimaced.

"I guess I do. This is cold."

He held up a hand and a curvy brunette with a scarred name tag proclaiming "JoBeth" bumped an ample hip against his shoulder. That she was the "Jo" in "Cuppa Jo's," a grandmother who spent all of her free time clucking over the much younger kitchen and wait staff and would do the same to him if he'd allowed it, didn't keep her from the expected flirtation. Though she glanced at his stylish companion, she was careful to keep any hint of questions out of her gaze.

"Hiya, Chaney. Long time. The usual? High octane chased with a Sweet'n Low?"

"Sounds good. And a warm-up for the lady."

"Got peach pie hot out of the oven. Marcy'll take it as an insult if you don't let her trot a piece out to you."

Jack grinned. "I'll pass for now but have her save a slice for the road."

"Gotcha, doll."

After she sashayed back to the counter, Jack faced his would-be client and got right to business.

"I'm sorry about your father."

Tessa D'Angelo inhaled a sudden breath as if his condolences struck like another unfair punch. She let it out slow and shaky, then, in her throaty rumble, said, "Thank you."

"I didn't know him but he had a reputation for being a straight-up kinda guy."

"And look where that reputation got him."

Her flat summation puzzled him until she reached up with an elegant sweep of her hand to remove the dark glasses. The baby blues they revealed were anything but sweet. They were bright with angry, unshed tears.

"My father was a good man, Mr. Chaney. He was honest

and decent and stood for justice all the way. Where was the justice in what happened to him?"

Casually he brought out the bulky tabloid he'd purchased on his way to the meeting. He laid it on the Formica-topped table where it covered the cup rings with words much more staining. She glanced at the glaring headlines and what little color her chiseled cheekbones retained all but drained away. She swayed slightly then gripped the edge of the table to regain her balance. Her delicate jaw worked a moment before she asked quietly, "If you believe that, why are you here?"

"I needed a cup of coffee. And I owe Stan. He asked me to take you seriously. This is pretty damned serious." His finger tapped the tabloid's banner: D.A.'s Suicide Tied To Drug Scandal.

"It's a lie."

"Most of the stuff you find in here is. But this sterling publication isn't the only one saying it."

"I don't care who is saying what. My father isn't guilty of anything. He wasn't making money off drug trafficking or by looking the other way. I'd think his death would be proof of that."

That was what Tessa had been trying to convince the police, according to her numerous calls, complaints and eventual condemnations.

Playing a calm devil's advocate, Jack murmured, "Or unfortunate proof that he got in over his head and couldn't face the consequences."

She was off her seat so fast he barely had time to catch her wrist before she bolted. Such fine, easily broken bones. He restrained her carefully but refused to go easy on her. After all, even though she was the one who'd placed the call, they were on his dime now.

"Sit down, Miss D'Angelo. Those opinions can't be news to you. They've been in every headline for weeks now. If you had thicker skin, you wouldn't bruise so easily." He felt a shiver go through her in reaction to her pain and rage.

"Hardly an amusing observation, considering," came her wry retort.

"Sit," he said again, and this time she did.

"It's not my place to make judgments, Miss D'Angelo. That's not what I do. I wasn't aware that my opinions were why you sought me out. So I guess it's time to ask, just why have you called me?"

"Justice, Mr. Chaney. For my father and me."

"Vigilante style?"

"Would it matter to you?"

Her sharp tone was a quick barb to a conscience he wasn't sure up until that very moment could be reached by mere words. His features stiffened.

"Obviously you think it shouldn't." She thought she was looking at a gun-for-hire, a quick, violent solution to her problems. What had Stan told her to give her that erroneous impression? Why come to him when the streets of the inner city were most likely teeming with guys who would kill for a quarter? That wasn't what he did and it was about time she found that out. "What do you want from me, Miss D'Angelo? You want to put a contract out on whomever you think is responsible for putting your father in the ground? You want me to pull the trigger, is that it?"

She never so much as twitched. "I plan to pull my own trigger, Mr. Chaney. That's not why I need you."

He blinked.

"I need you to teach me how to stay alive long enough to pull it."

She was blowing it.

Tessa could tell by the sudden blanking of his dark eyes. Gorgeous dark eyes that she bet could beg for forgiveness while making a woman forget what he had done wrong. Eyes that saw right through her tough outer shell to the marshmallow filling. It didn't help that with his smoldering George-

Clooney-like sex appeal, he looked more like a romantic leading man than the Rambo she'd been expecting. She had maybe a minute to plead her case or he was going to be gone. And with him, her last chance at finding out the truth.

"Stan said you could help me."

It was an emotional ploy but she could tell it was effective by the way his sensuously shaped mouth thinned into a disagreeable line.

"Stan told you I could make you into a killer?"

Now, she was surprised. "N-no. No, of course not."

Chaney relaxed ever so slightly. "Then I'm to assume we are speaking of a symbolic trigger."

"Yes. Oh, you thought—that I— No." Indignation stained her cheeks in hot points. "Mr. Chaney, my father gave his life to defend a system I will not abuse, even if it failed him. This isn't about vigilante justice, it's about truth. A truth someone doesn't want me to find."

"Isn't that what the police are for, Miss D'Angelo?"

It was hard to hang on to her patience. Just what did he think she'd *been* doing since the official report and its damning summation had been released to the press? But no one wanted to listen to a distraught daughter anxious to save her father's reputation with unsubstantiated tales right out of high-tech spy fiction.

"They don't want to look beyond the truth they think they've already found. Someone framed my father and now he can't defend himself against their lies. But I can and I will. But I can't do it…the way things stand now."

The coffee arrived and gave the tension between them time to ease to a manageable level. Tessa sipped her coffee, not caring that it burned her tongue and brought a swimming dampness to her eyes. She wasn't a stranger to pain or tears these days, but she wouldn't give in to either. Not any longer.

"Okay, I've heard your story. Now tell me how I fit into the next few chapters."

She took a shallow breath and made herself meet his steady stare. She couldn't let his sullen silent-screen-star looks distract her from what he was. He was a killer. A man who trained assassins for the government. A man so dangerous and beyond the laws she revered that she felt soiled just speaking to him. He had no respect for her cause or for honor; men like him never did. They had their own agendas, outside the rules that governed her world. But he was just the kind of man she needed to see those rules bent to her advantage.

"I've been threatened."

Her simple statement had the impact of a ten-pound sledge. The evasive glassy look was gone from his keen gaze, replaced by a sharp understanding. "Is that verbal or physical?" He was studying her battered features, betraying no reaction to the sight. She forced herself not to cover the ugly reminders. Better he look and judge for himself.

"Both." She didn't care to go into more details with a stranger. He didn't need to know that she lay awake at night listening for a telltale footstep, that if she was lucky enough to fall into a restless sleep, she always woke from it screaming and drenched in a sweat of dread. But he did need to know that the stakes were, as he'd said, serious.

"Just phone calls, lately. And I've been followed. Someone's been in my apartment. More than once. The second time I walked in on them. A robbery gone bad, the police called it." Her chin trembled slightly until she clenched her teeth. She could hear the voice whispering in the back of her mind and shook her head slightly to chase it away. Easy to do here in the light with noise and the companionable smells of coffee, grease and cigarette smoke to surround her. She fought to keep her own tone level.

"So far, it's just a game of intimidation but I don't like games with no rules, Mr. Chaney. I play to win. I always have. And to have any chance at all in this game, I have to be able to compete on their level."

He made no comment on that, no judgment. "Do you have a gun?"

"No."

"Get one."

"I will. But when I do, I need to know that no one is going to take it away from me. I've been a victim once and I didn't like it much. Next time they come for me, I want to be prepared. They hurt me and they scared me. And they killed my father. But they don't know me. I'm not going to run and hide, Mr. Chaney. And I'm not going to give up. That's why Stan sent me to you. I'm a sitting duck and I don't want to be. Teach me how to protect myself so that I can see justice done for my father and see those who killed him brought to trial."

Teach me how not to be afraid.

She didn't have to say that. She knew he saw it in her face, in the shaky hands that nested the bottom of her coffee cup seeking the warmth she lacked inside. But would he do something about it?

Would he make it his fight?

"You're wasting your time, Miss D'Angelo."

His crisply spoken summation struck the wind from her lungs, the hope from her heart. For a moment she couldn't respond, so he continued with that same detached calm.

"Go to the police. This is their job, not mine. I won't give you any false confidence so you can go out and get yourself killed. I train professionals who are already without fear to do a job they have no illusions about coming home from. I don't do Girl Scout camp. I'm sorry if Stan misled you."

He didn't look sorry.

He placed his hands on the table and started to rise. With nothing left to lose, she pulled out all stops.

"I don't suppose it would do any good to speak to your innate sense of decency. Men like you can't afford any, can they?"

A thin smile warped his lips. "No, ma'am. We're not do-gooders like your father. We're not flag wavers who think justice will always triumph. We know better. That's why people like you always come to people like me. I have no illusions left."

"I feel sorry for you, Mr. Chaney. How sad not to believe in anything worthwhile."

"I believe Detroit will have another crappy year despite a new billion-dollar home field. I believe the new fall season on television will end up in early midyear replacements. I believe a man can spit in the wind and have a better chance of not getting wet than you'll have in proving your father is innocent of the nasty things this paper says about him."

"I believe you're a coward, Mr. Chaney."

"Then you would be right, Miss D'Angelo, if being a coward means never taking on a fight you know you can't win."

He gathered up his heavy coat and laid two wadded bills on the tabletop. He no longer bothered with eye contact. He obviously didn't want to see her disgust.

"With or without you, I'm not giving up."

"Good luck, Miss D'Angelo."

And he was gone, just like that.

Tessa sat for a moment, struggling to take a decent breath. Now what was she going to do? All her bold statements blew apart like smoke in a sudden breeze when she thought of the darkened corners of her parking garage and the 2:00 a.m. ringing of the phone. There would be shadows and threatening silences. And she would experience, all over again, the crippling panic of being helpless.

To hell with Jack Chaney. He was about as useful as the Metro police. Both wanted to take the easy way out in spite of the very real danger she was in. So be it. Tomorrow she would buy a gun. And she would keep right on digging for the truth until someone stopped her with something more than whispers over the phone and footsteps in the dark.

With something more than a beating disguised to be a robbery.

It was cold outside. October bit with the force of January but she'd been cold even before she'd left the diner to traverse the near empty streets. When she'd arrived, the only space available had been three blocks away. Now, with the curbs abandoned and the sidewalks a wasteland of tumbling wind-tossed litter, it seemed like three miles.

Gripping her keys, she started down the walk, hurrying between the weak pools of light spilling out from liquor stores and places of dubious entertainment value. She didn't look around but stayed focused on her goal: a lone silver Lexus promising warmth and protection with the turn of a key and click of a latch.

Footsteps.

Her own quickened in pace with her heart. She fought the fatalistic desire to turn around, to confront the skulking threat head-on. What kind of weapon was a car key gripped in a sweaty palm against the fear that banged within her breast?

The footsteps grew bolder, closer, more determined in their cadence. The urge to run the length of that last block twisted within Tessa's belly and trembled down her legs. If she ran, there was a chance she would be pursued. Could she outrun whatever followed? Her breathing shivered noisily as she bunched her calves and cursed the heels she'd worn to impress Jack Chaney. Three inches of fashionable thinness. She might as well be on stilts.

Anxiety knotting through her, she held her coat together and readied to bolt for safety.

And just then, safety in the person of Jack Chaney separated itself from the shadow of her car ahead. A true professional, he'd checked her background to learn what she drove. He'd been leaning there, waiting for her. She didn't have to listen to know there were no longer footsteps behind her. Intimidation was a solitary business, not one meant for an audience.

"This is a dangerous neighborhood for a lady alone at night."

She smiled crookedly at his generic observation. "You have no idea." She came to a stop in front of him and was momentarily surprised. She thought he'd be taller. He'd seemed like a veritable giant seconds ago. Nervously she risked a look over her shoulder.

"He's gone."

Her gaze jumped back to him. "Who?"

"We didn't exchange names. I noticed him outside Jo's and wondered who he was waiting for while trying so hard not to be seen. Shall I try to catch up to him?"

"No." Her hand flashed out to fasten upon his coat sleeve just in case he might be serious about leaving her alone on the barren sidewalk. "It doesn't matter who he was. I know what he was."

Jack took the keys from her cold, cramped fingers and unlatched her door. He opened it for her and stepped aside as she slid in behind the wheel.

"Would you like me to follow you home?"

Yes!

She bit back that frantic cry and forced a competent smile. "I don't think I'll have any more problems tonight." At least not until she closed her eyes. But what could she do? Ask him to sleep at the foot of her bed like a faithful watchdog? He'd already said in so many words that her problems were her own. "Thank you, Mr. Chaney, but I've taken up enough of your time."

He didn't shut the door on their conversation. He draped his forearms over it and gave her a long, assessing look before asking, "And how much of your time are you willing to spend to see this thing through?"

"I beg your pardon?"

"A day, a week, until the thrill rubs off and the work gets too hard?"

"I don't understand."

"I don't think you have what it takes to take what I dish out."

She stared up at him, hope crowding into her throat. She forced a steady stare so he wouldn't know how close she was to believing what he said. Her words were heroic even though she quivered in frail doubt inside.

"I can take it."

"Really? Day in, day out, until I think you're ready? Not until you think you are? Do you have that kind of commitment, Miss D'Angelo? I run a boot camp, not a Club Med. What I do isn't a trendy gym class in pseudo-self-defense for bored housewives. I'll work you until you drop and push you until you beg for mercy."

"I won't beg, Mr. Chaney."

Begging hadn't helped her before.

Her fierce statement gave him pause. "Maybe, maybe not. But I guarantee it'll be on your mind every minute. You'll either cry uncle or I'll shape you into something that will make them think twice before sneaking up on you in the night."

"I want them to think twice, Mr. Chaney."

"Then you think twice, right now, while you can. If you come with me, I'll show you no mercy."

"I'm in your hands, Mr. Chaney."

His features tightened into a sudden impenetrable mask. "I don't want you in my hands. I've got enough on my hands to last a lifetime. I'll train you to survive, but no more than that. Don't expect me to get involved in your cause."

Tessa's elation took a grounding nosedive. Jack Chaney was no hero come to rescue her. He was a tool for her to use in her own rescue.

"Don't worry, Mr. Chaney, I know exactly what I can expect from you."

He nodded once. "Good. Pack a bag. I'll pick you up tomorrow at three. You're going to camp."

Chapter 2

Stan Kovacs looked worried.

As he watched Tessa pull the zippers up on her suitcase, his expression had all the forlorn characteristics of a droopy-faced basset hound.

"Stan, it was your idea," she reminded him as she set the case by the door of her apartment. She tried not to notice the significance of the chains and new dead bolt locks. "If you didn't trust him, why did you insist I call him?"

"Oh, I do trust him. With my ex-wife, my money, my life. But not necessarily with my best friend's daughter. Chaney can be…"

"Difficult," she supplied. "Yes, I know. But we're not dating, Stan. I don't care if he's difficult. Just as long as he's as good as you say he is."

Stan's features didn't alter at his mournful reply. "Oh, he is. No doubt about that."

She fussed with the tags on her luggage, trying to think of

how best to broach the subject. "I know in your business you've met all sorts of rather unsavory people."

"The dregs in the cup, so to speak," Stan agreed.

"How did you meet Jack Chaney?"

He smiled thinly. "Long story."

"The Cliff's Notes version. How did you get tight with a mercenary?"

That did manage to rearrange Kovacs's dour look. "What? Where did you get the idea that Chaney was a merc?"

"You."

"Oh." He glanced away sheepishly. "Guess I was trying to impress you or maybe scare you off from taking this particular path. Jack's a lot of things but he's not an indiscriminate killer."

"So he's the discriminating kind."

"He's the military kind. The Black Ops covert, no-record-of-his-name, disavow-all-knowledge-if-caught-or-killed kind. He's worked in a lot of places I'd never want to visit. His call sign was Lone Wolf. That'll tell you all you need to know about Jack Chaney."

"CIA?"

"I'm sure there are some initials involved but I don't want to know what they are. He's no angel but he's not the devil I obviously let you think he was, either. Sorry."

"For letting me think that or because he isn't?"

They shared smiles and a long silence. Realizing Stan had never exactly answered her question, which meant he had no intention of doing so, Tessa sighed.

"No matter his initials, I need him. And, Stan, I need you to keep on top of things while I'm gone. I can't let the trail to the real killers grow even colder."

"I plan to. I'm not giving up on your dad. He didn't give up on me when he had every reason to."

She touched his arm, eager to defuse his umbrage. "I never thought you would, Stan. Not for a second. I just want you to be extra, extra careful."

His face relaxed into a grin. "Yeah, like a fat, ex-alcoholic is going to put the fear of God into Martinez's men."

"I'm just a girl and I worried them plenty."

They both sobered. Stan nodded.

"I'll be quiet as a mouse. They won't even hear me scratching around."

She squeezed his beefy forearm through the truly ugly sport coat. "Good. Keep me posted. See if you can find out what Martinez had on Johnnie O' that was so bad he took jail time just to set up my father." That was the part of the case that had convinced the police to look hard at Robert D'Angelo. Johnnie O'Casey, three-time loser and small-time drug pusher, hadn't tried very hard to barter his way out of prison. He'd accepted the sentence and still named the district attorney as his accomplice. If saving his own worthless hide hadn't been the motive, something else had triggered his sudden desire to name names.

The wrong names.

But for what price and who had paid the bill?

"I'll look in on your mom, too."

"Oh. Thanks, Stan. I'm sure Dad would want you to." Her lack of enthusiasm implied that it wasn't her priority. Stan simply nodded. He never intruded on their family dynamics even though Tessa could tell by the pursing of his lips that he wanted to.

A knock at the door had Tessa taking a quick, involuntary breath as Stan reached for the knob. A silly reaction. Did she really expect one of Martinez's hired hit men to knock?

"Hey, Jack," Stan greeted jovially. "How's your dad?"

"Wondering when you're going to stop over for a little five-card." Jack Chaney stood in the hall looking dark and sleek and dangerous. Just the man she needed to see. Tessa released her breath in a relieved gust. She hadn't been sure he'd go through with it. *Take nothing for granted,* her father had always told her.

Stan laughed. "I haven't recovered from the last fleecing he gave me."

"It's your face, Stan. Your secrets are written all over it."

Pleasantries exchanged, Chaney looked down at Tessa's three-piece set of matched Gucci luggage without a blink. But he frowned at the sight of the cat carrier and the pair of glittering yellow eyes glaring out at him through the mesh door. Noting his disapproval, Tessa hoisted up the carrier, giving a defiant lift of one brow.

"Tinker goes with me. Love me, love my cat."

A dark brow arched. "An interesting but unlikely suggestion."

Wondering which part he found the most distasteful, Tessa stated, "I'm ready, Mr. Chaney." She picked up the medium-size suitcase. "Can you get the other two?"

"Yes, ma'am. Your chariot is out front. It's the Dodge Ram. Just toss your stuff in the back."

Frowning to think he meant Tinker, as well, she was distracted by Stan's quick hug and peck on her cheek.

"Behave," he warned in a whisper.

"I will if he will."

After Tessa started toward the stairwell, Stan confronted the younger man candidly.

"She's tougher than she looks."

"I hope so, for her sake."

"You behave, too."

Jack offered a lopsided smile. "Don't I always."

Stan rolled his eyes. Then the merriment was gone. "Watch over her, Jack. Keep her under wraps until I can find out if there's any truth to what she's saying."

Jack gave a snort. "Or to what she wants to believe."

"Somebody beat the hell out of her. I'm not willing to take any chances that it wasn't just a coincidence."

"You think her father is innocent, Stan?"

The P.I. frowned a minute then answered. "Right now, I don't care. Rob D'Angelo is beyond their reach, but she isn't. I don't want anything else to hurt her, Jack."

"What about the truth?"

"By the time I find it, she'll be ready to hear it. Like I said, she's tougher than she looks."

Jack shrugged noncommittally. "If you say so."

"What shall I tell anyone who asks about her?"

"Tell them she's going to camp."

"Saying your goodbyes to the old homestead?"

Tessa, who'd been staring up at the curtain-covered windows of her apartment, gave a start then a rueful smile. Saying goodbye to the sleepless nights, to the insidious terror that had her checking behind doors and under the bed in a manic cycle of fear? Good riddance was more like it. Whatever she was heading toward had to be better than that.

She suddenly realized that she didn't want to return to the rooms with the upscale address she'd so proudly decorated with trendy furnishings that toted her independence. She now saw the shadowed corners of the second-floor rooms as a prison when they'd once represented her freedom. She couldn't open the front door without seeing the glass glittering on the floor, without hearing the sinister whisper of her attacker's voice.

No, she would never put her belongings back in that place where she no longer belonged.

For now, she was making her home with Jack Chaney. And after that... Well, she'd just have to improvise.

"Let's go, Mr. Chaney."

"Before you change your mind?"

She met his smug assertion with a cool glance. "Or you change yours."

He opened the door for her to climb up into the four-wheel-drive vehicle, then scowled at the sight of the cat carrier on the floor of the passenger side.

"Not an animal lover, I take it."

"Sure. I love them with gravy and potatoes on the side."
He shut her inside the truck before she could manage a curt
reply.

Sticking her fingers through the wire grid, Tessa murmured, "Don't mind him, Tinker. He's just being…difficult."
A wet nose touched her fingertips in seeming agreement.

Chaney dropped behind the wheel and started the vehicle,
provoking the engine into a series of coughs and grumbles.
The smell of something scorching filled the cab.

"We could have taken my car," she posed diplomatically.

"Your car is easily traced to you. Just swallow your pride
and enjoy the ride." He shifted and the beater shuddered
away from the curb with a roar. "From now on, you're offi-
cially undercover."

And off the face of the known world, she mused, staring
out the window as familiar scenery whizzed by. She let it go
without regret.

"You never asked where we were headed," her driver observed as he checked the crooked rearview before blending
into freeway traffic.

"It doesn't matter," was her philosophical reply. Then,
after a pause, she asked, "Where are we headed?"

"No place you could ever find on your own, even if a map
existed. No man's land."

No woman's land, she'd be willing to bet as she studied
his profile. A nice profile. Clean, strong, good bones, firm
chin. Handsome in a dark, effortless way. Like a pirate.

He was the kind of guy who would have had girls lining
the street in front of his house when he was a teen. With his
easy confidence and dark, melting eyes, he could have been
anything from class president to class clown, star quarterback
to under-the-bleachers bad boy. But studying him more
closely, she figured him for the cool, sardonic loner who
could have had anything he wanted and shunned all of it.

She'd hated guys like that, the ones who never lived up to their potential. Had Jack Chaney grown up knowing he wanted to be a government hit man? Had he planned from an early age to skirt the fringe of acceptability with a wry, indifferent scorn?

She could see ex-military in him. In the way he carried himself, erect, alert, even when he seemed relaxed behind the wheel. She saw it in the crisp cut of his glossy black hair and squared-away look of his clothing. Efficient, without an extra inch or ounce on him. His dark eyes were always on the move, cutting between the mirrors in a precise circuit that allowed for no surprises.

And it disturbed her to find that he made her feel safe.

Suddenly uncomfortable with the turn of her thoughts, she tried distracting them with conversation.

"So how do you know Stan?"

"What did he tell you?"

"He did a lot of talking but never really answered my question."

Jack nodded his approval and for a minute Tessa didn't think he would answer. Then, with a casual shrug, he said, "He and my father were partners on the force a lot of years ago."

"The police force?" Why did the notion of Jack coming from a law enforcement family surprise her so? Because usually law and order was passed on as a tradition. Apparently not in his family.

"You said you owed him."

"I said too much," he muttered, but he didn't withhold the information. "About twenty years ago they got caught in a cross fire. My dad was hit. Bad. Stan could have left him and gotten to safety but he didn't. He stayed at my dad's side, keeping him from bleeding to death, keeping the scumbags off until reinforcements showed up. He rode with him to the hospital and later broke the news to us that Dad had been shot and would never walk again. Stan stayed with my dad through therapy and bankruptcy—with a whole lot more loyalty than my mom who figured the going wasn't going to get any better so she got going and never looked back. They don't come any better than Stan Kovacs in my book. That answer your question?"

And then some.

"Stan said your call sign was Lone Wolf. That sounds a little…"

"Unfriendly? Aboriginal?" he finished for her. His tone hadn't changed but a certain tightness sharpened the edges of his swarthy features until she could see the hint of American Indian in the sculpted highs and lows. "On my mother's side, way back. Just enough so I could run a casino if I wanted to. But that's not where I got the moniker. Lone Wolf isn't my Indian name, if that's what you're wondering."

"Where did you get it?"

"From my enemies, because I prefer to hunt alone. And I prefer my own company to those who never seem to run out of nosy questions that are none of their business."

Well, he didn't need to put a finer point on it than that.

The rest of their drive passed in a taut silence.

In the lull, it was easy for Tessa to drift into a sleep-deprived REM state. She'd only meant to close her eyes for a moment but when she blinked them open, it was to find that man-made structures had given way to soaring examples of nature's architecture. Spreading oaks ablaze with color, ramrod-straight pines standing at attention and ghostly poplars with their pale white trunks and flutter of graceful yellow leaves lined a two-lane highway upon which they were the only travelers. She'd fallen asleep in the inner city and had awakened to a deeply forested Oz.

Tessa leaned away from the window where her cheek had left a circular print and immediately checked for any trace of embarrassing drool. Chaney caught the movement and quirked a smile in her direction.

"You snore."

Great. Just the kind of intimate details she wanted known from the maddeningly enigmatic man beside her.

"Not usually."

"You should never let your guard down so completely, even around those you think you can trust."

His remark needled more than it instructed. Her reply was curt.

"I'll keep one eye open from now on."

"I always do." Then he added ominously, "I would if I were in your position."

All sense of security fell away at that cool observation. She wasn't safe. Not even here with this man she'd hired to protect her and to teach her to protect herself.

He was right. She trusted too easily, in unfamiliar situations, with unknown strangers. She'd grown up to privilege, private schools, safe streets and a good job. The closest she ever came to the seamier side of life was in the courtroom. She'd never had reason to check her back seat before getting in or to glance into shadowed alleyways anticipating a threat.

Until now.

Sitting stiff and duly chastised, she looked around, observing her surroundings. She was Little Red Riding Hood to his huntsman and there was no grandmother's house in sight.

"Are we—"

"There yet?" he finished for her. "Almost. It takes about fifteen minutes to the front door once we leave the highway."

Fifteen minutes to reach what? Exactly where was he taking her? Her lack of preparatory knowledge came back to haunt her. She'd been in such a hurry to leave her fears behind, she'd forgotten to ask what she'd be walking into. Or driving into. And since she'd seen fit to naively snooze the better part of the drive away, she had no idea where "there" might be. North, he'd said. There was a lot of North in Michigan.

When Chaney finally left the highway for the fifteen-minute last leg of the journey, it wasn't to pull onto a paved street. At first glance she hadn't even seen a break in the trees to indicate there was a road. Two-track, she believed best described the spine-jarring roller coaster of dust and sudden dips. Stray branches scraped against the sides of the vehicle as they bounced along the twin ruts cut deeply into uneven ground. It wasn't an obstacle course her Lexus would have appreciated.

Tessa clung to the door handle with one hand and braced her other palm against the dash as Tinker's carrier slid back and forth between her firmly planted feet. She locked her ankles tight on either side of the case hoping the suspiciously silent tabby hadn't already had the stuffings shaken out of him.

Then the Ram made a sudden turn and Chaney's compound appeared as if hewn out of the forest. Her mouth dropped open in helpless awe.

North woods had conjured up the image of rustic in her mind's eye. A log cabin, hopefully with indoor plumbing. But Jack Chaney's retreat was a veritable fortress in the wilderness. Squares and turrets of stone and log collided with huge ultramodern walls of glass and steel in what should have been a jarring juxtaposition. It wasn't. Pulled together under long sloping roofs of rough-hewn wood shingles, the massive structure seemed to blend with the rugged surroundings, easing the stark modernistic elements back to the basics of quarried rock and peeled timber. Only the high-tech satellite dish broke the harmony of new age and natural beauty. Tessa perked up. Not Club Med, perhaps, but certainly a far cry from the dour cabins she remembered from camp. Chaney's dwelling was huge, impressive, and as Jack wheeled the vehicle to the left, obviously not her destination.

They jounced down another dirt-and-gravel track until they reached a footbridge that spanned a winding stream. On the other side squatted a single-story barracks of log and stone. No soaring vistas, no dish TV. Just the raw basics of survival.

Welcome back, Camp Minnetonka.

Prepared to grin and bear it, Tessa climbed out of the truck and took a minute to twist and stretch her back. There was a brief stab of discomfort where a rib was still healing. She made the movements easier, babying the hurt. As she glanced to the right, through a parting of the trees, she could just make out one of the massive stone porches running along the side of the main house. She blinked and began to frown in uncertainty of what she was seeing.

There on the porch, just on the edge of the shadows, stood a small, slender girl of about twelve years old. In the muting tones of near twilight, all she could make out was the fact that the girl was Hispanic. As Tessa stared in surprise at finding a child in Jack Chaney's home, her astonishment doubled as a woman appeared to place her hands on the girl's shoulders to steer her back inside.

Just as it had never occurred to Tessa that Jack might live in a forest paradise, she'd never once considered that he might not live alone.

Chapter 3

Stark and utilitarian. Scout camp revisited.

Tessa tried to keep the dismay from her features as she surveyed her new home away from home.

There was a main room furnished with mission-style chairs around a slab-topped table. One wall held a projection screen, the opposite a large dry-erase board and cork wall studded with idle pushpins. Obviously a com center for covert planning. She could see Chaney heading up a briefing session while equally hard-eyed operatives sat attentively around the table. She couldn't see herself curled up comfortably with a novel and there was no television in sight. On the rear wall, a countertop housed a microwave, minifridge and small sink. So much for luxuries.

While watching her for any telltale misgivings, Jack gestured to the right and left. "Take any room. They're all the same. Connie will bring you some dinner. Until then, make yourself at home."

Her home was here. His home was there. With the woman and child.

"I will," she said with as much enthusiasm as she could muster. She said it to deaf ears because Jack Chaney was already gone. And she was alone.

Setting the carrier next to her luggage on the floor, Tessa sighed. "Just you and me, Tinker. Like always."

The big tabby came out of the carrier hissing and puffed up in an affronted bristle. After sniffing the air, he immediately began yowling. Tessa wasted no time setting up his litter box in the spartan bathroom. With his business tidily covered, Tinker plopped beneath the table to groom and calm his distressed nerves. Tessa picked up a bag and went to pick a room.

It really didn't matter which one she picked. All were equally unwelcoming. Half a dozen on one side of the war room and half a dozen on the other. For its convenience to the bathroom, she took the first door on the right.

Now she understood Chaney's amusement over her baggage.

The room contained a twin-size bed covered with a brown chenille spread. There was a drawerless night table hosting a homemade lamp with a glass base filled with beer bottle caps. A nice decorative touch. The only one. The small single window was covered by heavy brown curtains. There was one chair, as ugly and uninviting as the rest of the room, and a closet. The closet was a recessed hole in the wall featuring a clothes bar with a baker's dozen wire hangers and two plank shelves, one above and one a foot off the plain brown rug. She could envision steel-toed boots lined up neatly beneath a stack of olive drab chinos, a line of T-shirts on the hangers and who knows what on the top shelf. Certainly not her designer exercise wear and brand new Nikes.

She was in the wrong place. Chaney had tried to tell her. Stan had tried to tell her. Maybe she should have listened to one or both of them.

Too late now. Too late to do anything but make the best of it. And make herself at home.

She unpacked one bag. There didn't seem to be any point in emptying the others. She'd obviously have no use for the more civilized outfits she'd packed. She set her toiletries on the baseless sink in the bathroom and after checking for hot water and towels, returned to her cubicle.

Tinker had deposited himself on the foot of the bed to finish up the meticulous currying of his tail. He paused to eye her irritably then continued the task, not breaking the rhythm as she sat beside him on the bed. The mattress gave slightly, promising unexpected comfort. She lay back, only meaning to test the springs. Her exhausted body and soul had other ideas.

The soft sound of a door closing woke her to complete blackness. Two things about the north woods became abundantly clear. It was quiet and it was dark. Not the need-to-adjust-the-eyes-to-get-around kind of darkness that one had in the city but the pitch, unadulterated inkiness of nothing but stars and a sliver of a moon. No neons, no streetlights, no glancing headlights from passing cars, no glow from the telephone number pad or TV remote. Nothing. Nada. Darkness.

She crept from the room, her hand on the wall to guide her. And then the smell of something absolutely delectable provided a beacon into the main living area. After fumbling around, she located a light switch to illuminate the big, empty room. A casserole dish sat next to the microwave on the counter. Her stomach rumbled in encouragement. She and Tinker sat to a hearty beef and rice mixture washed down with several glasses of the milk she found in the minifridge.

Fed, rested, and with dishes rinsed, Tessa allowed herself to be drawn back to the puzzle of the main house. Shutting a disgruntled Tinker inside, Tessa slipped out onto the narrow front porch. Immediately taken by the chill and the isolation, she wrapped her arms around herself and looked toward the only light in the vast black backdrop surrounding her.

She'd never spent any quality time with nature. Her short jaunt at camp when she was nine had ended when a chicken pox epidemic sent all the girls scurrying home in their anxious parents' Mercedes after just one afternoon. What she knew of trees and other woodland fauna, she'd discovered at carefully arranged gardens under protective domes or in sculpted backyards for the occasional summer party. She'd had one plant, a dieffenbachia she'd been assured could endure any hardship or neglect. It had lasted a month under her care. Cut flowers in a vase was as close as she got to appreciating the great outdoors. And now she was wondering if she should have kept it that way.

Warmth and welcome, however, glowed behind the massive walls of glass and steel. But not a welcome for her. She wasn't sure why the idea of Jack Chaney having a family unsettled her so. Perhaps because she was uncomfortable with bringing possible danger to their door. Possibly because of the more basic things that had stirred her when she'd looked at her teacher and protector. Things one shouldn't admit to when the man had a family.

A wife and child threw all her conceptions about Chaney off balance. Lone Wolf. Stan had summed him up with that moniker and she'd liked the deadly and fiercely independent image it evoked. That was the image she'd bought into when she'd hired him: the skilled assassin, capable of slipping in anywhere to get the most unpleasant of jobs done. Just because he moved with government approval didn't change the basic makeup of the man. He was a killer. The kind of man her father made a career of putting away for as long as legally possible as a danger to society. The kind of man she now turned to to preserve all that her father had stood for. She smiled grimly at the irony, not sure straight-arrow Robert D'Angelo would have appreciated it.

A brief movement behind the backlit vista of glass caught her notice. A single figure stopped and stood in bold silhouette, staring—if the creepy sensation along the hairs on her arms was correct—right at her.

Jack.

He was watching her watching him. And he probably wasn't liking it.

Abruptly the shadow was gone and Tessa was alone once more. At least she felt alone. As alone and abandoned as she'd felt at her father's graveside. Without direction. Without purpose—except for one driving goal. To prove that everything her father embodied wasn't a lie.

"You shouldn't be outside. It makes you a target."

A squeak of surprise escaped her as Chaney's voice sounded practically at her elbow. After a few panicked blinks of her eyes, she could make out his shape in the darkness on the other side of the porch rail. She'd never heard his approach. It infused her with the debilitating sense of vulnerability again.

"I thought you said I'd be safe here."

"Safe implies a certain amount of common sense. You don't stand out in the open unless you want to draw attention to yourself."

Then what had he been doing up at the main house in front of the window? But of course he'd wanted her to see him then. Just as he hadn't wanted her to see him until his disembodied voice nearly scared the beef-and-rice casserole out of her. He was making a point.

Point taken. She wouldn't be safe anywhere until her father's murderer was caught. And the only one who could protect her was herself. Those were the skills Chaney was going to teach her.

"When do we get started tomorrow?"

"So early you'll still think it's today so I'd suggest you get some shut-eye. I guarantee, tomorrow night you'll hurt too bad to sleep."

She thought he was kidding.

He wasn't.

His voice came out of the darkness.

"If you have comfortable shoes, get them on."

Tessa dragged herself up out of the bed where it felt as though she'd only laid her head minutes ago. She'd left the door to her room ajar so Tinker could use his box and it was from the other side of the door that Chaney issued his orders.

"We do five miles every morning at sunup, rain or shine. Get ready."

"Before coffee?" she muttered, shoving her fingers through tangled hair. "How uncivilized."

"If you were waiting for breakfast in bed, you should have checked into a hotel. Let's go."

Fifteen minutes later she was yawning her way out onto the front porch where Jack's stern gaze was as bracing as the chill morning air.

"Tomorrow you get five minutes. No more. You don't need to put on makeup for a run. No one you're going to meet out here cares how you look."

She looked as though she'd been hauled out of the sheets and stuffed into the first piece of clothing available.

Jack thought she made breakfast in bed too damned inviting. And that made him testy.

She wore a black warm-up suit with pink racing stripes and some high-dollar name brand embroidered on the back. Her blond hair was swept back from the delicate bones of her face and secured in a no-nonsense plastic clip. Her shoes were expensive and made to take the abuse he planned to put her through. By the next morning she'd meet him with a belligerent hostility instead of bleary-eyed confusion…or she'd be begging him to take her home.

She's tougher than she looks, Stan had said.
Well, they'd soon find out.

The sun slanted through the trees, irregularly illuminating the winding path through the woods and, often as not, failing to warn of hazards until she'd stumbled over them. Twisting roots, loose stone, unexpected holes. This was no nature hike. It was her first exercise in survival. And she wasn't sure she was going to make it.

Tessa believed herself to be in shape. She'd played volleyball and tennis in high school and competitive tennis in college. She had a gym membership that garnered less and less of her time as her work took up more of it. She religiously used the stationary bike in the bedroom of her apartment. But she'd never punished her body the way this morning run behind Jack Chaney was meant to.

The first mile had gone fairly well. She'd kept up a decent pace that didn't embarrass her too badly. The air was crisp and the cool temperature made the vigorous exercise bearable. Somewhere between the second and third mile, her calves had started to burn in anticipation of things to come. By the time she plodded toward mile four, a stitch in her side made taking each breath a near sob for mercy.

But no mercy came from the man trotting in front of her with his long relentless strides. He never once looked back to see if she followed. He could probably hear her floundering and gasping and groaning as she staggered in his wake. By the approach of mile five, she was in a hazy fugue state fueled by pain and caffeine deprivation. The only thing that kept her going was the notion that Chaney was smiling at the thought of her distress. That, and the sight of his tight butt creating a visual carrot dangling in front of her.

He wore a black hooded sweatshirt and nylon running shorts. The kind designed to breathe and follow each movement. And following the movement of the skimpy fabric as it pulled and sighed over the bunch and stretch of his rump did funny things to Tessa's breathing, too. If she could manage to take a breath. Her cracked rib was screaming obscenities but she refused to listen. The man truly had buns of steel, while hers felt more like jelly-filled doughnuts. All her focus funneled into the mesmerizing flex of that amazing rear end until he abruptly stopped. She staggered into the back of him, wheezing, blinded by sweat. When she realized they stood outside her cabin door, she just wanted to crawl inside, feeling as though she'd completed a Boston marathon.

Holding her aching side, she gasped, "Can I have my cup of coffee now?"

"Water," he offered stingily. "While you're moving. As the song goes, we've only just begun."

By nightfall Tessa was sure she'd been plunged into a vicious hell devised by Jack Chaney to break her will. And he'd come perilously close to doing his job.

They'd spent the day on his homemade fitness course where he pushed her until her muscles screamed and her lungs cried for a moment's rest all in the name of evaluating her level of fitness. By the time she dragged herself to her single bunk to flop down still fully dressed, she knew he'd branded her with a big F.

Chin-ups, push-ups, rope climb, hand-over-hand ladder crossing. She was surprised he hadn't had her down on her belly wriggling under barbed wire as live rounds burst overhead. Live rounds felt like they were bursting inside her head as she managed to roll over onto her back and hoist one leg up onto the bed. The other continued to hang over the side. She knew she should shower. She hadn't had anything to eat except an apple and power bar for lunch. How many hours ago? She had swished down a couple of painkillers for supper before toppling onto the sheets. When Tinker jumped up onto the bed, the movement of the mattress made her groan. She was whipped, wasted, totally wiped out.

But if Chaney thought she was going to quit, he was mistaken.

And if she could ever get her rubbery legs to support her again, she'd prove it to him.

Tomorrow.

Tomorrow, where he probably had all sorts of other fiendish things planned to force her to cry uncle.

But she'd made it through the first day, even if just barely. And she'd make it through tomorrow, too. And the next day and the next. Jack couldn't make her quit. And he couldn't make her cry.

But what Chaney could do was exhaust her into a good night's sleep. No dreams. No restless tossings and turnings that left her wringing with sweat and limp with despair when she woke to find the nightmare was real. The nightmare that ended her father's life and her neatly planned future with a gunshot.

Tessa opened her eyes to the first gray streaks of dawn and lay for a moment, thinking with a bittersweet anguish that even after his death, Robert D'Angelo still controlled the mechanics of her day.

She had worked for him part-time to put herself through college, planning to follow his footsteps into the legal realm where justice triumphed and one determined individual could make a difference. At least, that's what she'd believed at the time. Her father had encouraged those beliefs with his unflagging work ethic, with his stirring speeches, with a firm handshake and firmer declaration that he would do whatever it took—within the limits of the law—to see one more criminal off the streets. His demeanor held the voting public, even the fickle press, in thrall. No one could say a bad word about the dynamic D.A., until he'd been found slumped over his desk with a pistol in his hand.

And she would do whatever it took, without complaint, to

restore the good opinion the world once held of District Attorney Robert D'Angelo.

And that vow gave her the strength to drag herself out of bed. Another brutal day in paradise.

She survived the run that day, and on the next eight that followed, with legs trembling and the image of Jack's tight ass bouncing in front of her like one of those beckoning balls leading from one word to the next in a karaoke sing-along. *Whatever gets you through it,* Stan used to say. Her new mantra. She couldn't remember what day it was and the thirst for daily news of the outside world made her feel as though she'd been incarcerated in solitary confinement. In a way, she was, isolated from the reality of nine-to-five and the eleven o'clock recap of the day. Her day never deviated. And the sameness made all else a blur. She was stuck in a Twilight Zone of her own making.

So she focused her energy into Jack's regimented schedule, looking no further than the next exercise, the next meal, the next exhausted night's sleep. And for the present, it was enough to get her by from one brutal day to the next. Muscles and tendons she never knew existed now complained like old friends. Where she'd been and where she was going faded into limbo. Only the moment mattered. And Jack Chaney ruled those moments with a dictatorial fervor. He expected her to break or get bored. She saw it in his cynical smile every time she asked how she was doing. "Still here and that's saying a lot," he would answer.

Still here. Damn right.

He didn't believe in her and he didn't believe in what she was doing. A deep stubborn streak surfaced to defy him. She didn't need his encouragement or his coddling. She'd come into his hands a house pet, domesticated right out of any natural instincts to survive, and his uncompromisingly harsh treatment was making her into a lean, mean junkyard dog. That's why she was here. Not to hide, not to ogle his fabulous butt, not to give in to the fears that ruled her every waking hour. She was here to get in touch with that inner she-wolf. And then she would make them howl for mercy.

After a scarfed-down breakfast of a surprisingly delicious scrambled egg burrito and juice chased with crude-weight coffee, Tessa confronted Jack's fitness course with a bring-it-on attitude. After all, what could Jack put in her way that was worse than finally breaking down the door and stepping into her father's office where the metallic scent of blood and gun discharge hung in the air? What could he do that would reduce her to the quivering, pleading mass she'd been on the floor of her apartment? Nothing. Nada. Nothing he could put her through could rival those life-altering experiences. Oh, he could make her hurt, he could make her curse him under her breath, he could make her long for a breath that didn't tear up through the lining of her lungs, but he couldn't shatter her world the way those two events had. So, bring it on, Jack Chaney. She would take whatever he could dish and she would grow stronger, more confident, more dangerous a foe than her unseen enemies bargained for.

Because she was Robert D'Angelo's daughter and odds didn't matter when justice was the reward.

What made a woman like Tessa D'Angelo tick? Jack wondered as she wound her lithe body through his obstacle course. Seeing her at Jo's, trembling like a fragile flower on the end of a delicate vine, he was sure she'd wilt before the end of the first day at his Wolf's Den. She belonged in a world of expensive silk suits, high heels and perfumed evenings, not grunting and sputtering her way through a break-of-dawn run or sweating to calisthenics that would have a made a newbie marine falter.

Tougher than she looks. No kidding.

And he was kidding himself if that didn't impress him out of his usual detachment.

He frowned as his gaze followed her graceful crossing of the balance beam. Even though she must have been exhausted from the morning run, she managed to move with the agile strength of a dancer, arms seesawing in fluid sweeps as she hurried across the narrow plank. With a hopping dismount, she sped without hesitation toward the tires and tiptoed through them like a child playing hopscotch. Her pale blond ponytail bobbed with girlish energy but there was nothing childish in the bounce of her breasts beneath her zippered jacket. He glanced at the stopwatch in his hand to give his imagination a time-out.

Everything about Tessa nudged uncomfortably against the barriers he'd created to keep the outside world at bay. Her determination combined with the wounded-bird protectiveness she'd stirred the moment she peeled down her sunglasses to bare an unwavering stare above all those assorted bruises convinced him to take her under his wing. And that made her a threat. A threat to all he'd built here in his isolated, insulated wilderness. A threat to his "Don't involve me" motto.

He hated causes, knowing that starry-eyed do-gooders like Tessa and her father often fell victim to them. He could have told her that her father was probably guilty of everything the papers accused. He knew, firsthand, that good men sometimes got mixed up in bad things through no fault of their own. But it wasn't his job to educate the mulish and high-minded Ms. D'Angelo in that area. Her unrealistic ideals were not his problem.

Whatever information Stan was bound to discover once he put his nose to the ground wasn't going to clear Robert D'Angelo's good name. It was going to show his naive daughter an ugly truth, that when he was pressed into a situation he couldn't escape, the D.A. had taken the coward's way out by putting a gun to his head, leaving his family to clean up the mess.

Well, who was he to condemn D'Angelo? Hadn't he done the same thing on a less fatal level?

Tessa swung across the ladder, going rung to rung like a twenty-first-century Jane in his own private jungle.

Coward, she had called him. Who was he to argue? As long as she believed him to be a man without honor, a coward who trained then sent others to carry out deeds he refused to champion, she would keep a safe distance. Stan would ferret out the facts and make her face them. Then she'd be gone to piece her world back together and he could go on living day to day in his. Without complications. Without risk. And he'd be happy as a clam about it, closed up in his impenetrable shell.

Tessa D'Angelo and her cause was not his concern.

He clicked the stem on the watch as she sprinted past him. Purposefully he didn't look her way as she bent over, hands braced on her knees, her sweet little derriere pointed in his direction. He was glowering when she came over to peer down at the sheet tacked to his clipboard.

"How'd I do, coach?"

Her voice was breathy, slightly ragged, the way he'd imagine it would be after an exuberant bout of sex. His own growled in response.

"Better by five point two seconds."

She looked ridiculously pleased at that, as if she'd won some prestigious court case or the lottery.

"But don't start booking your Olympic berth just yet."

Even his surly retort couldn't dim the sudden flash of her smile.

His gut twisted.

Then her bright, curious eyes lifted to a spot past his shoulder and her tawny brows arched in unspoken question. He glanced behind him to see Constanza carrying linens across the footbridge to the barracks. Even before she asked, he suddenly realized the conclusion Tessa had drawn.

"Are she and the little girl—"

Jack cut her off. "What they are, is none of your business. You were not invited here as a guest and I'll allow for no intrusions into my private life. Clear?"

She blinked, startled and hurt, but the fiery pride was quick to resurface. Her tone was equally chilled. "Like my mother's fine crystal."

She caught the book he tossed her way without checking the cover. Her gaze still skewered his, letting him know how unforgivably rude he'd just been.

Knowing she was right didn't improve his mood.

"Homework. Read lessons one through four. We'll be going over them at fourteen hundred hours. And I don't mean in a lecture hall."

She rolled the self-defense manual in her grip and, without another word, started for the barracks. As she passed the South American woman at the bridge, Tessa never acknowledged her with so much as a glance.

A long, hot shower helped unknot Tessa's muscles but did little for the tension twisting through her. With a towel turbaned around her damp hair, she reclined on her bunk against a brace of pillows borrowed from the empty rooms and flipped open the manual that she noted was written by a former SEAL. Poet laureates didn't teach unarmed combat.

While Tinker leaned into her hip to fastidiously wash his hind leg, Tessa began to study with the concentration she'd applied to her bar exam. Taking notes in a spiral pad, she jotted down the essentials of stance, footwork, making a proper fist and basic hand techniques for pummeling your assailant. Tinker paused to glare at her as she practiced the rudiments of the jab-punch, hook-and-elbow strike. She smiled faintly. Okay, a little like her Tae-Bo classes. She could do this. She continued through the detailed mechanics of knee strikes and round kicks, picturing Jackie Chan then, annoyingly, Jack Chaney, illustrating the moves in her mind's eye. Thinking of Chaney inspired her to restless movement.

With the book open on her bedspread, Tessa ran through the drills, combining punches and kicks with swift, potentially lethal intent. She pictured Jack's carved-in-stone features as he told her not to intrude in his personal life. Pow. Right jab. As if she'd find anything fascinating there.

He could keep his oh-so-important secrets. Chaney's life, no matter how intriguing, was not the reason she was here— here in the bunkhouse as a student, not in the main house as a guest, where the mysterious woman and child who may or may not belong to him lived.

A sudden surge of melancholy stole her aggressive thunder. He didn't have to be so mean about it.

Closing the book, she flopped down on the bed and gathered a briefly resistant Tinker up in her arms. As she stroked his scarred head, he magnanimously issued his rumbling purr of approval.

Even in the daytime it was quiet. She was a city girl, born and bred, used to the city's vibrant, jarring cadences. It was the music that scored her daily activities. She'd always been in a hurry, darting from the office to the court to dinner meetings and social galas. Working, always working, even in her pajamas late at night, curled on the couch in front of "David Letterman," a volume of appellate law on her lap, absently shooing Tinker out of her bowl of Frosted Cheerios.

Her planner was always full, her voice message light blinking and her bathroom mirror covered with multicolored sticky notes reminding her of errands to be prioritized. And what fueled most of her hours, nearly 24/7, was her father. Arranging his schedule, proofing his speeches, writing his motions, picking up his dry cleaning, always busy behind the scenes so he would look together and unharried. What was she going to do without him in her life to provide that driving force?

Even now she couldn't believe she would never hear his voice over the intercom asking if she knew where to find the Pellingham brief. Her days, her nights, her focus all funneled into Robert D'Angelo and his charismatic climb from prosecutor to D.A. and on into a political arena. Phones ringing, cabs honking, file cabinet doors rattling open, the constant gurgle of coffee being brewed. Those were the sounds that had filled her life with meaning.

Here, in this isolated silence, her thoughts echoed. And the last thing she wanted was time to think, time to second-guess, time to doubt. Was she doing the right thing? Would her father approve of the steps she was taking? If he was innocent, he would.

If?

She hadn't meant if. The Freudian slip horrified her.

She was the only one who knew for certain that her father wasn't guilty. Even if she hadn't heard another man's voice— The Voice—in the inner office just before the fateful shot, she'd have been sure. How could her father turn against all the things that mattered to them, all the things that pulled them together, as close as father and daughter could be when striving for the same cause?

But that wasn't quite true, was it?

They'd never been close as father and daughter. She'd put her own ambitions aside, pushed her way into his world, tried to find a place for herself in his busy professional life since he'd never had time for her in his personal one.

Why hadn't she been able to earn his love the way she'd claimed his respect?

Closing her eyes against the fresh pain stemming back through her childhood, Tessa braced her forearm across her brow as if to hold the hurt away. And with eyes closed, cocooned in silence, her weary body surrendered while her tormented mind continued to spin.

You won't like what you find. Stop now...

She surged into an upright position, the cry of panic and pleading still on her lips. Hands caught her wrists as her arms flailed, gently restraining her. Fingers cupped the back of her head, pulling it in against the warm, sheltered lee of a broad shoulder. Once released, her arms whipped around the solid support of the last man she'd expected to find upon waking in her bed.

"Daddy?"

But the voice that soothed away all the agony and terror of her dreams belonged to Jack Chaney.

"It's all right. I'm not going to let anyone hurt you."

Too late.

He wore a black T-shirt, heated by the filtered sun and by the skin beneath it. He smelled of the woods, fresh laundry soap and some deeply masculine aftershave. For a time she was oddly content to ride the comforting rise and fall of his breaths. He held her carefully, as if he feared she might break, or as if he was afraid too tight an embrace would serve to frighten her more. And for the first time in longer than she could remember, she felt protected and safe.

Her father had never come into her room to chase away the fragments of childish nightmares. Her mother had.

And now here was a man she wouldn't have thought had any soft edges, soothing her hair and quieting her hitching sobs.

Her hands opened, spreading wide and not coming close to encompassing the breadth of his shoulders. Soft edges? Hardly. He might well have been hewn of warm granite under the snug pull of cotton. Her thumbs shifted, tracing the swell of muscle and in one breath, her sob dissolved into something suspiciously like a sigh.

Fearing he'd heard it, Tessa started looking for a graceful way to escape his arms. How could she let him see her so achingly vulnerable and still demand his respect? She rubbed her face against his chest to erase the tears before struggling to lean away. His arms gave gradually, almost with reluctance. She couldn't quite meet his gaze, afraid of what she'd see there.

"I'm sorry. Just a nightmare."

"I heard you cry out. I came down when you didn't show up for your lesson." His words petered out until an awkward silence pushed between them more forcefully than physical distance. She snagged a quick breath as he rubbed away the last damp trail of evidence from her cheek with the slow drag of his thumb. Calloused yet unbearably tender. She sat back so fast the top of her head came up under his jaw, snapping his teeth together like a trap. She did glance up then, fatalistically drawn to see the quizzical knitting of his dark brows. He seemed bemused. Somehow, that was all too intimate.

"You shouldn't be here. What if your wife—"

She hauled in the blurted statement when his expression froze over.

"I don't have a wife," he said at last, enunciating with surgical precision. "I don't belong to any woman or any career. I am my own man, Ms. D'Angelo, and I like it that way."

The strange choking sensation building up from her chest to wad in her throat made her next words rumble.

"That's the way I like it, too, Mr. Chaney. You've made it perfectly clear that the only thing on your agenda is not to get involved, with my mission or my motives. And I will not allow any intrusions into my search for justice, especially from a man who knows nothing about honor."

For a moment he said nothing, then, oddly, he smiled. "Well, since it seems you're so eager to get started with full contact, let's get to it."

Chapter 4

For a moment she saw stars.

"Don't drop your hand."

Tessa sent out a punch and within a heartbeat her jaw numbed from the shock of another impact.

"What did I just tell you?"

"Don't drop your hand," she muttered through her mouth guard.

"Relax."

She stepped back and rolled her shoulders to ease the tension in them.

"Make a fist. Thumbs to your temples. Move them out about six inches from your body and at nose level. Elbows and fists at a forty-five degree. Good. Now keep that guard up. Your opponent is not going to stand there and let you hit them. They will hit you back. Concentrate. What are you thinking?"

She was thinking that he wasn't married.

She probably deserved every jab he shot through her weak defense because of the odd elation that scrambled her timing and most likely her brain.

Why should she care if Jack Chaney was single?

Maybe she'd taken one too many punches.

Looking at him in the fading daylight, dark, tough, aggressive in his baggy gray sweatsuit, all she could think of was the tenderness in his touch. *I won't let anyone hurt you.* She believed him and for the first time in over a month, the crushing panic was gone from inside her chest. *I won't let anyone hurt you.* Funny how such a simple claim from a near stranger could release her fears.

But Jack wasn't going to be there to protect her once she left his forest retreat, so she'd better listen and learn how to do it for herself.

"Never assume every opponent is going to respond the same way to a kick or a punch. Some you can drop, some will just shake it off and keep coming. Winning involves timing, speed, coordination and technique but none of those mean anything if you don't keep fighting. When it's time to fight, go at it one hundred and ten percent. You do whatever is necessary until your opponent is neutralized. Once you commit to fighting back, use surprise. React quickly when your opponent doesn't expect it and do it with force. No hesitation. Be prepared to hit and keep on hitting until your opponent is no longer a threat. Then break off. That's the difference between reasonable and excessive force. Be alert, decisive and aggressive. SEALs call that the warrior mind-set. Be aware of your surroundings. Be ready to act when you need to and be ready to commit that hundred and ten percent."

She'd started to nod when she saw the blur of his right hook coming. And surprisingly, instinctively, her hand was there to deflect it. In the same motion, her right jabbed out to connect solidly with his chin. It wasn't a hard pop or a damaging one. It didn't stagger him or even cause him to flinch.

But she'd made contact. Quickly, decisively and with aggression.

Jack grinned. "That's what I'm talking about. Ready to mix it up some more?"

"Bring it on, Chaney."

As they sat at the war room table eating a delicious meal laid out by the silent and nearly invisible Constanza, Jack continued to instruct and Tessa listened. Still flushed with the accomplishment of landing her first blow, she allowed herself the illusion of being one of his capable trainees preparing to do battle. In a way, she was. The men who'd framed and murdered her father were still out there and they'd made it clear they weren't going to accept her interference quietly.

"There are four levels of readiness," Jack was saying as he forked rice and beans into a warm tortilla. "Most people wander around in the white level, totally oblivious to what's going on around them. It's in this unaware comfort zone that people are the most vulnerable and when they'll most likely be attacked."

Tessa could see herself entering her apartment, as white as the rice on the table, seeing warning signs all around her yet clueless as to the danger. She'd been vulnerable, a victim.

"Every average citizen needs to increase their awareness to the yellow level. This isn't a state of paranoia. It's a state of preparedness. Awareness is a tremendously powerful tool that uses all your senses. You take the time to notice your surroundings so you can foresee potential problems. Watch people for verbal cues and body language. Learn the names of the security people who work in your building and make sure they know you. Know where the alarm buttons are, where the exits are, just like on an airplane. When you're going someplace new, plan your transportation routes in advance. Walk closer to the street than to alleys and doorways. Ask yourself, if you were an attacker, where would you hide? Carry your body confidently. Walk or stand erect in a way that conveys assertiveness. When you pass someone, look them in the eye. Let them know you see them but maintain your personal space of at least two arm lengths. That's your safety zone."

It made sense. Tessa nodded. She'd been a victim. She'd walked right into a situation, blindly, trustingly. She understood the analogy. When you're on an airplane that's going down, it's too late to look in the seat back flyer to locate exits and safety equipment. She rolled another tortilla and munched thoughtfully, passing a piece of the delicately spiced chicken down to Tinker.

"Once you're in the yellow zone, proceeding with caution, and you know something isn't right, that something bad might happen, you slip into the orange level of readiness. At this point, you know some action is necessary on your part. You either have to get away from the situation or be prepared to confront it. Moving quickly and decisively from yellow to orange is vital to your personal safety and self-defense. You have to be prepared to weigh your options and make your move. Be ready to jump into red if necessary. That's where you hit first, where you do whatever you need to do, and do it immediately, for your safety or the protection of your loved ones."

She felt a twinge of remorse. Too late. She'd been too slow to action, to even suspect. She could hear the muted voices in her father's office, behind his closed door, but she still hadn't reacted with more than puzzlement. Then the shot. She'd been paralyzed for how long, for how many vital seconds, while the perpetrator escaped?

Jack was studying her, his features impassive. Did he see her guilt, her grief? He could have said something to lessen her sense of blame but he didn't. There was no way to do that now. She'd buried her father. But she wasn't about to let her mother bury her. Instead of telling her to forgive herself, Jack explained away her culpability with a simple statement.

"We live in a passive society. We depend on other people to protect us. We see ourselves as having no control over our surroundings. We're victims before the fact, accidents waiting to happen. But it doesn't have to happen if you're ready for it. Be prepared to fight. Be prepared to get in that first punch. Once you let your opponent take control, you're in trouble. If you let them take you away from the initial point of attack, statistics show you only have a three percent chance of survival. Don't give them that control. Be ready. Don't hesitate. Be proud and indignant. They can't do this to you. The strong and aggressive survive, Tessa. I didn't make up those rules but you'd better learn to follow them."

And she would.

Peripherally, she realized he'd called her by her first name. She wondered if he'd meant to or if he was unaware of it. Going from Ms. D'Angelo to Tessa put them on a new level of intimacy, and because of it, she found herself saying, "He hurt me, Jack. He surprised me and hurt me in my own home. I never saw it coming and I couldn't get away. He wanted to scare me and he did. He terrorized me for I don't know how long. I'd come around and think he was gone and then I'd hear him and see those creased trousers. And he'd hit me…"

She felt it all over again, the terror, the pain, the awful feeling of having no control. Coldness shuddered out from her belly, radiating outward to chill her heart, to freeze her blood, to immobilize her muscles.

And then Jack's big, warm hand settled firmly over hers. His expression was intense, his features inscrutable. He didn't try to tell her it would be all right. He didn't try to tell her to let it go. He made her face it, head-on, right back into the hell of that night.

"What was he doing there, Tessa? What did he want?"

She blinked up at him through the glaze of her tears, trying to focus on what he was asking. "What was he doing?"

"The police report said it was a robbery. Was anything missing?"

"No." Her tone steadied. "It wasn't a robbery."

"Then what was he doing there? Why did he stay after you walked in on him? Tessa, did he do anything else to you?" Though his tone didn't actually change, it was suddenly infused with a harsh grittiness. The voice of a truly dangerous man.

"He was in my room." She could hear the sounds from the bedroom, the sounds of drawers being opened and shut. The shuffle of papers, the sounds of her belongings being tossed carelessly to the floor. "He was looking for something."

"What? What did he think you had?"

The fear fell away before a new cool logic. "Evidence. Evidence against him or his boss. Whatever my father was planning to use to indict them."

"Did your father usually send files home with you?"

"I took things home with me all the time. My work day didn't end at five."

"What cases were you working on? What was big enough for them to resort to murder?"

"We were in the middle of a lot of cases but just one big, ugly confrontation. Councilman Rachel Martinez. She and my father were planning to run for the same congressional seat. Only, when we started digging into her background, unpleasant things started popping up. Things my father believed linked her to drug trafficking and an overseas pipeline."

"The same things your father was accused of." He said it flatly, noncommittally.

"Fancy that."

"Mmm."

"I think Martinez had him killed."

"You can think what you like but proving it is another thing. What did your father have on her?"

Tessa rubbed her brow in frustration. "I don't know. That's

the problem. Usually we worked on everything together, a team effort. But he wouldn't confide in me on this one. He was putting together a solid case, was all he'd say."

"Whatever he had, they didn't find it when they killed him or maybe you chased them off before they had the chance. If they had found it, they wouldn't have come after you. The police never found any link between drugs and Martinez."

"They weren't looking in that direction." Her tone snapped like brittle ice. "They gave their report based on the testimony of some sniveling junkie looking to cut a deal. They took his word, a three-time loser, over my father's. All the good he'd done, all the criminals he'd put away, and they took the word of a felon."

"Our system loves to condemn its own heroes," was Jack's philosophical response.

"Yeah, well, it stinks. It really stinks. And now the real villain is still out there because there's no one like my father willing to hunt him down."

"Yes there is."

Her. He meant her.

"Like father, like daughter," he summed up succinctly. "Isn't that why you're doing this? Because just like him, you couldn't let it go, you couldn't let them go unpunished?"

Her reply was soft, humbled. "Something like that."

"Then don't let them get away with it."

Fear unexpectedly stabbed through her insides, making her go all cold again. "I can still hear his voice, Jack."

Walk away while you can. My next visit won't be quite so pleasant.

"And you're afraid of what he said."

She didn't have to answer.

Jack wanted to curse. He wanted to shake her. He wanted to crush her close in his arms and never let her go. Didn't she realize the danger she was in if any of what she suspected was true? Why couldn't she be like ninety-nine point nine percent of the populace and give up and let it go? Like father, like daughter. She'd sunk in her teeth and she wouldn't release that bite, not ever. Not even after they struck her and threatened her. Not even when the system that was set up to protect her, failed her. Didn't she know how easily professional men—men like him—could break her delicate bones?

He'd been crazy to bring her here, to train her, to give her the illusion that she'd actually have a chance against some thug bent on destroying that which made her so unique in his eyes. But if he sent her away as unprepared as she was now, she wouldn't have a chance at all. And he'd be reading her obituary in the paper.

Damned if he did, damned if he didn't. Already damned, truth be told.

"He meant to scare you with what he said to you. If you cower in fear every time you think of his words, he's won and you might as well give up. Right here, right now. Is that what you want to do?"

He knew the effect his goading words would have. She bristled, the glistening panic in her eyes becoming a steely sheen of determination.

"No."

"Then get mad. Play that voice in your head and get mad as hell. He was in your home. He hurt you to intimidate you, to warn you away. If he thought you were a real threat, he would have killed you. He expects you to hide. He expects you to shiver every time you think of him and what he did, what he might do. Is he right?"

"No." A faint yet steady conclusion.

"Then turn that anger into power, into aggression, into focus. How dare he? Who does he think he is to steal control of your life? Are you going to let him?"

"No."

"Who's going to stop him?"

"I am."

"Who is?"

"I am."

"Attagirl." He pushed back from the table. "Read lessons five through eight and get ready to rumble right after tomorrow's run."

"I'll be ready."

"Not if you let him sneak into your dreams and keep you up all night."

"I won't let him."

"Good."

He left her sitting at the table, filled with an aggressiveness that he'd spoonfed to her. Tessa D'Angelo, his fierce, fragile avenging angel. And what did that make him? The protective guardian watching over her? He stepped out into the cool night and inhaled a deep breath. It would be emotional suicide to think he could be anything else.

Her world was black and white, right and wrong, while his had always been shifting shades of gray. He mocked the sense of fair play and justice she stood for and she scorned his lack of convictions. He tried to shrug it off. Why should her opinion matter to him?

Maybe because of the way she'd felt in his arms. A man could get used to that feeling real fast.

He snorted. What was he thinking? That Tessa was going to throw herself into his arms? Throw a right hook was more like it. He'd made it clear that his life was off-limits so why was he even entertaining the idea of finding a place to fit within hers? He liked his life the way it was—simple, direct, uncomplicated.

Lonely.

He'd cut himself off from the things that mattered to Tessa, things such as involvement and caring and honor. He'd been there, done that and still had the scars to prove it. Scars that burned every time he looked into a little girl's eyes and saw her mother there.

He started back to the house, his Fortress of Solitude. If it was good enough for a superhero, it was good enough for him. He'd surrounded himself with things that were important to him: comfort, beauty, peace and quiet. And then he'd let Tessa elbow her way in, demanding he reprioritize. Well, he wasn't going to. Not for a woman who was going to be here and gone. Not for a woman who asked him to take up her cause and get burned by it. Not for a maddeningly independent woman who believed he had a conscience for hire.

He climbed up onto his porch but the usual feeling of welcome was missing. He turned to look down at the barracks, with its one light burning, and a sense of belonging began to tug annoyingly at the edges of his heart and mind. Tessa D'Angelo, the woman who filled his thoughts with foolish, heroic ideas he'd long outgrown, the woman who made him ache with desires he'd long pushed from his life, called to a conscience he didn't want to claim.

"How's she doing?"

"Tougher than she looks," Jack admitted reluctantly.

Stan laughed on the other end of the connection. "Warned you, didn't I? Told you she wasn't going to be easy to discourage."

"Point taken." He hesitated then figured he might as well plunge right in. "Did you find out anything on your end yet?"

Stan was silent, probably surprised into swallowing his tongue. Finally he recovered. "Are you asking out of idle curiosity or because you really want to know?"

"Don't get cute, Kovacs. It was just a question."

Stan's sigh was heavy. "And that's all I've found. A lot of unanswered questions. Rob always called me in to do his investigative legwork. Always. But not this time. He was playing this one close to the cuff. If I didn't know better, I'd say it was personal."

"Because he was planning to run against Martinez?"

"No. That would be business and to Rob, business was business. Only family was personal."

"If he had information on Rachel Martinez that he wasn't ready to let anyone see, where would he keep it?"

"In the office, but I've been over everything. I've gone through every piece of paper, every computer file. There's nothing on Martinez. Just a file on his potential campaign strategy against her."

"Would he have won?"

"Won what?"

"The election," Jack asked out of interest. He was rabidly apolitical but this wasn't about party lines. It was about the lines of anxiety that tightened around Tessa's mouth and eyes.

"Polls gave him sixty-three percent to Martinez's thirty-seven."

"Is Martinez the kind of woman who would murder over that twenty-six-percent margin?"

"Don't know. She grew up in the school of hard knocks. Got elected because of it. You know, wrong-side-of-the-tracks girl with motivation escapes dead end of gangs and drugs to make good. Horatio Alger stuff. The public eats it up. Maybe she didn't disassociate herself from some of that bad company she grew up with. Maybe she was owed some favors and called them in. Politics is a dirty business."

"But is it a killing business?" That's what he needed to know.

Stan mused for moment then said, "You sound like you're starting to believe her."

"Just an overly active imagination, Stan. I like a good brain teaser. You know me."

"Yeah, Jack. I do. And this isn't like you. She getting to you?"

Jack didn't like what that question implied. "Yeah, she got to me with a right jab this afternoon. Stung like a son of a gun."

Stan laughed but he wouldn't be dissuaded. "She's a pistol, our little Tessa. And she grows on you, whether you like it or not."

"She's not putting down any roots here, Kovacs. So you'd better get out there and find out something fast. Because if you don't, she's going to wade right back into the middle of a whole lot of hurt."

"I hear you," Stan replied glumly.

Then something else occurred to Jack. "Did D'Angelo have a home office?"

Stan considered this then admitted, "I don't know. He might have. He didn't like leaving Barbara alone for very long."

"Barbara?"

"The missus."

Jack recalled the elegant woman standing at D'Angelo's side opposite Tessa. "Have you looked there?"

"I didn't want to intrude yet. She was pretty broken up about…everything. Her two boys have been staying with her, helping her get things in order. They're flying out on Friday. I was planning to make a call then."

Good. Until Friday, the D'Angelo home was secure and Barbara D'Angelo safe in the company of her sons. Why wasn't her daughter there to keep her company, as well, instead of out chasing after vague hopes and suspicions?

None of his business.

"Let me know what you find out, Stan."

"Will do. And, Jack…keep her safe."

"Don't make her my problem, Stan," Jack warned as the claustrophobic sense of commitment crowded in.

"She already is."

Get mad and get even. Tessa liked the sound of that but thinking about it and realizing it were two different animals. Adopting a tough pose in front of Jack wasn't the same thing as fighting off the suffocating panic that fell over her in the night.

I won't let him, she'd told Jack so boldly. Did she have the courage to push her assailant out of her mind, out of her dreams? He'd taken control of her life for long enough. He'd stolen her sense of security, of trust, of control. He'd left her trembling and shattered on the floor of her apartment. He'd left her shivering and weak with dread beneath her covers. And now, he'd left her…stronger.

The notion surprised her. Yes, stronger. He'd shaken her from her complacency. He'd shown her a cruelty she never thought she'd have to experience. The fear, the pain, prepared her to fight back. To get mad. Damn him for taking her life away from her. Well, she was going to take it back. And she was not going to let his boss smear her father's name and spit on everything he stood for, on everything she believed in.

The truth was out there. The hard, cold facts that would restore her father's good name. No one else was going to do it. The police had turned away, case closed. Even his legal associates winced from the whole affair as if Robert D'Angelo had tarnished their institution. Only Stan stuck by him, remembering the man her father was, not the greedy abomination the press had created circumstantially.

If only he'd lived to prove himself innocent.

The man with the sinister voice had stolen that opportunity. Along with her chance of ever realizing a father's love.

Too restless to endure her own company in the big, empty barracks, Tessa slipped carefully out onto the porch. The night air caressed her fevered cheeks, cooled her rage, soothed her pain. With the moon shining ripe and heavy overhead, the surroundings were illuminated by a soft, silvery glow. Mindful of Jack's warning, she stepped off the porch and onto the path that led along the edge of the stream. It would have been easy to lose herself in thought but she'd never wander in that placid white zone again. She moved purposefully, surveying her environment and listening to the night. And amazingly, she noticed that it wasn't quiet at all.

Frogs sounded from somewhere in the thick pads where

the stream angled in its serpentine course. Crickets chirped their last songs of the season. Somewhere a distant dog howled. Or was it a coyote? She'd heard there were coyotes in the north woods. The occasional screech of night birds, of owls and hawks punctuated the subtle music of the forest. And suddenly she didn't feel so alone.

She heard another sound, one not of nature or its creatures. A twig snapped behind her.

Tessa immediately shifted into a level orange.

She'd gone a lot farther from the barracks than she'd planned. Through the thick stand of pines, she could faintly make out the light she'd left burning. She couldn't even see the main house. She'd let herself get separated from her safe zone, an easy target, a victim.

Or was that what Jack was hoping?

Irritation spiked. Of course. He'd seen her leave the porch even after he'd laid down Chaney's Law. So, to teach her another lesson in consequence, he'd come creeping after her in the dark, hoping to jump out at her, catching her unaware and thus prove his point.

Well, maybe that was what he'd planned but it wasn't going to happen.

Sweeping the ground with a glance, she found a substantial branch about a yard in length and as big around as her wrist. She picked it up, hefting it to gage its effectiveness as a weapon. It probably wouldn't incapacitate him but it would certainly get his attention. Smiling grimly at the thought of Jack's unexpected welcome, she stepped off the path into the deep shadow of an oak tree. There, she waited, quieting her breathing so she could hear every scuffle of leaves, every stir of stones. Until her stalker was upon her.

"Hiyyya!"

She leaped out from behind the tree, brandishing her makeshift cudgel, ready to smack him senseless for thinking to scare her.

But instead of Jack Chaney, she confronted a much smaller form, a figure that fell back and down the slope to the stream. With a very feminine squeal.

Chapter 5

A dismayed Tessa found herself staring down, not at a duly chastened Jack Chaney who would have deserved the indignity but at the young girl from the main house. A young girl who wailed in pain when she tried to get up.

Tessa scrambled down the steep embankment, uttering apologies and assurances. Surely the child must have thought her some kind of mad woman to leap out at her in the dark. Guilt tore at her when she saw the girl clasp her ankle, her features pulled tight in misery.

"I'm sorry I frightened you. I thought it was Jack. I'm Tessa. I'm not going to hurt you."

She knelt so they were on the same level and was relieved to see no fear in the child's large dark eyes. Just pain. Tessa's remorse notched tighter.

"I'm not supposed to be here but my aunt said you had a kitty. Mr. Jack is going to be very angry." Her velvety-dark eyes glistened. She was a lovely girl with a heart-shaped face and flawless bronzed skin. Her bob of thick black hair was hidden under a Pistons ball cap and she was wearing an Orlando Bloom T-shirt. But she was no All-American girl. Her voice held the melodic cadence of South America.

Mr. Jack. He wasn't her father.

"I'm not supposed to be out here, either, so I guess he'll be angry with both of us."

The girl responded faintly to her smile and offered, "My name is Rose. I'm almost twelve."

Such a tiny little thing, all spindly arms and legs and huge eyes.

"Well, Rose, we'd better get you back where you belong. Do you think you can stand up?"

She gnawed her lip for a moment. "I will try."

She weighed next to nothing. Tessa had no trouble lifting her but the girl grimaced when she tried to put weight on her left ankle. A tiny whimper escaped her. Tessa immediately scooped her up into her arms and started toward the house.

"My cat's name is Tinker." She chatted to distract Rose from her discomfort.

"A funny name for a kitty."

Tessa didn't explain it was short for Tinker's Damn because whoever had tossed him out onto a freeway median in the middle of February hadn't given one. No one except her when she'd seen him shivering there in a blizzard. "You can come down and meet him. He's a fat, grumpy old guy."

"I'm not supposed to cross the bridge," Rose replied. And Tessa could see the wisdom there. A young girl had no place among whatever sort of men Chaney usually housed. But then, she wasn't exactly his usual sort of trainee.

"I'll talk to Mr. Jack and see what we can do."

The child clutched at her and let her dark head rest on Tessa's shoulder. A surprising sense of maternal instinct ran amuck within her. She didn't have much experience with children. Her middle brother Todd had twin boys who were

six and had more energy then a whole outfield of battery-pow-
ered bunnies. They were too wiggly to be held for longer than
a hug. But since Todd and his family lived on the West Coast,
where he worked for a computer firm, she only saw them on
holidays and in photos. Not up close and personal. Ram-
bunctious little boys didn't smell sweet and feel soft like this.

"Does your aunt work for Mr. Jack?" Tessa asked, partly
to keep up the conversation and partly because she'd been curious about the two of them, as well. They'd reached the
gravel drive of the main house. Up close, it was even more
impressive.

"*Sí.* She work for him and he take care of me. He brought
us to live with him here in the U.S. after my mother died."

That presented more questions than answers. But Tessa
didn't have time to ask them, for suddenly Jack was there on
the porch above them, backlit from the open front door.

"What happened?" he demanded tersely as Tessa climbed
the steps.

"She hurt her ankle. Just a sprain, I hope."

"It was my fault," Rose cut in quickly to save Tessa the
awkwardness of explaining. "I slipped down by the creek
and the lady heard me cry out."

No retelling of the madwoman who'd jumped out to
threaten her with a big stick.

"And which side of the creek were you on, little monkey?" Jack asked as he reached to take Rose from Tessa's
arms. She gave the girl up reluctantly. Jack enfolded the child
with the same practiced care Tessa had seen her brother use
when one of his sons scraped their knee. The thin arms went
easily around Jack's neck.

"On my side, like you tell me, Mr. Jack," she said sweetly
as she glanced over his shoulder to wink at her coconspirator.

"Mmm. I'm sure you were." No sign of an angry Jack
Chaney. His voice held a touch of amused tolerance as he carried her inside. And since he didn't shut the door behind

them, Tessa followed, as eager to see the interior as she was to learn the severity of Rose's injury.

She stood in the soaring foyer and simply gawked.

To create the illusion of a floating timber frame and unfettered height, the living room Jack carried Rose into consisted of a wraparound wall of windows on three sides with sturdy beams high above to anchor the floor-to-ceiling multipaned glass together. The focal point was a stone fireplace on the far end, built into the window wall so the massive chimney was visible outside.

Arranged comfortably in front of the yawning hearth on a black-and-white, cow-print wool rug were plump suede chairs facing an ultramodern couch of dark ebony wood with a unique trim of rope across its arms and back. In the center of the rug was a low table of the same dark wood, its top made of woven leather strips. An eclectic selection of art books were stacked to one side next to a hand-beaten brass bowl.

And standing in the corner surrounded by glass was a high-powered camera on a tripod with a lens big enough to see the rings around Saturn. Only Tessa had a sneaking suspicion that Jack wasn't studying the stars. It was pointed toward the stream…and her living quarters.

With consummate care, Jack sat Rose on one of the overstuffed chairs and knelt in front of her on the rug. With the gentleness Tessa well remembered, he unlaced the girl's hiking boot and rolled down her sock. He probed the already swelling ankle, stopping when the child sucked in a pained breath.

"Well, I don't think it's broken," he pronounced. "Some ice and some pillows underneath it ought to do the trick. And no sneaking out after dark to spy on our company."

"Miss Tessa isn't company. And she has a kitty."

Even Jack couldn't think of a logical way to argue around that.

Just then Constanza rushed into the room in a flurry of hur-

ried Spanish and anxious clucking. She was older up close
than Tessa had supposed, her features a sepia network of hard
work and premature worries beneath her severely styled hair.
Her simple blue skirt and beige cotton blouse were spotless
and crisply pressed. And she wore the scent of beeswax and
lemon Lysol like a fine cologne. But as proudly as she wore
the badges of her profession, it clearly wasn't her priority.
There was no mistaking the love she had for the child who
was not her own.

"It's all right, Connie. It's nothing serious. Just a twisted
ankle," Jack explained with a calm he hoped to pass to the
agitated woman.

"Tweestd?" Her eyebrows puckered as she wrung her
detergent-chafed hands in pantomime. "Ah. Tweested. Yes?"

"Yes. She'll be fine as soon as you tuck her into bed."

"No," Rose wailed. "Mr. Jack, you take me." She empha-
sized her demand by flinging her arms around his neck in a
tight squeeze.

And then Tessa saw it and her heart broke for the child.
Although his embrace was gentle and he didn't push away,
Tessa watched Jack freeze by slow degrees. It started in his
eyes, their soulful darkness taking on a flat opaque sheen.
Though he was still smiling, his lips were thin and the gesture without warmth. Though he hadn't physically moved, he
was suddenly a world away. And Tessa wasn't the only one
who felt that abrupt and intentional distancing.

"Let Connie take you. I need to talk to Ms. Tessa."

Without looking up into that austere face, Rose leaned
back, releasing her hold on him as if she'd done something
unforgivable but wasn't quite certain what it was. As the girl
allowed Constanza to lift her up, Tessa got a brief yet unfor-
gettable glimpse of a pain that mirrored her own childhood,
an unrequited longing for the loving tenderness her own father lavished on his sons and wife but never displayed toward

her. And she'd never known what she'd done to provoke that chilly almost imperceptible barrier.

Why hadn't her father loved her?

Why couldn't Jack love this needy little girl he'd brought to live in his home?

As Constanza carried the girl away and Jack straightened, his features a mask over whatever emotions he felt, Tessa risked pushing into the off-limits of his personal life.

"She's a beautiful child."

His mouth quirked into a faint enigmatic smile. "A bit too precocious for her own good sometimes." Then he turned to Tessa and an unexpected heat lit his dark gaze. The difference between it and the chill of moments before was like a sudden geothermal thaw. "A bit like you, Ms. D'Angelo."

A criticism or compliment? Hard to tell.

Tessa stood at the edge of the communal area. She hadn't been invited inside Jack's home and to make herself comfortable was a bit presumptuous. But still, she wasn't ready to leave. She'd agreed to stay out of his personal business but now that she was here, she meant to take advantage of the intrusion. She smiled back.

"And you like that about us, don't you?"

He didn't answer but he didn't deny it, either. "Want to tell me how the two of you chanced to meet?"

"You might say we were both testing our boundaries."

"Aren't boundaries placed for a reason?"

She pursed her lips. "Perhaps. But if they're not tested every once in a while, how do we know they're needed?"

That dark smoldery stare passed leisurely over her body leaving a blistery trail of warmth in its wake.

"I thought a nice girl like you respected boundaries and played by the rules?"

"What makes you think I'm such a nice girl?"

He laughed, a big, booming sound filled with an insulting amount of mirth. "Oh, I think you're the poster child for nice girl. You work hard, you play fair, you don't cheat on your taxes. You probably don't even take the little shampoo bottles from the hotel."

She didn't. Her eyes narrowed. He made it sound so…unappealing. "That's me in a nutshell. How perceptive of you, Mr. Chaney. A nice boring girl leading her straight-arrow dull life." It was her life. That's why she suddenly felt so angry with him for pushing it into her face.

Another laugh, this one low and provocative, perhaps. "I said nice, not boring. You, Tessa, are not boring. Not by a long shot." That last was said in a slightly deeper register, creating a curious response in her belly.

What was she thinking? She *was* a nice girl and Jack Chaney was definitely not the kind of guy with whom she should be parrying innuendoes. Was that what they were doing? The notion shocked her from her indignation. Jack was flirting with her and she was enjoying it. Immensely.

How long had it been since she'd had a playful exchange with a man? Her brutal, all-inclusive hours had precluded a social life unless it was business-oriented. And when she was on the job, whether behind the desk or a glass of champagne, she was working. No time for fun for this nice dull girl. The men in her field were too caught up in their own ambitions and those who weren't were intimidated by hers. The rest were on the other side of the aisle in the courtroom. She didn't date. She didn't flirt. She didn't even think about those things. And she didn't know what she was missing until this gorgeous man with his mercenary heart challenged her placid existence and revved up her libido into a growling overdrive.

It was fun, this verbal sparring. And she bet if Jack Chaney ever decided to shed his cloak of uninvolvement where she was concerned, they could have a whole lot of fun, indeed. She thought of his big, warm hands and the things he might be persuaded to do with them. Her thighs clenched. Her breasts tingled. Good Lord, she was ripe for a little naughty fun. And with Chaney, there was no question that it would be no strings attached. Maybe that's what she needed right now. To connect physically, if not permanently, with another human being. She was so tired of being alone, of being excluded. The idea of closeness, even on this most basic of levels, was an unbearable enticement. If only the man could be convinced to mix business with pleasure.

She was lousy at seduction. Her idea of sexy was shoes that didn't pinch and a writ of habeas corpus. Her experience in the field of intimacy consisted of two one-night stands and too much alcohol to think better of it. And neither of those forays had impressed her enough to coax her back for a second round. But Jack, she knew instinctively, would be impressive. And then she would walk away. They were both adults and if it was what they both wanted for the moment, why not?

Why not, indeed?

Thinking of Jack beneath the starchy sheets in her narrow bunkhouse bed lacked romance but… She glanced covertly down the hall, wondering what his room might look like. Wondering what Jack might look like without the black T-shirt and chinos he wore. Sleek, controlled, she imagined. Hard. She shivered.

The sound of Jack's cell phone ringing made her jump right out of those mentally tangled sheets. He took one beat, then two, to look away from her, his gaze not quite impassive. Speculative, maybe, but still cautious. Then he whipped out the cell and flipped it open.

"Chaney."

Tessa expelled the breath she hadn't known she was holding. Her heart hammered, sending tidal surges of need and desire through her system. Even her toes were curling. As soon as he finished his call, she would test her inexperienced powers of seduction. And if Jack was willing…

"Stan? I can hardly hear you. Bad connection. Where are you calling from?"

Stan. Tessa's mind snapped immediately back to business. "What's going on?"

Jack angled away from her, cupping his free hand over the phone as if to amplify the reception. "Stan? What was that? I can't—"

A long, tense pause, then Jack closed the phone. When he turned to her, Tessa's skin broke out in a cold gooseflesh. The intensity in his expression warned of bad things, of things she wasn't prepared to hear.

"What?" she whispered.

"I'm not sure." His tone was terse, professional and frightening. "Stan was calling from Jackson."

"The prison?" Where the man who condemned her father was cooling his heels for the next ten to fifteen. "Is this about Johnnie O'?"

"I didn't get much. Other than Stan said there was some trouble. I don't know what kind, but we'd better prepare for it anyway."

Before she could ask what he had planned, he strode briskly down the hall only to return moments later with a sleepy Rose in his arms and an anxious Constanza trailing behind him.

"Follow me," he ordered Tessa. She fell in without question.

He marched them through the house to a room with field-stone walls and a high, wood-beamed turret ceiling from which hung an impressive bronze wagon-wheel chandelier. Sectional leather seating made a cozy horseshoe and the opposite wall was solid books. Everything from leather-bound classics to Sam Spade and Louis L'Amour. Though there was plenty of light, Tessa noted that there was no window.

Jack carefully deposited Rose on one of the sofa sections and pulled a colorful woven blanket around her. She snuggled down against the rolled arm of the couch and was instantly asleep. The bliss of youth.

But Tessa was wide awake and wired.

"What's going on?"

"Stay here while I find out."

He stepped outside the doorway and pulled a no-nonsense steel pocket door across the opening, shutting the three of them behind it. There was no dramatic click but Tessa was certain they were sealed in just the same. Was this his version of a panic room? But then, Jack didn't panic, he prepared. When Jack Chaney prepared for trouble, he went all the way.

Constanza settled on the seat next to the sleeping child, placing a reassuring hand upon the girl's shoulder. She didn't look alarmed. She began to hum a low melodic tune. That calm didn't reassure Tessa. Too restless to sit, the space too small for her to pace, she positioned herself in front of the floor-to-ceiling library and made herself read each and every title: Steinbeck, Hemingway, Erica Jong. Okay, it was an interesting collection. *Just read and don't think and let Chaney do his job.* Which at the moment, she realized, was to protect them.

Had O'Casey escaped? Had threats been made against her?

Don't second-guess. Wait for facts. Her father's famous saying. Wait for the facts.

Even when the facts remained maddeningly out of reach?

She wished for a little of Robert D'Angelo's patience as she hugged her arms around herself. That was one of the skills she'd never quite mastered to his satisfaction. *If you hurry, you miss something,* he was always chastising. She glanced at the solid steel door. Well, she was missing something now and she needed to know what it was and how it concerned her.

Minutes ticked by. She was on the fifth row of titles. He had them separated by both subject and author name. Another time she might have delighted in selecting from the wealth of fiction and biographies. But for now, her concentration was strained just focusing on the few words on each well-tended spine. Margaret Mitchell? Her brows soared.

The pocket door opened, sliding almost soundlessly back into the wall. Jack met her questioning gaze briefly before turning his attention to Rose's aunt.

"Take her back to her room, Connie."

The woman was satisfied, but Tessa, chafing with curiosity, could barely contain it until the two of them were alone. Jack wasn't much for explanations when there were orders to be given.

"Get your things together."

"Why?"

"You're moving up here to the main house."

"Why?"

The delay her insistent questions caused made him frown. He wasn't used to being asked for reasons and pausing to give them obviously irritated him.

"Stan was meeting with Johnnie O'Casey tonight. He'd been trying to wrangle a face-to-face all week."

"What did Johnnie O' tell him? Did he say who paid him to frame my father?"

"O'Casey won't be telling anyone anything. He was found hanging in his cell ten minutes before he was supposed to meet Stan."

Tessa processed that information, her features shifting from anger to frustration and finally to a fearful understanding. Someone hadn't wanted O'Casey to talk. That meant he'd had something to say. Tessa realized that to Jack, that meant one thing.

The danger she was in was very real.

Chapter 6

She woke from a deep, sound sleep to a flood of daylight. Where was she?

Clutching the bright Navaho blanket to her chest, Tessa sat up and peered around, memory clearing like the fog from the stand of pines outside her window. She was in the cowboy room at Chaney's main house. Her last thought, as she'd fallen wearily into the embracing feather sea floating on a carved-wood bed frame, was that Roy Rogers would have felt right at home. The rustic Western influence she'd noticed in the other rooms was distilled in the small corner guest room, right down to its hand-hewn square log walls, red, beige and black quilt-patterned woven rug and rack of antlers. Her belongings were stacked on a barrel-style chair in the corner. She'd been too exhausted in mind and body to put them away last night.

Johnnie O'Casey, the man who might have shed light on her father's murder, was dead.

She remembered him from his trial for possession with intent to distribute. It had been his third strike and he'd known
he was going down. He'd sat at the defense table, his scrawny
body swimming in an orange jumpsuit. But even knowing he
was headed for hard time, he'd smiled. He'd stared defiantly
at her father as he'd made his opening arguments and he'd
smiled like a Cheshire cat. An I-know-something-you-don't-
know smile. There had been solid evidence against him and
that smirk had bothered Tessa throughout the first few days
of testimony.

Then she'd understood when O'Casey took the stand. He
hadn't been smiling. He'd looked nervous and contrite and
wired from the lack of narcotics. As his slick defense attorney led him through the unfortunate choices he'd made to end
up where he was, he'd dropped the other shoe. He'd been
speaking quietly about the network that had provided him
with a cut version of the high-end cocaine he could only
dream of moving on the shadowed streets where his custom-
ers hid in hallways. He'd told slowly, succinctly, how he'd
been waiting for a delivery when he happened to witness a
drop-off and pay-off. The pay-off was made by parties he
hadn't recognized. No amount of bargaining could make him
name that name. But as a smile crept out to tease and dance
around his thin lips, his red-rimmed gaze had flickered to the
prosecutor's table and he'd admitted to getting a good look
at the man who'd delivered the China White. He'd know that
man anywhere. In fact, he'd been looking right at him.

To prevent a mistrial, Tessa's father had withdrawn from
the case. Immediately their lives had become a media circus
with Johnnie O' as gleeful ringmaster. They hadn't been able
to break his insistent story, especially when his pregnant
junkie girlfriend had backed up peripheral details. She hadn't
seen the exchange but she'd provided collaborative testimony.
Having had his say, O'Casey had gone docilely to prison and
the girlfriend had disappeared to places unknown.

But it had been enough to bring down Robert D'Angelo's pristine career.

Despair swamped over Tessa. What now? How was she going to make a case when the witness who gave perjured testimony could never recant his damning tale? No coincidence that his "suicide" should happen just before he was to meet with Stan. Suicide. Like her father. Assisted suicide, no doubt.

A scratching on the slightly open bedroom door had her patting the mattress. She expected Tinker to come bounding in, eager for breakfast. She didn't expect him to arrive wrapped in a child's cradling embrace. He looked fat and sassy, well fed and well content with the attention.

"*Hola,* Miss Tessa. I find your kitty. I give him his breakfast already."

Tension flowed out of Tessa at the sight of the girl's beautiful smile. "Good morning. I'm sure Tinker was glad for the company."

As Rose nestled her cheek into the cat's soft fur, Tessa could see that Tinker wasn't the only one hungry for companionship. She thought about the child out here in the middle of nowhere and wondered.

"How's your ankle this morning?"

"It feels better." And to prove it, she moved across the room, slowly, haltingly, but without any obvious signs of pain. She perched on the edge of the bed, reluctant to set Tinker down even for an instant. Content with the situation himself, the big cat purred like a jackhammer.

"Your English is very good, Rose. How long have you been in the States?"

"I come here with Mr. Jack six years ago. I was just a little girl then."

Tessa smiled. Oh, yes, and she was so old and mature now. "What about school?"

"I do my lessons on the Internet. And sometimes a teacher comes to stay here for a while, like Mrs. Walker who taught

me how to do my numbers. I am a good student, she tells me.
I get all As on my homework. Mr. Jack checks it for me every
night. He says if I want to be a teacher, I have to work very
hard at my lessons."

"Is that what you want to be? A teacher?"

"*Sí.* They have need for teachers in my country. I will
learn here then help my people. I am very lucky to be in such
a place when so many have so little."

Tessa's heart took a twisting turn. She could have been listening to herself talk at that age. Only she'd wanted to be a
lawyer, saving the world in a one-woman crusade for justice.
Though jaded and a bit tarnished, those were still her ideals.

"I think that's a wonderful plan. You will make a good
teacher. What will you teach your people?"

"How to get better jobs. How not to be afraid."

It was hard to swallow the emotion in her throat. "Were
you afraid when you were there?"

"Not all the time, Miss Tessa. Sometimes my friends and
I would pretend that we were models in New York City and
we would have pretty clothes and little dogs and live way up
high in an apartment building. But that was when I was little. I will never be a model because my legs are too short. But
teachers can have short legs, so I will be a teacher."

"I think you've made a very wise career decision." Tessa
pulled up her knees and wrapped her arms around them as she
regarded the preteen. "What about friends, Rose? Who do you
play with here?"

"I am too old to play."

Tessa's smile was bittersweet. "You're never too old to play."

"I have my aunt and Mr. Jack. And I have met other girls
in the chatroom through my online school."

But no flesh-and-blood friends. No peers. No girls to gig-
gle and gossip with. Aren't you lonely? Tessa wanted to ask,
but just looking at the girl, at the way she stroked Tinker with
such gentle concentration, she had her answer.

"Should you be in here, little monkey?"

Rose responded to Jack's scolding tone with a beaming affection. "I was telling Miss Tessa about learning to be a teacher."

"Then show her that you've learned some manners and let her get up and get dressed for breakfast."

With cat in arms, Rose slid off the bed and hobbled obediently to the door. As she passed Jack, he rumpled her hair. A brief fondness crossed his features but was gone too quickly for the girl to notice as she glanced up at him.

"Tell Connie we'll be ready to eat in a few minutes."

"*Sí,* Mr. Jack."

And then it was just Jack in her doorway and Tessa beneath her covers.

He filled the frame with a dangerous and dreamy presence, the latter making the former all the more apparent. This morning, wearing tan Dockers and a navy-blue polo shirt, he looked more like an investment banker than a mercenary trainer. The scent of his aftershave teased up images of soft pine needles and walks hand-in-hand. And the all too observant look he gave her conjured up other images, including Jack Chaney beneath the covers with her.

Very aware that she was clad only in her underwear, Tessa tugged the bedspread higher. Catching the movement, Jack grinned. A heart-stopping, pulse-tripping flash of brilliant white and charm.

"Guess I'd better show some manners, too, and let you get dressed." He still made no attempt to move.

She inclined her head in deference to his mode of attire. "No run this morning?"

"Day off. We've got other work to do."

That vague reply told her nothing. But the sudden tension that crept into his posture said it had something to do with a man hanging in a prison cell.

"Give me five minutes."

Jack nodded.

As he started to turn, Tessa called, "Where's breakfast?"

"Follow your nose."

Thinking she'd be following the crisp scent of his after-shave, as Tessa moved down the wide hallway she was enticed by another mouthwatering aroma. The delicious smell led her into another sun-drenched portion of the house where a slanted, glass-paneled ceiling angled to meet a windowed wall over the kitchen area. And again she was struck by the innovative architectural choices that blended the cozy feeling of a lodge with modern efficiency.

Circling a butcher-block island, the large cook area was a vista of shiny stainless steel, rugged concrete countertops and painted glass-fronted cabinets. Gleaming cookware dangled from an exposed beam above the island and a garden of fresh herbs flourished along the wall of windows. Constanza worked at the industrial-size stovetop, flipping tortillas and an egg mixture filled with flavorful chorizo sausage and peppers. She didn't seem to mind Tinker weaving figure eights around her ankles.

"*Hola,* Miss Tess," she called without missing a toss. "There is juice and coffee on the table."

"Thank you. That smells fabulous."

"*Gracias.*"

Rose already waited in the breakfast nook where a table topped with colorful blue, yellow and white calla lily tiles was flanked by booth seating. Tessa slid in opposite her, gravitating toward the hot carafe of coffee. The only thing that could distract her from that rich fragrance was the sight of Jack Chaney peering over Constanza's shoulder to check on their meal. The fit of the tan Dockers did wonders for his backside.

"Go easy on the sauce, Connie. We don't want to set our guest on fire."

So, she was a guest now. When had that change occurred?

When he'd hustled her up from the bunkhouse without so much as a word? When she'd sat down in the middle of family territory wearing a civilized nubby maroon sweater, black slacks and gold jewelry instead of jogging clothes? She wondered how being Jack's guest differed from being his student and how the change in living quarters would figure into the mix.

"Don't worry, Constanza," she called amiably. "I like it hot."

Jack turned to regard her with raised brows. "Really? A cool cucumber like you? I never would have guessed."

"The tonnage of what you will never guess about me would amaze you," she countered, vigorously stirring cream into her coffee.

His grin flashed wickedly. "I look forward to being constantly amazed then."

Anxious to divert their conversation toward something a little less heated, she remarked, "What I find amazing is this house."

"Thank you. The architects were great at interpreting my ideas."

"You designed this?" Now she was amazed.

"Not completely." He slid in next to Rose in the booth and helped himself to coffee. Tessa couldn't help notice how big and brown his hands were, how quick and efficient his every move. "I put together bits and pieces of places that had impressed me during my travels and they fit it all together. A lot of the inspiration came from a ranch in Montana where I spent a few weeks recovering from…an injury to my leg."

Tessa read between the lines. Probably a gunshot wound.

"I liked the way that place related to nature but I wanted things practical and convenient, too. I wanted lots of private space, lots of glass and wood and good old honest concrete mixed in with raw timber, plaster and Cor-Ten steel. You get the open feeling without sacrificing security."

Hence, all the glass. She surveyed the slanted windows with a new appreciation. The better to see you coming, my dear. "I bet nothing's coming through that, is it?"

His steady stare was her answer.

Bulletproof glass. A sealed panic room. Probably hidden cameras and trip alarms galore. A paranoiac's dream. Was Chaney trying to keep the world out or his own private haven in? Fine for him but was it fair to the little girl?

Plates filled with breakfast burritos smothered in a smoky chipotle sauce with a side of refried black beans and fresh fruit wedges ended conversation until dishes were scoured and stomachs full. Jack leaned back to pat his flat belly.

"Connie, if you cooked like this every day I'd be content to sleep in the sun and do nothing, just like a plough horse out to pasture." He glanced at the floor. "Or this lazy, pampered cat."

"Tinker deserves to be lazy and pampered." Tessa jumped in on the defensive. "He led a hard life in his rather wild misspent youth."

"So did I, but it didn't turn me into a fat domestic content to let the mice come to me."

"That is because you are a cougar not a house cat, Mr. Jack," Rose piped in, enjoying the banter between the two of them.

"A cougar," he mused, liking the sound of that. "Well, this cougar's going to get his claws out if some little girl doesn't get to her studies."

With a squeal of laughter, Rose scrambled across his lap, pausing to hug Constanza on her hurry from the room.

"Cougar," Tessa snorted, sipping her doctored coffee.

"You prefer the timber wolf analogy. Either works for me."

They sat in companionable silence, drinking their coffee while the sun warmed them. Finally, Jack ruined the moment.

"What are you going to do now that O'Casey is dead?"

She stared into her cup while her insides went cold. "Are you suggesting it's time I just give up and leave things the way they are?"

"I'm asking if you have any other solid leads."

"I have some, so you're not off the hook yet, Chaney."

"What are they?"

"Leads."

"What kind of leads?"

"Solid leads."

Jack smiled thinly. "If you had good leads, the police would still be investigating."

"Okay, there are no other leads. O'Casey was my last hope. Happy now?"

He didn't look happy. He looked contemplative. "Because the threats haven't let up, whatever evidence your father had is still out there."

"You act as if you actually care." Frustration lent a bite to her tone. It was petty and unfair to blame him for her dead end but she felt petty and nothing about her father's case was fair.

"Not really," was his dismissive reply. "Just making conversation to entertain my guest."

"Guest, my rear end."

"And a very nice hind end it is, too."

"You're acting like a hind end."

"That's the thanks I get for trying to be helpful."

"Try harder, why don't you? You're the expert in these sorts of things."

"But you didn't hire me for those skills and as I recall, I advised you at the time that they were not for sale."

"I think we need to go practice our sparring. I'd like very much to hit you."

He laughed and leaned his elbows on the back of the booth, annoyingly relaxed and even enjoying himself. At her expense.

"Did your father have a home office?"

Knocked off track, Tessa regrouped some quickly collected thoughts. "Um, sort of. My mother didn't like him bringing work home but I think he'd sneak his laptop in if he was into something…big. Like this case."

"Would he have kept papers there?"

"Not hard copies."

"Disks maybe?"

"Disks maybe."

Why hadn't she considered that? Surely, Martinez's men had by now. And if the information was there…

"I need you to take me to my father's house."

"Stan was going to stop by as soon as your brothers left this morning."

Tessa waved an impatient hand. "She won't let him in. She has no use for Stan or any of the 'street people' we worked with. She might meet him politely at the door but she'd never let him inside her palace. And she'd never let him go through Dad's things."

"And she'd let you?"

"That's what I need to find out."

She sat tense and silent on the passenger side of the Dodge Ram. A quick call to Stan had informed him that they were on their way to the Bloomfield Hills estate. Relieved of that duty, Stan promised to find out all he could about O'Casey's supposed suicide. The coroner would have him on the table later that day and, seeing as how he was an old friend of Stan's, the P.I. was going to hang around in case something useful happened to slip out. Such as signs of forced inducement.

Jack was used to Tessa's headlong enthusiasm when it came to matters of proving her father innocent. Yet she was oddly restrained at the notion of returning to her family home. Too many memories? He wondered but he didn't ask. That was her business and none of his. It was just odd. To get a better feel for the situation, he decided to prompt a little conversation.

"Would your father have left some clue with your mother?"

Tessa laugh was sharp. "I don't think so. My mother is fairly clueless about everything except fashion sense and how to throw the perfect fund-raiser. Like I said, she never took an interest in my father's career except in how it could improve her social status."

That didn't jibe with the pictures Jack had seen of Barbara D'Angelo at her husband's side. She'd been aglow with pride and energy. True, most of the press revolved around her adeptness as a hostess but then not every woman was cut out to be a workaholic dynamo, like her daughter. An oil-and-vinegar situation? Or did rivalry over D'Angelo's attention divide them? Again, none of his concern. He didn't come from an Ozzie and Harriet background so he couldn't cast any stones. Nor could he even guess at what passed for normal behind closed doors. For the last three years of their marriage, his parents hadn't exchanged a word that wasn't two or three decibels above the sound barrier. But he couldn't picture the D'Angelos as yellers. Probably just cool and civil and proper as all get-out.

"Will your brothers still be with your mom?"

"They left for their respective parts of the country early this morning."

"I'm surprised you didn't want to be there to see them off."

"They weren't here to see me." He didn't detect any hostility there, just candid fact. "They were here mostly to do damage control to smooth over all the fuss I made. They share the popular conclusion that I created a conspiracy out of grief. I don't blame them really. They've got their own lives and have been distanced from what's been going on. I didn't want to drag them into it." She paused. "They were also here to make sure our mother didn't fall apart. She collapsed when she heard my father was dead and I don't think she's said a coherent sentence since. I'm surprised she didn't throw herself into the open grave on top of the casket. But that would have meant getting her Chanel suit dirty."

Jack raised a brow at that bit of bitterness but again made no comment. "So his death hit her hard?"

"My mother has spent her life on a pedestal. The thought of not having someone to worship her every move was probably devastating. She's never had to do anything useful or productive unless the media was there to take pictures. I imagine she's at quite a loss without anyone to adore her and out of her depth at the thought of having to balance her own credit card statements. That is if her doctor doesn't have her drugged into a stupor."

"Don't you think that attitude is just a little uncharitable?" He said the words as if it didn't matter one way or the other to him what she thought.

"You don't know her. You didn't have to grow up being measured to the standard of her perfection."

Which made Jack wonder who was doing the measuring, Tessa or her mother? Or was it Robert D'Angelo? He cast a quick sidelong glance at her stony profile and couldn't figure how she might have fallen short. She had looks, brains, tenacity and character by the truckloads. Unless she lost points for Miss Congeniality. Tessa D'Angelo was nobody's vapid party girl. He couldn't picture her batting her eyes and stoking an ego to wheedle a pledge for some innocuous charity. She was all business. Did she think that made her less feminine? Less appealing? Not to any living, breathing male. But maybe it did to her own fragile self-esteem.

Something had inspired the resentment that practically oozed from her pores when her mother was the subject matter.

"It's that one, the Tudor on the right."

They'd entered an exclusive gated community and were

cruising down a manicured boulevard taking sour looks from the yard crews working at the palatial estates. Obviously they didn't feel the big noisy four-by-four belonged in the Lifestyles of the Rich and Almost Famous setting.

Palace was an understatement.

The D'Angelo homestead was an impressive stucco-and-timber three-story in a tax bracket so far above his it might as well have been on Jupiter. A plush lawn sloped gracefully up to meet a circular drive and landscaping out of some home-and-garden magazine. As he approached, he caught a hint of a pool and tennis courts out back, behind the four-stall garage. Though showy and pretentious in scale and address, just like the others in the exclusive cul-de-sac, there was no sign that anyone actually lived here. Had that occurred when Robert D'Angelo died or had it always been a showplace rather than a home?

If she'd been tense before, Tessa was now like one of the white Carrara marble statues gracing the side gardens. Her features were perfectly composed and completely lifeless as if just being here drained the vitality and personality from her. The only movement was her hands, which were winding and twisting the leather strap of her handbag into tortuous knots. Mimicking her insides, perhaps.

He parked the bulky truck at the front door, half expecting some liveried house servant to rush out and chase him away. Or to direct him to the servants' entrance. But the house was quiet with the appearance of being empty. In fact or just in spirit, he wondered.

"Home sweet home," he commented.

Tessa didn't smile or even blink. "Let's get this over with."

He came around the vehicle but she didn't wait for him to open the door. She hopped down and began to approach the double doors with the enthusiasm of going to a tax audit. He fell in beside her. The desire to touch her arm or the small of her back in a show of support was nearly overwhelming but he didn't extend the gesture. He didn't think she was even aware of his presence. Her focus was on the front steps and the foyer beyond. Would she knock or just open the door as if she belonged? *Mother, I'm home.* Somehow he couldn't picture that fond scenario.

The door opened before they reached it and they were met, not by some snooty servant, but by Barbara D'Angelo herself.

Jack wasn't sure what he expected but it certainly wasn't the gorgeous, composed and overjoyed woman standing there. She leaped forward with a glad cry to embrace her daughter.

"Oh, Tessa. Tessa, sweetheart. What a surprise! I'm so happy to see you!"

And from the way Tessa stood rigidly within those perfumed arms, the feeling was definitely not mutual.

Chapter 7

"More coffee, Mr. Chaney?"

Jack shook his head at the elegant woman proffering a silver pot. "No, thank you, ma'am."

Everything about Barbara D'Angelo was elegant and composed and genteel. From Tessa's descriptions he'd expected to find a swollen-eyed wailer draped immobile upon her mourning couch. Though signs of weariness and past weeping were evident, Barbara's smile was genuine.

"I appreciate you bringing Tess home, Mr. Chaney. I see too little of her as it is and under the circumstances…" She drifted off, looking uncomfortable and not wanting to place her guests in the same awkward position. "Stan mentioned on the phone that you thought I might have some evidence of what Robert was working on."

"You spoke to Stan?" Funny, he'd been given the very distinct impression that the private investigator was not welcome in the D'Angelo home. He glanced at Tessa, who was amazingly stoic.

"Oh, we talk at least once a day. Dear man, he's so worried about me. The feeling's mutual, you know. I would hate to think that Robert's death would have any…any adverse effects on him."

She meant sending him back to the bottle. "No, ma'am. I don't see that as happening."

"He speaks very highly of you, Mr. Chaney, and of your father. I remember Michael from when Robert was working his way up and used to spend night and day between the station house and court. I used to take sandwiches down to them."

He blinked, trying to picture the Barbara D'Angelo who sat across from him, in cashmere and silk, carrying food to the overworked at the precinct. But then he looked beyond the perfect makeup and professionally touched-up hair, the designer clothes and jeweled setting, beyond all the surface things, and he saw the kindness in her soft brown eyes, the humanity in her gentle smile. And he could see a woman toting a baby and a parcel of sandwiches. And he saw strength, the deep core determination he saw when he looked at her daughter. Where had Tessa gotten such a skewed idea of her mother?

Even now Tessa was doing everything she could to isolate herself from the gracefully grieving woman. The moment she'd been freed from her mother's hug, she'd led the way into the living room to select a purposefully distant and single chair. Barbara chose the posh white leather sofa and Jack sat opposite on the edge of a flimsy brocaded settee. With Tessa wrapped up in her hostility and Barbara adrift on the huge couch, Jack was at a loss as to how to relate to the two women. So he concentrated on the widow.

"I know questions can be difficult…" he began.

"How can I help you, Mr. Chaney? I told everything I knew, which wasn't much, to the police."

"What was your husband working on before he died?"

"It had to do with that councilwoman he was going to be running against, Ms. Martinez. Robert was a very private man when it came to his work. He preferred to leave it at the office. But I could tell this was really bothering him. He wasn't sleeping well. He'd make phone calls at odd hours of the night. I think they were overseas calls. I heard him speaking Vietnamese. He was terribly upset about something but when I'd ask him, he'd tell me it was nothing. He was lying, Mr. Chaney. There was something very wrong."

"Do you have your phone records?"

"I kept a copy. The police took the originals for their investigation."

"I'll have Stan pick them up. What about the money, Mrs. D'Angelo?"

She shook her head in a disbelieving fashion. "A quarter of a million dollars. It just appeared in our account. It was a wire transfer, but the police were unable to trace the source. We're comfortably set in our lifestyle, Mr. Chaney. Robert doesn't—didn't bring money problems to me but I think he would have mentioned if we'd had a sudden windfall."

"Where do you think it came from?"

"I don't know. We thought it might be an anonymous campaign contribution at first, but when all this nasty business surfaced, all sorts of nasty things were implied. Blackmail, drug money, hush money. Ridiculous, of course. Robert would never have involved himself in any of those things. My husband was ambitious but his integrity was above reproach. He was an honest man and those were the things he spent his career attacking." She took a deep breath and her composure faltered. She stared down at the hands knotted in her lap, where the huge diamond ring she wore reflected the light, and her eyes filled with tears just as dazzling.

Giving her a moment to pull herself together, Jack looked away, to where Tessa sat stiff and unmoved by her mother's pain. And she was the one who finally spoke in a remote, all-business tone.

"Mother, did he bring anything home with him? Papers? A disk?"

Again she shook her head. "It wasn't work he was obsessed with those last few days. It was the past. He was going through his old Special Forces mementos. I thought it odd because he never looked back at that particular time and he never talked about it. His campaign manager was always trying to get him to play up the medals he'd brought home with him. He thought a war hero would sell big. But Robert wouldn't let him. He said to leave the past in the past, that his current record was enough to get him to whatever his future held."

"And yet he went back to the past himself."

Barbara looked up at Jack. "Yes. You're military. You know how impossible it is to get that part of your life completely closed away."

Jack's features tensed. He nodded.

"Robert was very good at it. He never fit in with the military lifestyle but he saw it as a stepping-stone to where he wanted to go. They were in their first year of college, Robert and his roommates Chet Allen and Tag McGee. The war was winding down when Tag's number came up. And just like that, the other two enlisted. They were inseparable back then. I was finishing high school when they went for training and by the time I graduated, I was married to Robert and they were in some jungle a world away. Robert wrote faithfully but he never mentioned the war or what he was doing over there. For all I knew, he could have been on some grand vacation. He wrote about the future, about his plans for us after he got out of law school. It was as if the tour he did in Nam never happened."

"What did happen?"

"He was wounded, nothing serious but enough to send him Stateside, in the same action that killed his friend Chet.

Tag went into some special program and we never heard from him again. I used to look for his name among the casualties and MIAs. I even read the Wall but I never did find out what happened to him. 'He came home,' was all Robert would say. And then he put that part of his life behind him. Until recently."

As delicately as he could, he broached what could not be ignored. "I know it's classified but it's rumored that your husband did a lot of missions across borders we weren't supposed to cross. There were rumors that he made drug connections while he was over there."

"My father would never be involved in drugs." Tessa jumped up from her chair and began to pace the room with a restless energy. Barbara watched her through pain-filled eyes while struggling to restrain her need to go to her, probably realizing the offer of comfort would be rebuffed.

"She's right, Mr. Chaney. Robert would never have done the things they suggested. He saw things in one of two ways. Right or wrong. Drug trafficking was an evil he never would have condoned. Never."

Tessa paused in front of a large, decorative fireplace. There, she studied the photos arranged upon the mantel in varying-size silver frames. They were of family. Portraits of them posed together and candids through their growing-up years. An attractive all-American family. She looked but didn't touch. "Never," she reaffirmed softly.

Jack cleared his throat to get out what he needed to ask. "Mrs. D'Angelo, could your husband have taken his own life?"

He heard Tessa's sharp intake of breath but his focus was on the woman across from him, the woman whose features suddenly aged and twisted with an intense inner anguish. But she answered with a quiet truthfulness.

"Robert was a man to whom image, integrity and respect was everything. He didn't just do a job. He was the job. If he thought those things were compromised, if he thought he couldn't do his job—"

"What are you saying?" Tessa demanded.

Barbara didn't flinch from her daughter's furious outburst. "The thought of the investigation, the knowledge that his career was ruined... Even if he was proven innocent, he'd never successfully run a political campaign. His name would always be linked to scandal and that destroyed every dream he'd ever held. And it destroyed him, too, Mr. Chaney. The idea that people would believe such lies about him, it broke his spirit. Could he have taken his own life? Yes."

Without a word Tessa stormed out of the house. Barbara watched her go, a heartbreaking sadness imprinted upon her perfect features. Then she returned her attention to Jack.

"Do I believe he did? No, Mr. Chaney. Tessa is very much like her father. They're not quitters. Robert was down but he wasn't out. He would have regrouped and he would have fought one spectacular battle. If there was a way for someone else to have been in that room with him, to have pulled that trigger, I would have believed everything my daughter claimed. But it wasn't possible. His office was on the fourteenth floor of a sky-rise. The door was locked from the inside. There was no other way out of it. He was alone in that room when the shot that killed him was fired, no matter what Tess wants to believe." She studied Jack's face. "But you believe her, don't you?"

"Your daughter has a lot of passion behind her purpose. I believe she believes it. I believe someone else believes it, too. Mrs. D'Angelo, are you safe in this house alone?"

She blinked. "Yes, I think so. The community has guards who patrol at night. Robert had a top-notch security system installed. I used to tease him about living in Fort Knox but he'd say he was just protecting his family jewel." The tears returned and she wiped them determinedly away. "Forgive me, Mr. Chaney."

"Yes, ma'am."

"You think I'm in danger?"

"I think I'd feel better if Stan stayed here with you for a little while."

"Mr. Chaney, I don't think that's necessary."

"It would make you feel better, too, Mrs. D'Angelo. You don't want to be alone right now." He put forth his most charming, empathetic smile. "And I'd like you to show Stan everything your husband was looking through."

"Of course." Then her brows lowered. "Is my daughter in danger? Tessa swore to me that the incident at her apartment was just a coincidence. Was it?"

"No, ma'am. I don't believe it was. I think someone believes she has information regarding your husband's death. But I think you might have it and not know it."

Barbara was silent for a long moment. When she spoke, there was no alarm, no fright, in her tone. Just concern. "I'll do whatever I can if you'll make me one promise."

"And what's that, Mrs. D'Angelo?"

"You take care of Tess. You keep my daughter safe."

Now he was the one alarmed. But he kept that discomfort behind his impassive game face. "Yes, ma'am. I plan to."

She was sitting in his truck with all the animation of a crash test dummy.

Take care of Tess. Yes, ma'am.

What was he thinking? Taking care of Tessa wasn't in his job description. And neither was searching out clues to her father's death. She wasn't his problem. He had problems of his own. He jerked open the door to the driver's side with unnecessary force but she never glanced his way as he swung up behind the wheel. The engine growled to life just like his frustrations snarling inside him.

He didn't want to be responsible for this woman.

He took a breath to calm his thinking but unfortunately that inhalation sucked up the scent of her beside him. Warm, desirable female. Vulnerable. Dependent upon him.

He swore softly and put the truck in gear. He'd take her back to the compound. He'd do what he'd been coerced into doing. He'd get her fit and competent and ready for trouble. And he'd send her out into the thick of it without a second thought. No matter what Barbara D'Angelo had made him promise.

He swore again. Tessa D'Angelo was not going to get under his skin.

"You must think I'm a spoiled brat the way I acted back there."

Her quiet self-deprecating tone startled him out of his grim mood.

"You're not paying me to think."

He thought she was gorgeous, gutsy, fierce and...well, yes, a brat.

She rubbed trembling hands over her face. "I don't know what it is about her that brings out the very worst in me."

"Must be a mother-daughter thing." A woman thing. Two women pulling a man between them, both vying for attention he didn't have time to give. At least that's what he'd think if he had any business coming to conclusions.

"She thinks he killed himself. Who'd know better than the grieving widow, right?"

He didn't answer. He felt her gaze but wouldn't meet it. *Stay objective, Chaney. Don't compromise the mission by getting involved. There's no percentage in it.*

"What do you think?"

"Why ask me?" His voice was a little sharper than necessary.

"Because I want to know. Because I need a little perspective right about now."

She was still staring at him. What did she expect? Some sage advice that might just get her killed? Oh, no. No way he was getting pulled into that trap. If he said, *Back down, I think you're spinning your wheels on emotion,* and then a killer went free, she'd blame him for an eternity. If he said, *Stick to your guns,* and those guns turned in her direction…well, hell, he couldn't be damned for more than one eternity, could he? This one was already taken.

"I think I'd like to see his office."

The words just came out, surprising both of them.

"I mean, this whole thing hangs on whether or not someone else had access to your father in that room, doesn't it?"

He hadn't expected her to balk. "The police said it was impossible. I don't know what you think you might find."

"I'm a little bit better than the police when it comes to this sort of thing. But it's up to you. Take a left or a right?"

A left would take them toward the freeway and his refuge. A right would pull them downtown, to the scene of the crime, so to speak.

He glanced at her. Her features were a mask of indecision and something more.

Fear.

"We don't have to—"

But she brushed off his easy out.

"Take a right, Jack. It's time to get back on the horse."

She hadn't been back to the office since the night it happened. She'd made excuses for not returning, logical reasons to stay away. Didn't want to compromise a police investigation. There was nothing there to find. Nothing there to see.

But there was.

She was afraid she was going to see it all again and her fragile soul wasn't ready to endure that agony.

They entered the front lobby. Her heart started beating faster, in a frantic little flutter.

"What's the guard's name?"

Jack's question distracted her from the marquee by the elevator doors. *D'Angelo, Robert.* She glanced at the burly black man in uniform standing at attention behind his desk.

"Maurice."

"And when Maurice isn't here?"

"Gary. He works nights." He'd been working the night she'd gone up in the elevator alone. "The police already questioned them."

"Is this elevator the only way up?"

"There's a service elevator in back that the cleaning crew uses but it has a key lock."

"How about stairs?"

"Two sets." She pointed across the lobby. "There and in back. But the doors are locked at night. Just like the main doors are locked. The guard has to let you in. Only tenants and employees have a key to the garage entrance."

"And you always speak to the guards by name?"

"Yes."

"Good. Always make sure they know you're in the building, especially after hours."

"We have to sign in and out once the doors are locked."

"But not during the day."

"No. Not during the day." She nodded toward the guard. "Hello, Maurice."

"Nice to see you, Ms. D'Angelo," he responded with a polite smile. And that look in his eyes. That sympathetic, you-poor-thing look that she got from those who didn't know what else to say. What could he say? "Sorry your life went down the toilet"? "Don't forget to wash your hands"?

Jack was pressing for the fourteenth floor. "What about alarms?"

"What?"

"What kind of alarms do you have in the building?"

"The usual, I guess. Fire. The one in the elevator."

"Make sure you know where they are so if you need to get some attention, some help, you can make a lot of noise."

Then she understood his questions weren't purely concerned with her father's case. It was to shift her thinking into yellow alert. She stood a bit straighter and swept the lobby with a glance that really noticed who else was in it, to assess potential threat.

"And there are cameras," she added. "Here in the lobby and at the elevators in the parking structure. The police have the tapes from the night my father died."

The doors opened and again Tessa felt the grip of reluctance to go in, to go up to the rooms where such great, ambitious plans had come crashing down. She hesitated, just for an instant, but it was long enough for Jack to notice. He didn't say anything. He didn't offer any of the pat statements meant to comfort and assure that things would be all right. He touched his hand to the small of her back. A simple gesture, one that didn't impel her forward or extend sympathy. The connection was basic, bracing, just like the words he spoke so matter-of-factly.

"Get angry."

Someone had killed her father and, so far, had gotten away with it. They expected her to give up, to back down, to crawl away and hide. Part of her, when faced with what waited on the fourteenth floor, wanted to do just that. But the other part of her began to get mad. She stepped into the elevator car and stabbed the correct button. Jack followed. He hadn't moved his hand from where his fingertips pressed lightly just above the waistband of her pants. Heat and strength flowed from that point of contact. Though they didn't speak as they went smoothly, quickly upward, that continued touch told her what she'd needed to know for a very long time.

She wasn't alone.

The crime scene tape and smudges of fingerprint powder were gone. The door to Suite 1410 looked deceivingly undisturbed, as if it was just another day at the office and as if when she opened it, all would be as it should be inside. The phones would be ringing. Reporters would be waiting, hoping to get a few minutes with the candidate. Hal Storey, their political analyst, would be going over poll sheets planning the next wave to swamp public opinion in their favor. And Robert D'Angelo would be behind his desk, signing paperwork for a harried court clerk while talking plea bargains with the defense team on his speakerphone. His bag lunch would be spread across the files, sandwich still uneaten and going stale. He'd look up and wave her in, into his world, his life, his dreams.

She unlocked the door and opened it to silence.

The lights were off. The smell of an efficient cleaning crew hung in the climate-controlled air. And then Jack asked the impossible.

"Walk me through what happened that night."

She reached out and flipped on the lights, illuminating the scene of her nightmares.

"It was about eight o'clock. I'd signed in downstairs and asked Gary, the guard, about his little girl. She had the measles. It was quiet. I don't remember seeing anyone else. We had a trial the following week, nothing exciting but I had a motion to prepare for the judge and figured I'd draft it before going home. I'd gone out to dinner with the junior partner from another firm."

"His name?"

"Jeff Boetright from Engle, Steiger & Steiger. It was just dinner."

She didn't mention she'd had hopes it could be more. Jeff Boetright, junior partner from Engle, Steiger & Steiger. Out of the blue, he'd called, asking her to take him up on a quiet meal and some conversation. He was handsome, ambitious, funny and she'd needed the distraction from the pressure cooker of campaigning and long hours of paperwork. And, face it, her social calendar hadn't exactly been running over with offers.

But the dinner had been a disaster. Jeff ate, drank and drank and drank office politics. He'd talked about himself and when he'd exhausted that subject ad nauseam, he'd talked about her father. She might well have been an extra place setting for all the use she got during that painfully long meal. Jeff had had no interest in her on any level and apparently had asked her out just to pump her for information on her father's campaign plans. It seems Engle, Steiger & Steiger had just picked up a fat account from Councilman Martinez and the always-scheming Jeff had been looking to score a few points. Well, he hadn't scored any with her. She'd had him drop her off at the office and written off the dinner in her mind as an unpleasant business expense.

"I didn't know anyone was still here. The lights were off and the door to my father's office was closed. Then I heard his voice. I figured he was dictating. He did some of his best thinking after hours, and my mother had gone to some charity event that night so he didn't have to be home. I didn't want to disturb him so I went to my desk and got out the paperwork I needed."

She walked to her big ultramodern command center, a horseshoe of desktop, crowded with computer and communications equipment and file bins. The file she'd come for that night still rested on her blotter, unopened, the case unresolved while substitution of attorney motions were being submitted. She touched the red folder but for the life of her couldn't remember a single detail about the case. Odd. With her near-photographic memory, she could usually recite the trial brief verbatim. She hadn't thought about any of their cases since that night, since the owner of that voice had sent their caseload spiraling off her priority docket. The only case she was interested in was one no one else wanted to take. She closed her eyes and took a breath, letting the sounds of that night come back to her. Her father, his tone sharpening, growing

louder in agitation. And then the other man whose low words
were indistinguishable but still made her go cold with dread
at their implicit threat.

"They were arguing. I couldn't hear what they were saying but my father was very upset. He never raised his voice
in the office or at home but he was shouting."

"Could he have been talking to someone on the speakerphone?"

"I wondered that myself. It was late and he never made ap-
pointments after hours in the office. Over cocktails at his
club, but not here. This was his private sanctuary after five."

But not his and hers. He never encouraged her to stay to
burn the midnight oil with him.

"Then what?" came Jack's soft prompt.

Eyes closed, her senses filled with the atmosphere of that
night, Tessa jerked abruptly. "The gunshot. It was so loud. For
the longest time I couldn't move. I couldn't make myself
consider the significance of that sound. There was a clatter
and a thump then silence. Just silence."

She'd run to the door and found it locked. She'd been calling then, screaming her father's name with only more of that
damning silence to answer. She'd tried using her shoulder as
a battering ram but the panel was solid oak and as she'd discovered, painfully, quite impervious. She'd been sobbing by
then, great gulping sobs that had heaved up from her belly to
claw her throat raw.

An accident. It had to have been an accident. But if he was
all right and was sitting behind his desk chagrined because
he'd foolishly discharged his pistol, why hadn't he answered
her frantic cries?

"I called Gary. I told him to come up with the keys. I
didn't say why. I guess I hoped it wouldn't be necessary to
call the police. My father was a staunch supporter of gun control. Imagine how it would have looked in the paper if he'd
injured himself with his own handgun. That's what I was

thinking at the time. I was thinking of how to protect his image, not how to save his life." Her recriminating words came to an awful grinding halt.

"There was no way you could have known, Tessa." He said it with a simple, get-over-it directness. And somehow she was able to take hold of her galloping emotions. She glanced at him through eyes bright with pain and confused horror.

"No, I had no idea. Never in a million years could I have guessed what we'd find when Gary opened that door." Her words choked but she was able to swallow and continue almost matter-of-factly. "There was so much blood. I was shocked. I remember thinking my father would never have left such a mess. He was always so meticulous about his work space. Funny the things you think about."

"Yes, it is," he agreed gently. He continued in the same tone. "Where was the gun, Tessa?"

"He had it in his hand. I knew he owned one. He'd bought it for my mother but she'd refused to learn how to use it or to have it in the house. So he kept it here in his desk."

"Did anyone else know he had it?"

"I don't know, Jack. It wasn't something that just came up in conversation. He wasn't the kind of man who would have a gun, or who would advertise that he had one. It would have been on record somewhere that it was in his possession. He wouldn't have had it in the building without going through the proper channels."

"But he knew how to use one."

"Oh, yes. He was a marksman in the service."

"Did you stay with him until the police arrived?" Another quiet yet firmly asked question.

"Yes. Gary went into the outer office to call 9-1-1. I didn't want to leave my father alone."

"Did you move anything? Did you notice anything out of place?"

She thought a moment, forcing her mind to go over the gruesome scene incrementally. "No."

"Tessa, was the speakerphone on?"

She met his gaze fully. "No."

"Think carefully. Had there been any repair work done in the building in the month before your father died? Not just in your office but anywhere."

"I don't remember."

"Who would know?"

"Maurice would have a list of any repair or maintenance crews that were in after hours."

"It wouldn't have to be after hours."

Then he simply stood, taking in the room. Floor, ceiling, walls, windows. And she could see him thinking, *If I were a predator, where would I hide?*

"How could he have gotten out of the room, Jack? There's only one door and he didn't go past me. The windows don't open and the duct work is too small. How the hell did he get out of the room?"

His gaze cut from the single door to the rectangular air vent to the large windows looking down over the city. He went to that clear vista to place fingertips against the glass as he surveyed the world below. He made no comment, offered no suggestion. Frustrated, Tessa threw up her hands.

"A ghost. That's what the police said. I was chasing ghosts. Well, I don't believe in them."

"I do," was Jack's surprising reply. "I've seen them and what they can do." He turned away from the window, his expression tightly shut down, his stare intense. "Can you get a list of any workers who were in the building?"

"Sure." Hope and excitement surged inside her. "What are you thinking, Jack?"

"I'm thinking plenty. I'm saying nothing. Not yet. Let's get that list. I want to drop it off with someone."

Pumped with expectation, Tessa never thought to ask whom.

* * *

"What do you think? Think you can do a little homework for me?"

"You never asked for help when you were a kid. I'd almost given up on ever being of any use to you."

"Cry me a river, Pop. Just figured you'd jump at the chance to put that new computer of yours through its paces."

"Not much makes me jump these days." Michael Chaney patted the arms of his wheelchair and grinned. "Kind of out of practice." He leaned around his son to study Tessa where she stood just inside the doorway to his apartment. He lived in a tidy single bedroom unit with full handicapped access. Pictures of his son in military uniform marched proudly across the painted walls. They shared the same broad white smile meant to charm ladies out of their panties. That smile softened. "You look like her."

Tessa gave a start of surprise. "Who?"

"Your mother. A fine lady. Made great tuna on rye."

Tessa said nothing to interfere with his memories of Saint Barbara who hadn't touched a can of tuna in twenty-five years and probably couldn't find the bread drawer. Nor did she correct his lack of visual perception.

"I was sorry to hear about your dad," he continued with real feeling. "What a waste. I'm glad Jack's going to help you make things right."

"Actually, you and Stan will be doing that," his son amended.

"The legwork?" Again, the grin at Jack's exasperation. "Happy to do anything I can to help out one of the good guys. Robby D'Angelo was one of the best and it makes me sick to hear what they've been saying about him. You give us a couple of days and we'll come up with what you need. And don't you worry, little lady. My boy will take good care of you. He's one of the good guys, too, even though he tends to forget that once in a while."

"I'm working for her, Pop, not married to her."

The elder Chaney winked at Tessa. "Same thing. And you could do worse."

"He's teaching me to take care of myself, Mr. Chaney. And then I'm going to take care of whoever killed my father."

After considering her tough talk, Michael Chaney nodded. "Vengeance is mine."

"Not vengeance. Justice."

"Sometimes that's the same thing. Jack will watch your back just like Stan watched mine. You give 'em hell, little lady."

"Why are you getting yourself and now your family so involved in this, Jack?"

Busy negotiating traffic, Jack didn't spare her a glance. "Is that what I'm doing?"

"It's not that I don't appreciate—"

The rest of her planned dismissal was cut off as Jack looked into the rearview mirror and froze. His sudden low curse was followed by a curt warning.

"Hang on."

The impact to the rear of the truck threw her against the wrap of her seat belt and knocked the breath from her. Almost immediately they were struck again. Jack fought the wheel and managed to swing them into the next lane of rush-hour motorists. A big sedan pulled up alongside them. The windows were darkly tinted. Tessa couldn't see the driver. She cried out, gripping the dash as the other vehicle purposefully slammed into the passenger door. Hemmed in on all three sides, Jack had no maneuvering room and struggled to stay in their lane as they were battered twice more. Then, with an exit fast approaching, he gave the wheel a yank to the right.

The Ram lived up to its name, bashing into the sedan with enough power to shove the vehicle off onto the shoulder, smoke billowing out from under the hood. The truck barreled up the off-ramp but instead of making good their escape, Jack cranked the wheel, spinning the Ram in a tight one-eighty to confront their assailant. He revved the motor meaningfully.

Seeing the tables turned, the driver of the crumpled car gunned the engine, sending the vehicle careening back into traffic. In a near suicidal move, the car executed a U-turn and amid the screech of brakes and blare of horns merged with southbound traffic.

Tessa expelled her breath noisily.

For a moment they idled on the exit ramp facing the wrong way. Then Jack edged back onto the highway much to the surprise of several drivers starting up the ramp. As he blended into the flow of bumper-to-bumper he muttered, "Damn rush-hour traffic. Now you know why I don't live in the city."

Chapter 8

They didn't discuss the vehicular assault. It didn't need to be brought out in the open. Someone had been watching either Tessa's mother's house or the office. They'd seen her with Jack and had followed, waiting for a chance to use traffic as their weapon. With a less skilled driver behind the wheel, they might have succeeded. If Tessa and Jack had been in her Lexus, they would have been a highway statistic and no one would have been the wiser as to the cause. Another convenient accident and problem eliminated. What they didn't yet realize, Tessa decided, is that not only did they fail, they had created a much bigger, more dangerous problem. They had tangled with the wrong guy.

Rubbing her shoulder where it ached from the cut of the seat belt, Tessa glanced at her somber-faced driver. His features could have been cut from a block of ice with a chain saw. She knew he had never wanted her troubles to become his and yet they'd encroached upon him steadily, bringing her under his care, into his house and now to her rescue. And the tightness in his squared jaw said he didn't like having any of those situations forced upon him. Whether it was out of obligation to Stan or because, as his father said, he was one of the good guys and couldn't help himself, he'd given up his intensely private life to try to make some sense out of the chaos that was her own. And he didn't like it. In fact, he probably resented the hell out of it and her. She wouldn't blame him. This wasn't what he'd signed on for.

"I want to start training again in the morning."

He didn't look at her. His response was as flat as the press of his lips. "Fine."

And that was the last that was said until they pulled in at the compound. Jack got out to inspect the damage to his already battered truck. The bumper had a new wrinkle but her door was as creased as his aggravated brow. Without a word, he went around to the back of the truck once more and returned with the dented license plate in hand. At her questioning look, he finally relented.

"They can't trace this here. It's registered to my office address. I've been meaning to get a more upscale location anyway."

What did he mean? That he suspected they would vandalize his place in the city in hopes of intimidation? They didn't know Chaney. Tessa sensed that when they messed with something of his, it was like poking a sleeping predator with a stick. And he wouldn't be content to go back to sleep until he'd had every last one of them for dinner.

"Maybe I should leave."

"Now there's a smart idea." He started for the house in great angry strides. After a moment's hesitation, she ran after him.

"I just don't like the idea of putting Rose in danger by my being here."

"Well, I don't like it, either."

"So maybe I should—"

"What?" He spun to face her. The fierceness in his expression set her back a step. "Run around in circles with a target on your back until they take you out like they did your old man? I never thought you were stupid. Was I wrong?"

"No. I'm not stupid." But he made her feel that way. All she wanted to do was to protect him. "I was just trying to give you an out."

"Damned decent of you. But it's a little late for that." He started away again then turned back to explain with a terse simplicity. "It doesn't matter now. They've seen me. If they're professionals, and I know they are, they'll recognize one of their own. They're going through military databases right now trying to figure out who I am. But unless their clearance is higher than God's, they're not going to find me. And they're not going to find this place. And unless you do something stupid, they're not going to find you."

"I'm sorry, Jack."

Her soft-spoken words derailed his anger. "For what?"

"For intruding. It wasn't my intention."

He stared at her, his dark gaze engulfing her. Then he threw her best intentions back at her. "Wasn't it?"

She let him go, watching his determined retreat without the means to argue against his accusation. She had hoped he'd get involved. She needed his help, his expertise. She needed, desperately, the sense of balance and security he brought, even reluctantly, into her life. Now she had what she wanted. Too late to bemoan the fact that she hadn't earned his trust or gained his permission first.

She'd have to live with his disapproval. And with her own doubts.

"Ms. D'Angelo, you come up now for dinner," Constanza called from the porch.

Dragging the weight of both disappointment and doubt with her, Tessa went up to the house. Constanza led her to the dining room where a huge walnut table and its surrounding bent-willow chairs commanded a view of the tangled forest through a wall of glass panels. The atmosphere was again that soothing mix of rustic comfort and modern simplicity. Rose sat in one of the hand-crafted chairs with Tinker in her lap. Her expression lit up in welcome.

"*Buenas noches,* Miss Tessa."

"*Hola,* Rose." She slipped into the seat across from the girl and her fickle pet. Her glance touched on the empty chair at the head of the table. "Where's Mr. Jack?"

"He is making some phone calls. He said he would join us soon. Must be important business for him to miss Aunt Connie's *vindo de pescado.* It's a fish stew she cooks on the grill and is his favorite."

"Must be important," Tessa agreed. And most likely, it involved her.

A silent Constanza carried in a fragrant bowl and ladled up portions for the three of them while Rose chattered on about her day.

"I have been writing a report on tornadoes. Have you ever seen a tornado, Miss Tessa? Me neither, but winds knocked down some of our trees last year and took away our power for a week. They say one touched down just north of here. Would you like to read my report?"

"Rose, Ms. Tessa doesn't have time for that," Jack's smooth tone intruded. He slid into his seat and began to dish up his stew. "Smells great, Connie."

"Of course I have time," Tessa assured the crestfallen youngster. And immediately Rose perked up and attacked her dinner with enthusiasm. The poor lonely thing was as hungry for the attention as she was for the delicious meal. Both filled necessary parts of her growing body and soul. "You can show me after we finish eating." She glanced up. "If it's all right with Mr. Jack."

Jack waved his permission. He seemed distracted, no doubt

by his telephone conversation, and spent the rest of the meal in silent thought. She understood his desire to keep such things from Rose but would that also apply to her? A man like Chaney dealt in secrets and knew how to keep them well. If he didn't consider her as need-to-know, she would never know. And she didn't like being kept out of the loop.

Once the meal was finished and Tinker was contentedly lapping up the remains, Rose caught her hand and tugged until Tessa followed her upstairs to her room. Was Jack's up here, as well? Tessa wondered, noting several other closed doors.

Stepping into the child's room was another refreshing surprise, like wandering unexpectedly into a jungle paradise. The wallpaper was bright topical colors, vivid green banana tree fronds and vines blossoming with splashes of yellow, orange and crimson. Toucans, spider monkeys, pythons and panthers frolicked on the dazzling canopy over the bed. The wall behind the bed was a mural of a waterfall complete with rainbow and brilliant birds in flight. Mobiles hung from the ceiling and the movement of air from the opening door had the egrets, flamingos and parrots dancing and wheeling around.

"You like?" Rose asked, delighted by her reaction. "Mr. Jack made it for me so I wouldn't miss home so much."

"Do you miss it?"

"Sometimes but not so much anymore. The time I was there is like these walls, pretty but not real."

And Tessa's heart softened to think Jack would expend so much effort to make a lost little girl less afraid.

What was Rose to the cold-eyed ex-operative? Why would her happiness matter so much to a man who preferred to keep the world at a careful distance? A more pertinent question would be, what had Rose's mother been to him? Obviously someone important enough to obligate bringing her child into his home, if not into his heart.

What kept Jack from loving the precocious little girl?

Tessa couldn't believe it was disinterest. She had seen affection in his gestures and in his reactions before his self-protective mechanisms slammed into place. And how sad for Jack that he felt he had to hold himself away from caring about the one individual who so obviously adored him completely, without reservation.

Was that what his profession had taught him or was it something deeper, more personal? Such as the abandonment of his own mother?

Determined to give the girl the full benefit of her attention, Tessa perched on the edge of the canopy bed and listened with real interest as Rose read her report. The girl didn't just read. She taught. Tessa observed a future educator in the bud, one who would blossom beautifully with the right encouragement. Would she find it here, in this unconventional household where her only companions were a somber aunt, a taciturn guardian and a computer?

That computer, the link to her playmates and schoolmates, gave an impatient beeping from its place of honor on the far wall.

"I have a study group chat in five minutes," Rose announced, then appeared to struggle with a dilemma. She glanced at the nineteen-inch flat screen then at the living, breathing company seated on her bed, torn between the two.

Tessa smiled gently. "You have fun with your friends. I'll see you later."

That was all it took to send the girl bounding to her desk to hurriedly sort through her books and papers and switch on the screen.

Tessa slipped from the room unobserved and found her way back to the dining room. Jack was standing in front of the windows, cup of coffee in hand, staring out into the night. He heard her approach and waited while she poured a cup of fragrant brew for herself.

"She's a bright little girl," Tessa began as a neutral overture to conversation. But Jack wasn't in a conversational mood.

"It's not good for her to get too attached to you."

"Better that she be here all alone, detached from you?" She struck back, hurt by his not-so-subtle warning to back off.

"Rose is not your concern."

"Is she yours? Are you her legal guardian?"

She saw him flinch slightly and pressed ahead ruthlessly. "How did you get her out of South America?"

"No one was there to miss her."

"So you just took her? You smuggled her in like some artifact or undeclared merchandise?"

"I gave her a home, something she wouldn't have gotten down there."

"Is this her home…or just someplace you let her stay?"

He looked at her then and the fury in his dark eyes was as palpable as a destructive force of nature. "That, again, is none of your business. Rose is my responsibility and I've seen to her every need."

"Except for love. Do you love her, Jack? How could you not? Or was it her mother that you cared for?"

His hand closed around her upper arms in a move so fast and unexpected it made her gasp. But it was his tone, low and icy, that frightened her.

"Look. I haven't butted in to your business. I haven't asked any awkward questions about your relationship with your family, have I? So have a little respect for mine or I'll send you packing so quick you'll be meeting that pretty little backside of yours on the way out. Understand?"

"Perfectly."

Whether prompted by her frigid reply or the realization that he'd stepped over the line, Jack released her with a final warning. "This is not your family or your house. You have no say in what goes on here. You have the right to an opinion and the right to keep it to yourself. Exercise it."

* * *

Exercise it.

The words burned in Tessa's brain as her stride gobbled up the five-mile run. She didn't look at Jack's delectable backside. Her stare skewered between his shoulder blades.

How dare he come on strong to her? Did he think to scare her? To intimidate her? Or was he just trying to bluntly put her in her place, a place that didn't involve living in his house, sitting at his table and daring to criticize his rules or, heaven forbid, break them? The omnipotent Jack Chaney, above reproach, beyond the reach of real emotion.

Well, she didn't want a place in his life nor did she want to wake up whatever might substitute for feeling within his ice-cold interior. She wanted to learn to stay alive. To not be afraid. To stay angry.

And she was still burning when they faced one another on the mats.

Jack was all competent instructor as he explained, "When you're in close with an opponent, body leverage should do most of the work in a basic takedown."

All calm and cool as if he'd never grabbed her. As if he'd never gotten in her face to issue a fierce ultimatum.

"Throw a punch."

With pleasure.

Jack parried her jab easily. His right hand caught the back of her neck, propelling her down into the pretend pump of his knee kick.

"Bring your left forearm under his right arm and bring it up to a twelve o'clock position. At the same time, keep his head down with your right hand at six. He's stretched out and helpless and it's time to take him down. Turn him inside and drop him to the ground."

With little effort, he had her on her back. When she was face-up and vulnerable, he kept her arm pinned against his shin and simulated a knee strike to the body and elbow strike to the head.

"You want to bring your opponent under control, not roll around with them for ten or fifteen minutes. When you've got him on his back, place yourself at a ninety-degree angle with your upper body on his chest. Lock your right arm behind his head and place the bone of your left forearm across his neck for a choke hold. Make sure your head is down and in tight to your elbow so he can't reverse the hold. Got it?"

As soon as the pressure was off, Tessa pushed him to the side and trapped his right arm under her bottom leg and their bodies tight together. She whipped her arm around his head and locked it in place by gripping her opposite forearm.

"I read ahead," she told him smugly.

His surprise was monumental but only momentary. With a toss of his shoulders for leverage, he was on top of her, chest-to-chest at a ninety-degree angle. He had her left wrist in his right hand, his left arm snaking under her upper arm so that he could secure her with the slightest pressure. No matter how much she wiggled, she couldn't get free without bringing exquisite pain shooting through her left arm.

She stopped wriggling beneath him. The moment she went still, so did he and awareness of their proximity stole their wind more effectively than a straight blast punch from the sternum. His grip eased gradually from her wrist as if he wasn't sure she wouldn't try another attack. Attacking wasn't foremost in her thoughts. She was at a shameless white level and vulnerable to whatever he might attempt while lost in his dark, smoldering gaze. Her mouth softened and began to part.

Then he was up and off her. By the time he put down his hand, her senses had returned.

Get angry.

She saw the creased pant legs stepping into her field of vision.

She saw her father's impassive face as he closed the door to his office, shutting her out time and time again.

She saw the gun in his hand and the gore on his desk.

She saw the faces of the police investigators as they listened to her story and tried to politely hide their disbelief.

She saw Jack's hard features levering close to her own.

Exercise it. Take every advantage.

He pulled her to her feet but before he could release her hand, Tessa twisted hers so her fingers closed around his wrist. She leaned ahead slightly just until he was off balance then jerked his arm toward her. At the same time her other palm flashed up to catch him under the chin and her fingers hooked toward his eyes. She heard his exclamation but momentum drove her. Momentum and just plain anger. Her elbow was already swinging a wicked arc toward his temple. She'd meant to pull it back at the last minute but she'd underestimated the adrenaline pumping through her system. She connected with an eyeball-rolling force that actually staggered him. He was too good at hand-to-hand for her to ever bring him to his knees so she relished this small victory for its full female empowering value.

Until she stepped back and saw his eyes all squinty and teared up.

"Oh, no! I didn't mean to poke you."

He blinked repeatedly and massaged the rapidly discoloring orbits. "Don't apologize, Tess. You did good. I've never had a student get through before. I'd applaud but I think you blinded me."

Ravaged with guilt, she pulled his hands down and leaned close to assess the damage. "Look at me. Oh, you big baby. I didn't hurt you that badly."

His hands twisted to capture her wrists and before she knew it, she was on her back with the breath knocked from her.

And then his mouth was on hers and she couldn't have taken a breath if she'd wanted to.

Chapter 9

Though Tessa hadn't known it a heartbeat before, the kiss was exactly what she'd wanted. Needed. Longed for.

And just as she'd guessed, the man could kiss.

He sucked the oxygen from her lungs, the power of thought from her brain. All she could do was react and respond to the heat spreading wildly from the fluttering pit of her belly. Heat that felt so good, so right after being cold inside for so long. That's what Jack was—power, heat, the very symbol of control—and she clung to those things and to him with a greedy desperation. Perhaps a little too desperately, for Jack levered back to regard her through a shuttered stare. Cautious, oh, so cautious. The lone wolf once more.

"Is this how you reward all your students?" she quipped, hoping the levity would relieve the edgy tension she could feel building between them.

Taking the out like the coward he was, Jack grinned.

"Only the ones who look as good in a sports bra as you do."

Grateful for the chance to make a graceful escape, Jack rocked back onto his heels and stood, bringing Tessa up with him. She stood close, so close a man wasn't meant to maintain his sanity while the taste of her still lay moist and sweet upon his lips. If he reached out, she'd be in his arms. He could tell by the willing tilt of her head, by the tempting part of her mouth, by the sexy combination of conflict and desire swirling in her heavy-lidded gaze.

Oh, hell.

He took a saving step back, both physically and emotionally. Surprise became confusion and then a reluctant relief in her uplifted stare. She wasn't ready for this complication any more than he was. Somebody had to show some restraint. And dammit, it had to be him.

"Since you've been such a good girl and an overachiever by doing extra homework, I think it's time we moved on to another section."

Just as he'd hoped, thoughts of passion were pushed aside by anticipation.

"Feel up to handling a handgun?"

"I can handle anything you've got, Chaney."

His wolfish grin brought an appealing flush of color to her cheeks. "We'll see."

She was a natural. Once Tessa got over her inherent fear and distaste at handling the textured grip of the .40 Smith & Wesson, she found the 24.7 ounces of firepower a comfortable fit in her hand.

"We'll try a semiautomatic first. This is an autoloading pistol instead of a wheel gun revolver. They're a little more complicated and some women have a difficult time loading a magazine. Women aren't as strong as men and sometimes they have a hard time shoving the magazine in with enough force to get a good seating or have trouble pulling back the slide then releasing it smoothly."

Tessa smacked in the clip with the palm of her hand and worked the slide quickly. "No trouble."

He fought the urge to grin. She was showing off. But that wasn't a bad thing. It meant she felt confident and comfortable. A real Dirty Harriet. She was making his day.

"You've got ten rounds plus one as opposed to five in a wheel gun. Let's hope you don't have to use any of them."

"If I do, I want to make sure I can hit what I shoot at. And stop it."

"That's the plan. A lot of times when guns are purchased for self-protection, whether by a man or a woman, the new owners make the mistake of feeling safe just by having the gun tucked away in a drawer or purse and never bother really learning how to use it. You have to know how to control a gun or it controls you."

"Show me."

So he did. For the rest of the afternoon he went through a cleaning and reassembly drill half a dozen times before he'd let Tessa attempt it. She got it right the first time. Then they went to the range. With her percussion earphones draped at her neck, she listened to Jack explain correct stance and proper sighting before he passed the pistol to her.

"Now, slow down and breathe. There's never a rush. Do it right the first time and there won't be a second. No. Like this."

He stepped up behind her, shadowing her stance and the extension of her arm. His hand covered hers like a snug-fitting glove. His cheek nestled in against her hair. And her breath started chugging like crazy.

"Relax. Deep breath. Squeeze the trigger."

The recoil and sound were both bigger than she'd expected. Her body jerked back against Jack, finding him a solid, immovable force. She'd shut her eyes without realizing it and when she opened them, she got a surprise.

"I hit it."

"Not pretty but clean. Again."

She took a breath, expelled it and let the tension flow from her. Contrarily, her awareness of her instructor continued to increase.

"Concentrate. You've got a powerful tool in your hand. Control it."

His hand was still over hers. Her mind was adding tool and Jack into the same equation. Finding focus was more difficult with his hips wedged in behind hers. Finally she couldn't think of anything but the mesmerizing rhythm of his heartbeats.

"I've got it," she told him a bit testily. "If you could just step back a little."

He complied with more reluctance than she'd have expected after the hurried way he'd backed off from the unplanned kiss of that morning.

"Show me what you got," he prompted from a safe distance.

And after she'd gone through half a dozen clips, he was suitably impressed by what he saw. "Nice shooting there, Annie Oakley. You've got the makings of a lethal little lady."

She ejected the spent clip and eyed the tight pattern on the target with approval. She was thoughtful rather than exuberant. "It's not hard when you're staring down the barrel at a piece of paper that's not shooting back."

"And that's a lesson in itself. Don't get overconfident. Target shooting isn't like aiming at another human being no matter how much that piece of humanity may need to be shot. You're going to hesitate. You're going to be afraid you'll freeze up. That's why practice is so important. If the moves are second nature, your conscience won't have time to second-guess your brain. She who hesitates is—"

"Dead," she finished for him. "That's not going to be me. I won't freeze up." Not again. She slapped in a fresh clip and fired off a rapid spat of bullets. By now, she was used to the kick and relished the buck against her palm. The recoil made her feel empowered, in control, both things having been absent from her life for quite some time.

And instead of being threatened by or uncomfortable with her newfound confidence, Jack demanded it from her. He equated strength and femininity in a way no man she'd known before ever had. Those she'd met and considered dating had shied away if she allowed her ambitions to flare. Power and self-assuredness was an unattractive trait in their eyes. But not in Jack's. When he looked at her, she saw his respect, saw his admiration for the work she was doing. When she failed and had the courage to come back again, more determined, she earned his unspoken approval. And that encouragement was like an aphrodisiac to her long-starved sense of self.

She wanted no part of the kind of relationship her parents had shared, with her father in the limelight and her mother on a delicate pedestal. She'd always wanted a man who'd be her partner in all things—from the bedroom to the courtroom, supporting her emotional needs and her desire to achieve her own successes. But somehow, just like her mother, she'd let those dreams escape her to help the charismatic Robert D'Angelo attain his. It never occurred to her to resent him for it. They'd shared the same goals, the same quest for justice, and meeting them through him had been enough.

Then.

But how about now? Was she so insistent upon this hunt for his killer to forestall choosing the direction the rest of her life would take? Alone.

She wasn't afraid of the future, she told herself. But she had an unsettled score with the past to take care of first. She couldn't move ahead until she freed herself from the obligations she dragged behind her. Once that was done, once she'd seen her father's murderer in jail, she would be released to pursue whatever dreams might come her way. Her glance canted toward the devastatingly handsome Jack Chaney.

Even impossible dreams.

But she had no time for them now. Now she had to stay focused, to stay strong for her father's memory, even as the memory of Jack's kiss rattled through her like one of Rose's tornadic systems.

Jack was an enigma. He'd vowed to be indifferent to her cause yet had been pivotal in putting her unofficial investigation back on track. He'd saved her life with his expert handling of the truck on the freeway. Even now, he provided a safe haven in which she could hide to rebuild her battered confidence and strengthen mind and body. All he asked was that she stay out of his business, respect his privacy. Easy to agree to, hard to accomplish when everything about him sparked her professionally hewn curiosity.

What made a man like him, forged in combat and duty, step away from all the things that shaped him and gave him purpose? What brought him to this place to retreat from the world and the risks entailed by living in it? Was he hiding, too, or just healing?

Tessa glanced up toward the stone-and-cedar house, to where Rose had been watching them while she did her homework. She sensed the answer lay with the child and her aunt and with Jack's responsibility for them. He wanted her to believe all the unflattering preconceptions she'd brought with her. That he was a cold, detached killer intent on training other killers to do their job more efficiently. That he'd tolerate no intrusion of his work into his life. Yet he'd brought her up to live under his roof and to sit at his table. He'd said that he didn't care about her problems. Yet he'd put himself in harm's way to help in solving them. He'd said that he didn't care about her. Yet he'd given her a kiss that rocked her world.

Did he live by rules that only he was allowed to break?

She'd never been a rule breaker. She'd established her whole life, her career, her purpose around them. She played hard but she played fair. And so had her father. Now he was dead and she was being stalked by his killer. And the man to whom that mattered most didn't seem to care about anything.

She smiled tightly at the irony.

"I think we're done for the day, Annie O. Connie expects us to be at her table on time and to be smelling presentable."

"A shower sounds great. As soon as I clean Betsy."

"Betsy?"

She held up her pistol. "I feel like we're on a first-name basis now."

He chuckled and then his expression grew serious. "You did good today. Stan told me you could rise up to any challenge. He was right."

"And here you were hoping I'd be crying for my mamma after the first day." She smiled again, a bit ruefully. "You were almost right."

"Glad you were able to prove me wrong. Believe it or not, I always admit it when I am. And you thought I had no character at all."

She studied him, taking in his half-smiling smirk, his cocky stance, his I-dare-you attitude. Character? He oozed with it. It was as much a part of him as the innate sensuality that had her long-dormant fantasies spinning. Why try so hard to hide it behind the brusque indifference? Was he ashamed of being one of the good guys or did he believe he was no longer qualified to be among that number?

"You are definitely a character, Mr. Chaney. If you'll excuse me, I've got a gun to clean."

"What a turn-on. I love it when you talk dirty."

Did he? Was he even halfway serious? She couldn't tell. His dark gaze gleamed with amusement and more. It was the *more* that made her think again of his kiss and how good passion tasted on him. She was hungry for more but realized she would have to settle, at least for now, with whatever Constanza had simmering on the stove.

Dammit, Jack Chaney. Wanting you wasn't supposed to be part of the bargain.

* * *

With Betsy oiled and carefully stowed away, Tessa indulged in a long, steamy shower. She hurt. A spectacular bruise had formed below her shoulder blade from where she'd been thrown against the Ram's seat belt. The other aches and pains left no outward marks but betrayed her every time she tried to move. She felt like a punching bag.

And then there were the other aches and pains. The ones chafing out of sight but never out of mind as her sexuality rumbled back to life at this most inopportune time.

Jack was beating her up from the inside out.

With her hair bound in a towel and a short terry robe covering her scented and moisturized skin, she left the bathroom and ran smack into the object of her frustrations. He started right out with a rapid-fire dialogue.

"Your building had the heating and cooling systems checked a month before your father died. My dad authenticated that request. But no one authorized a recheck two weeks later. Whoever was crawling around inside the guts of your building that second time wasn't supposed to be there."

Tessa forgot all about her raging hormones. "And you think that second man was the killer?"

"Perhaps. Or just someone checking out the lay of the land. But I'm betting it's our boy. Pros like to do their own on-site walk-throughs. And if it was him, we might get lucky enough to catch him on tape. Stan's picking up the surveillance videos from the police department and a copy of the building schematics. I want to see what our friend saw when he was planning his little ghost walk. If we know how, we're closer to who."

Light-headed with excitement, Tessa whispered, "And when we know who—"

"We nail his ass."

"Yes!"

Without thinking, she whipped her arms around his neck

to hug him in jubilant celebration. They had clues. They were actually closer to pinning the crime upon the guilty party.

For a moment Tessa's elation surpassed every other emotion in Jack.

And then two realizations sank in.

Not only didn't Jack mind her impulsive embrace, parts of him were hugely in favor of it.

And he'd said *we*.

We.

What was he thinking?

He hadn't meant to jump on the D'Angelo bandwagon quite so completely but when he saw her coming out of the misty bathroom, her skin aglow with heat and nothing to separate it from his stare but a scrap of terry cloth, his mind went maddeningly blank.

When she'd bumped into him and those soft contours yielded to his tougher terrain, he'd started babbling like a schoolboy trying to score points with a favorite teacher. Of course, that wasn't the kind of scoring he wanted to do in this case.

We.

He might well have signed on the dotted line to enlist in her perhaps-not-so-foolhardy campaign. Foolhardy or not, justified or not, that still didn't make it his fight. He hadn't taken on a reckless challenge to impress a girl since…ever. But something about the brave yet vulnerable, fierce yet fragile Tessa made him want to strut just a little. Hell, a lot.

And with her pressed up tight against him, her damp cheek to his neck, and his hands curved carefully around the lift of her rib cage, he wanted a lot more. He wanted her without the terry cloth. He wanted her hot and moist and naked and eager to share a lot more of those soul-stealing kisses. He wanted her without the politics, without the soapbox, without the memory of her father standing between them.

And he guessed she wanted pretty much the same thing or she wouldn't have nudged her hips into him where he was ready and raging for release.

He didn't think anything could deflate that enthusiasm.

"Mr. Jack?"

Passion liquefied and swirled right down the drain. Just as quickly, Tessa hopped a neutral distance away, her flushed cheeks conveying an equal guilt.

Jack turned to face the perplexed girl. He could see her confusion, her need to hear him explain away what she'd seen but he couldn't find the words.

"What is it, Rose?"

"A phone call for you."

"I'll take it in my study." And he hurried away from both females who asked so much without saying a word.

Rose confronted the blushing and next-to-undressed Tessa with a blunt question.

"Are you Mr. Jack's girlfriend now?" The slightest hint of adolescent jealousy growled beneath those words.

"Goodness no." Her surprise was genuine enough to have the girl relaxing. "He just gave me some very exciting news and I guess I got a little carried away and hugged him. I'm here for the same reason as the others, to have Jack train me. I'm not a guest."

"No. But you're not like them, either. He would never have let any of them in the house. He never let them cross the stream."

Tessa almost said it was because she was a woman and therefore less of a threat. But would that make her twice the problem in the eyes of a young lady unwilling to share his reluctantly given affection? She considered her own desire to claim her father's notice. How well she could understand Rose's dilemma. On one hand, Tessa was the closest thing to a friend and confidante Rose had had in a long time. And on the other, Jack was definitely not indifferent to her presence.

"I'm not interested in Jack," she told the girl to ease the fears of abandonment crowding in her eyes. "I'll only be here for a few weeks. You'll be here for a lifetime."

That summation satisfied the girl just as it disheartened Tessa. She was just passing through Jack Chaney's life. And there was no reason to think that her passing would leave so much as a ripple.

"Mr. Chaney?"

"Mrs. D'Angelo? Where are you calling from?" A riotous mix of music and voices made him strain to hear her hushed tone.

"I'm on my cell phone."

"Are you at a party?" After he'd told Stan to keep her in the house and safe?

"It's a fund-raiser for a new youth center. I've been on the board for years. I couldn't not go. I didn't want to not go," she admitted in a stronger, almost defiant confession.

"Is Stan with you?"

She laughed. "Could you imagine Stan in black tie and tails?"

"Not even at his own funeral."

"I'm taking every precaution, Mr. Chaney. I'm not a careless woman."

No, he didn't think she was. He thought there were a lot of people who didn't give Barbara D'Angelo nearly enough credit.

"So why are you calling, if not to flaunt your rebellion against my authority?"

She didn't laugh again. She became suddenly alarmingly serious. "Rachel Martinez is here. She's one of the biggest contributors. She was very kind in coming over to give her condolences."

There was a razor edge to that comment. Obviously, Mrs. D'Angelo had her own suspicions regarding the death of her husband.

"I'm sure she's grateful that your husband is no longer a threat at the polls."

"That's not where my husband was the real threat. I guess I didn't realize that until tonight. I should have seen it but I didn't want to. There are some things you just don't want to know."

"What kind of things, Mrs. D'Angelo?"

"Things my husband was exposed to during his time in Vietnam. The killing, the corruption, the…temptations."

"Was he susceptible to those things?"

"I didn't want to think so. Now I don't know what to think. Rachel Martinez was over there, too. She was with the Catholic Relief Services as a civilian volunteer. Robert never mentioned that they'd met. It was a big war. But for as long as I can remember he never liked her, didn't trust her. I thought it was because of her political agenda or that he didn't think she was good for Paul—her late husband. But now I have to wonder if there's more he didn't tell me."

"What changed your mind?"

"Remember the friends my husband enlisted with? Taggert McGee and Chet Allen?"

"You mentioned them earlier."

"They were close as brothers but war can do strange things to men, even men who share almost every secret, every dream."

"I know that, ma'am. I've been there."

"Then perhaps you can explain how Chet Allen, who supposedly died in Cambodia, is in the other room, standing next to Rachel Martinez."

Chapter 10

"It was like seeing a ghost. I thought I was imagining it at first."

Tessa watched her mother pace the plush white rug. She'd never seen Barbara smoke before but she did it with a familiar ease. Nor had she ever seen her mother entertain even the UPS man without having her makeup flawless. This morning, her skin was unusually translucent, her eyes shadowed darkly by fatigue. And she looked her age.

"You're sure it was him?"

Barbara glanced at Jack long enough to smile thinly. "Oh, yes. I never liked Chet. There was something too high-strung, too intense about him. He took important things lightly and the trivial too seriously. He had a way of looking right through you that...well, it was unnerving. But he was Robert's friend, one of the Three Musketeers, so I tolerated him even though he made my skin crawl. When Robert told me he'd died, I remember thinking, horribly I know, that he was the sort of soldier that should never come home. He liked war. After basic, he told me he couldn't wait to get shipped out to start collecting trophies. I didn't know what he meant at the time." Her arms wrapped around herself to suppress a hard shiver. "I do now. He was a scary, dangerous man."

"I know the type."

Tessa glanced at Jack. Seeing him sitting comfortably in her mother's elegant living room dressed in dark slacks and shirt under a well-made tan sport coat, he seemed surprisingly domesticated. But paint his face in camo colors, put him in fatigues and send him into the jungle with an automatic weapon, what would he become then? Something very scary and dangerous. He knew the type because he was the type. The type the average citizen wanted to have in a foreign country to fight for their safety but not on their streets living among them. No wonder Jack preferred his wooded retreat. He'd never left the jungle behind, either.

"What did Robby tell you about how Allen died?" Stan asked from where he sat looking uncomfortable on one of the brocaded chairs. He'd picked Jack and Tessa up at daybreak to smuggle them into the D'Angelo home. At Jack's insistence, he'd made a spot for himself in one of the first-floor spare rooms where he could keep an eye on the surveillance equipment already in place and on the extra gadgets he'd added as per Jack's instructions.

"He didn't like talking about things that happened over there," Barbara answered. "Once he got home, he just wanted to put it all behind him. I didn't push. I didn't want to know what he'd gone through. I was just glad to have him back. He had the rest of our lives planned out and if he wanted to pretend nothing happened while he was away, I was willing to go along with it. But he did send me a peculiar letter, the last one I got before he was shipped Stateside. He sent some pictures, some clippings, but I didn't pay much attention to them. He told me in the letter he was coming home and that was the only thing that mattered to me. He also told me that Chet had died." She snubbed out her cigarette and immediately lit another one. Her hands were shaking. She inhaled deeply and expelled an impressive smoke ring.

"They'd been out on some hush-hush mission and Chet had been killed by enemy fire. Robert was wounded in the same firefight and couldn't bring Chet's body back with him. Robert was awfully upset about it. He'd never given up on Chet. He'd hoped that Chet would change once he came home again, you know, become the friend he'd gone drinking and fishing and cruising for girls with. But I know that wouldn't have happened. Whatever Chet became over there was the real Chet. What he'd been before was just a cover-up.

"Robert mentioned a drug problem. I guess it was pretty common over there. I thought he meant Chet was taking drugs, but now I think he was trafficking them. Robert was supposed to testify at some sort of inquiry that involved running opium from the jungles over there to the inner-city jungles over here. But after Chet died, I never heard any more about it. I think he was supposed to give evidence against Chet and was relieved that he died, honorably, before charges could be brought."

"And would that have pissed Allen off enough to have him come back from the grave to kill your husband more than thirty years later?"

Barbara gave Jack a long, cool stare. "Chet liked to plan his every move carefully. He never did anything on impulse. Tag and Robert used to tease him about being so methodical he'd draw up blueprints before using the toilet. Chet was patient. It didn't matter to him how much time it took to get something done, but he always finished what he started. It's what made him so good in the field."

"And your husband was unfinished business?"

"Maybe. Who knows how a man like that thinks."

Jack would know, Tessa guessed. He'd understand a man like Chet just fine.

"What was Chet Allen doing at an upscale fund-raiser?" he mused out loud.

"He was there to meet with Martinez, I think. One of her aides had come to pull her aside. She met with Chet in a back hallway. They argued. I don't think Chet was supposed to be there. They were very careful not to be seen together in public."

"Did they see you?"

"No. I was on the way to the powder room. I'd gotten a terrible headache and was looking for a quiet place to take something my doctor prescribed. I didn't want headlines to read 'D.A.'s Widow Caught Popping Pills At Society Party.' Those people still follow me. I don't know why. I'm no story."

Jack glanced at Tessa. Yes, she was, his steady gaze told her.

"Anyway, I'd slipped outside to go around back to the kitchen area. I was just about to come in when I saw the two of them. I couldn't hear what they were saying with the door shut and I didn't want to risk drawing attention to myself. I hurried back to the party. And that's when I called you, Mr. Chaney."

"You did the right thing."

Barbara didn't think so. She sighed heavily. "If I'd been smarter or braver, I would have found a way to listen in and see what they were up to. Tess would have found a way. She's always been so resourceful."

Tessa didn't respond to the admiring statement. Her thoughts were spinning.

Chet Allen, ex-Green Beret. Death on wheels. Capable of entering the fourteenth floor of a high-rise without being discovered, without leaving a trace, to kill the man who had forced him to go underground. Allen, a man involved in drug trafficking. But had revenge motivated him or was it something else? Something that linked him, a supposed dead man, to an influential councilwoman about to run for a higher government office? If she heard Allen's voice, would she recognize it from her nightmares?

"I ran a quick check on Allen," Stan was saying. "He doesn't exist."

Tessa looked to him for clarification. "You mean, he's dead?"

"No, I mean all traces of him are gone. Like he was never alive. His service record has vanished. There's no mention of his enlistment or his death."

"Mr. Allen obviously found other, more lucrative, employment," Jack surmised.

"How can we find someone who doesn't exist?" Tessa felt her frustration level begin to rise. Another dead end? All this and another dead end?

"I know a guy who knows a guy…" Jack began with a casual vagueness.

"Guys in the same type of employment?" Tessa pressed, hopes daring to notch up just a little.

Jack was resourceful, too.

"Let's just say they don't get W-2s. I'll see what he can find out about our buddy Allen and maybe get a line on who's pulling his strings. Allen wouldn't risk exposure for a personal vendetta. It might have been a perk but I doubt it was the only thing on his agenda."

"Martinez?" Barbara ventured. "Could they have met when she was doing humanitarian work?"

"We have to prove it," Tessa concluded. It all came down to proof. "I think it's time we confronted Councilwoman Martinez."

"No."

Jack's response was flat and inflexible.

"Why not? If we squeeze her enough—"

"She'll have us charged with harassment. And she'll know we know. She's not going to tell us anything because she's up to her eyeballs in this mess. If Allen goes down, she goes down and she's not about to take a fall after all the risks she's taken already. If you confront her, you're just going to give away our suspicions prematurely. If she thinks you know too much, she'll step up her efforts to get to you. And a man like Allen can get just about any place he wants."

"I thought you said I was safe with you." She was angry enough at the roadblock he'd just thrown in her path to lace that comment with sarcasm.

"Only if you don't paint a bull's-eye on your back and dance around in his sniper sites."

"Tess, please listen to Mr. Chaney," her mother urged with a quiet anxiousness. "Don't rush into anything that might get you hurt."

Tessa rounded on her like a cyclone. "I've been hurt. And I've been afraid and I'm tired of being those things. I'm tired of letting Martinez and your friend Allen make me those things. And unless someone puts a stop to them, they're just going to continue doing it to whoever gets in their way. My father gave his life trying to stop them."

"And now he's dead." Barbara summed it up that simply. And for her, it probably was just that simple. She didn't care about justice or duty. She didn't want the luxury liner of her life rocked. Poor spoiled Barbara D'Angelo with no one to keep her on her pedestal.

"For a cause." For Tessa, that was the only argument necessary.

"Causes get people killed," Jack concluded. "And you know what, there's always another cause and someone else to take it up. There'll always be more causes and none are worth dying for."

"That's a coward's claim."

Jack shrugged, unaffected by her scorn. "I'm not ashamed of it. You're dealing with a powerful woman, and men or women with power get dangerous when they get desperate. You're no match for those without conscience."

"You mean, like you?" She flung the words like a dagger.

"Yeah," he agreed somberly. "Like me."

Stan cleared his throat, growing uneasy with the heated exchange. "Tess, Jack's right. It takes time to make a good case. Your father taught me that. If we rush in unprepared, it'll give her time to hide her secrets deeper, maybe where we can never find them. If we creep around, not like cowards but like clever little mice—" he winked at Jack "—who knows what we can uncover before she gets wise. Right now, she thinks you're a nuisance. Don't make her think you're a threat."

"Tess," her mother said softly. "Rachel Martinez isn't going anywhere."

"And neither is my father."

Barbara looked away, wounded by the attack.

"Fine." Tessa threw up her hands. She couldn't fight them all and they were determined to be conservative to the hilt, while Ms. Martinez continued living her high life and smiling benevolently on her TV ads. "We'll be quiet little rodents scurrying around in the dark."

"Being very careful not to leave little reminders of where we've been," Stan added with a grin. "This little mouse found out a juicy tidbit this morning from the coroner's office."

Tessa's attention sharpened. "About Johnnie O'?"

"It seems our eager witness wouldn't have had a very lengthy future even if he hadn't taken a long drop on a short rope."

"What do you mean?"

"O'Casey had AIDS. Full-blown. He played with a lot of needles and finally got stuck. He was dying even as someone killed him."

Tessa processed this and was quick to find another missing piece. "His child. His girlfriend was pregnant."

"And HIV-positive, too. She gave birth to a baby boy with his father's eyes and his father's deadly disease."

A crushing sorrow for the innocent baby derailed Tessa's express train of suppositions. But Jack was there to hop on board.

"And where is the baby now?"

"Funny, the kid was born to an HIV-positive crack mother turning tricks on the street and suddenly he's in some exclusive care center getting every break available."

"And who's footing the bill?" Jack wanted to know.

"Daddy," Tessa stated. "Daddy made a deal to give his child a chance to survive. That's why Johnnie O' was willing to go down for the count. It didn't matter what they did to him. He was dead anyway. What mattered was the baby. Who would have thought O'Casey had a heart."

"Stan, find out where the money came from."

"It's from a private charity organization. They wouldn't give me any names."

"Maybe I could get them for you."

They all looked to Barbara in surprise. She met their incredulous expressions with one of cool competency. "I've served on just about every charity board in town. Could be I know a guy who knows a guy."

Silence. Then Jack chuckled. "That's how it works." He stood. "We've been here too long. Mrs. D'Angelo—"

"Barbara."

"Barbara, you keep trying to find what it was your husband was looking for and what he was trying to hide. I'll bet my gold crown it has something to do with Allen over in those China White jungles."

"I'll keep looking…Jack."

"I've got to go see a guy about a guy."

As they started for the door, Barbara stepped close to tentatively touch her daughter's arm. Tessa bristled but she didn't pull away.

"Tess, don't be a hero. Doing things the right way doesn't mean everything goes your way."

A ghost of a smile sketched across Tessa's lips. "Dad used to say that."

"He was right. He was right about a lot of things. He said you were a firecracker under a bucket, that when something set you off, the explosion would take everyone by surprise. Your father was like that, too. Calm, collected, then boom when you least expected it, when it mattered the most."

Tessa's brow furrowed. That wasn't like her father at all.

"He would be so proud of what you're doing. Just make sure you're doing it for the right reasons." And while her daughter stood, defenses down, her eyes misting with emotion, Barbara hugged her into a perfumed yet strong embrace. "Please be careful."

Tessa put her hands on her mother's arms, surprised to feel strength instead of the expected weakness. Gently she pushed away. "I will."

Barbara allowed herself to be levered to an impersonal distance. Her expression grew poignant and bittersweet. Then she glanced toward Jack where he and Stan were talking in the doorway. "Listen to him, Tess. He's a smart man. Stan trusts him and so do I. He's got your best interests at heart."

Tessa was going to refute that when she caught her mother's speculative smile. Barbara thought she and Jack… She thought they were…

"Mother, there's nothing between me and Jack." Unfortunately.

"Yet."

They left the house in Barbara's Mercedes. Its tinted windows gave no clue as to who was inside. If the house was being watched, they would assume it was Barbara leaving for one of her many functions. To keep up that pretense, Jack drove the smooth-handling vehicle, slowly, casually, taking them into the shopping district where the trendy salons and uniquely expensive designers Barbara patronized were located. Jack pulled into a parking garage, into a space and cut the engine. They waited, Jack watching, Tessa wound tight. Long minutes passed. Tessa didn't speak. She was still angry with him for his failure to back up her suggestions. And she was still mulling over her mother's insinuations.

Yet.

"Down."

"What?"

Jack gripped her by the shoulders and pulled her toward him until her face was in his lap. He layered his body over the top of hers in an uncomfortable press. Then she understood. Anyone driving by would think the vehicle was empty.

The sound of the idling engine of some large luxury gas hog purred by. Perhaps some blue-haired matron looking for the perfect parking spot. Perhaps not. Perhaps some big sedan with a crumpled left fender. With her head wedged between the steering wheel and Jack's amazingly hard abs, she couldn't see what was going on outside the vehicle. But even though neither of them moved, plenty was going on inside it.

She could feel the steady rock of Jack's breathing and the weight of his hand where it hit her leg just below the hem of her skirt. She'd dressed up for this meeting at her mother's. Always wanting to look her best in case someone was making comparisons. He rested his hand on her thigh in a light cuff, neutral and nonthreatening. Until his thumb briefly stroked along the underside of her knee. Being ticklish, it took all her willpower not to leap off the seat at that feather-like caress. Being a woman, her pulse leaped into a level of high alert. And once in that state of readiness, her senses filled with an awareness of him.

She wanted him. The tension of the moment only made that inappropriate desire sharper. Right here, right now, in the plush interior of her mother's car, in a parking garage where they could be discovered at any second by startled upscale shoppers or by carefully trained killers. Her breathing shivered at the thought of them, naked on the soft, beige-leather front seat, fogging up the windows like a pair of kids necking at the drive-in. If Jack thought her cleaning a gun was a turn-on, thrashing around a gearshift with him had her motor running.

Too soon, he straightened and coaxed her wordlessly to do the same. While she tried to rein in her respirations, he coaxed the engine to life and made a turn out of the space.

"You're going the wrong way, Jack."

"No doubt about it," was his rather raspy reply.

He guided them quickly down the twists and turns of the garage, around alarmed motorists who thankfully didn't have time to sound their horns and give them away. He pulled up to the ticket booth where the attendant met him with a scowl.

"Can't you follow the signs, buddy?"

Jack grinned as he passed over the correct change. "Sorry. Got a little distracted."

The pimply faced attendant leaned down to get a look at Tessa, who was trying to smooth down her hair and her skirt at the same time. The kid had the audacity to smirk and nod in wistful understanding.

"You fed his geek fantasies for the next few nights," Tessa mumbled as they merged into traffic.

"It was my pleasure." His tone was all husky inference, but the gaze fixed on the rearview was all business. After a few blocks, he relaxed. "Looks like we gave them the slip." He glanced at her, just a quick sexy aside. "And speaking of slips, how come you're not wearing one, a nice professional woman like you?"

"I didn't exactly pack business lingerie with my sweat suits."

"Too bad."

And that got her running on high octane for the rest of their silent drive.

They exchanged the sleek Mercedes for Jack's battered

truck outside one of Barbara's favorite restaurants. Stan would bring Barbara to pick it up later that afternoon. This time, as he drove, Tessa paid extra attention to where they were going, in case she had reason to find her way back here again. When they pulled up the gravel drive, she was puzzled by the strange sense of coming home that was as unwarranted as it was unlikely. She was just passing through. There was no permanence for her here.

Jack had made that abundantly clear.

He helped her down from the high seat then immediately disappeared into the house. To see a guy about a guy. Leaving her to approach more slowly, alone.

Constanza had prepared a light salad lunch that she shared with an unusually sedate Rose in the kitchen. Tessa was grateful for the silence. Her mind was turning full-tilt, veering away from the confusing sexual pull she felt for Chaney to the information they uncovered at her mother's.

On the day that he died, her father had been on his way to court. She'd been at her desk finishing up a stack of witness subpoenas. He'd stopped there, waiting until she'd lifted her head in question. For the longest time, he'd said nothing. He'd just stared at her through eyes so somber and…and sad that she'd been alarmed.

"Tessie, we need to talk."

He hadn't called her Tessie since grade school.

"Sure."

"I'm late for court. How about this afternoon?"

"Okay. What's up?" His oddly anxious mood had had her own prickling with dread. His discomfort had been so unusual that she couldn't help but be concerned.

"I need to talk to you, Tessa. There're some things I have to tell you. I've put it off for far too long."

"About one of our cases?" But she had known that it wasn't. It was something else. Something bigger.

He'd glanced at his Rolex and looked relieved. "I don't

have time right now but I'll call you when I get a break this afternoon. It's important, Tess." ·

"Okay. I'll make sure I'm free."

But his call had never come. The matter went to trial and the afternoon went by with no word from him. They'd never had their talk. She'd never know what was so important. Quite frankly, she'd forgotten about the conversation in the tragedy that had followed. Until now. Until she had a reason to rethink his intentions.

Chet Allen was her father's service buddy. Friends for life. One of the Three Musketeers, her mother had said. They'd shared everything and kept no secrets from one another. No secrets.

Had her father known Allen was still trafficking drugs in Asia? Was that why Allen killed him? Worse, had they been working together to blackmail Martinez over her involvement? That would explain the money in her father's account.

Had her father taken hush money to back off his investigation? Had he needed the money that badly to front his political campaign and to spoil his wife with more extravagant tokens of his esteem? Pain and envy had Tessa considering the unthinkable, the intolerable.

What if the last important thing he'd meant to tell her had been a confession?

Chapter 11

She'd just turned away from a spectacular fading sun as it dipped behind the treetops when she saw a man standing outside the living room window.

Jack had never reappeared after lunch, so left to her own devices, Tessa had picked a book from the library. In desperate need of some distraction, she'd discovered a cozy nook glassed in on two sides overlooking the porch. It was of a smaller, more intimate scale than the fireplace room, with a conversation area made up of an overstuffed white-linen sofa and several chairs of woven leather and brown corduroy surrounding a low, copper-topped table. Supporting the planked ceiling were peeled tree trunks spaced at intervals along the glass wall to give the impression of being lost in a forest. The view of the winding creek and low stone wall running down to it made a pictorial vista inviting rest and ease. Stretched out on the couch with chapter one, before she knew it, the afternoon was gone.

She never heard a sound. Some instinct had her glancing over the back of the couch to be momentarily blinded by the glare of the sun. Then there he was, standing an arm's length away with just the glass to separate them.

Too startled to move or to even cry out in her own defense, she stared like a paralyzed wild thing faced with a hunter's double barrel.

It was not Chet Allen. She weakened a bit with relief. The age was wrong. Allen was her father's contemporary. This intruder was Jack's age. Although he wore an expensive dark suit and a peach-colored silk shirt with fancy cuff links, a watch of heavy gold and a diamond winking in one earlobe, there was no way to dress up what he was. A dangerous man.

He wore the suit well. Obviously it was made for him, to encompass the impressive span of his shoulders and upper body bulk before tapering to narrow waist and hips. And to hide the added dimensions of his shoulder holster. His graceful hands were manicured and his grooming impeccable. But these things, including the metrosexual choice of shirt color, couldn't detract from the power of the man. With dark hair buzzed nearly to the scalp in a stubble to match the covering on his granite jaw, his features were hawkish rather than handsome. But his eyes gave him away. They were direct to the point of insulting, pinning her to the couch cushions with their steady stare. A dark and coldly opaque stare without a trace of emotion flickering behind it.

This was the guy Jack was seeing about a guy.

Tessa heard the front door open and glanced toward it. In the splinter of time it took for her to divert her attention, the man was gone. The porch was empty, as if she'd imagined ever seeing him.

With a shiver, Tessa dropped her book to the tabletop and jumped off the couch. Though only seconds passed before she reached the front door, there was no sign of the mysterious man or of Jack, who'd gone out to meet him. She could either rush around foolishly trying to find them when they obviously didn't want to be found or she could wait for their return to hear what information had surfaced along with Jack's spooky friend.

She hated to wait. She, who had once been so methodical, so calmly relentless, felt like screaming in frustration. This wasn't Jack's party, it was hers, and she was tired of his exclusionary tactics.

Especially when the information was so critical.

She paced the front foyer, growing more edgy and anxious with each turn on the stone floor. There was no doubt that Jack's friend was ex-military, probably Black Ops as he'd been. Would he have access to the kind of off-limits, need-to-know intel on Chet Allen that right now she needed to know? Things such as who he was working for, who he'd been working with, where he'd disappeared to when they'd erased him from the government database. Things such as whether his relationship with her father had continued after he'd supposedly died.

Did she really want to know these things?

What if they told her more than she was ready to hear? What if they told her the father she idolized was up to his wallet in dirty dealings? That he'd given in to the temptation offered by the dark side of humanity he strove to convict after she'd so rabidly protested his innocence? Was she the one being naive? A fool?

Damn. Where was Jack?

A soft scuffle of sound behind her had Tessa nearly jumping out of her skin.

"*Hola,* Miss Tessa."

"Constanza."

"Did Mr. Jack say whether or not Mr. Russell was staying for dinner?"

Russell. "No, he didn't. Mr. Russell comes here often?"

"Not so often. He comes to arrange for new groups of men to stay here."

"I see."

And perhaps she did see a little too clearly.

A pang of betrayal twisted low in her belly. Had Russell come bringing news of her father's case or was he here to set up Jack's next training session? Was Jack about to abandon her and her uninvited cause? He'd made it clear from the start that he wasn't going to join her crusade for justice. Did Russell's appearance offer the much-needed excuse to bail in favor of the detached work he preferred doing?

"Where can I find Jack and Mr. Russell?"

She climbed the spiral steps, her temper and anxiety rising apace. Jack's private study and his bedroom were in a second-story wing at the back of the house. She could hear voices as she neared the top of the stairs and she paused to listen to the direction of their conversation before interrupting.

"We could be in Afghanistan by the first of the year, if you think that would give you enough time to work with them."

That was Russell. He had a cultured voice with an English accent that took her by surprise.

"For what you have in mind, and the time frame, the training will have to be tremendously intense. You're talking about dropping into the middle of some nasty stuff over there."

"And I want my men prepared. I want the best, Jack. That's why I came to you. I could have them here by the end of the week. Would that give you time to get things ready?"

There was a pause. Tessa's heart clutched tightly as she waited for Jack's response. It was brutally vague.

"I'm not sure. I'm kind of in the middle of this thing."

"Jack, this is important."

And she wasn't.

"Mr. Chaney's schedule is clear," she announced as she climbed into sight. "I've taken up enough of his time."

Russell came immediately to his feet. Jack remained rooted where he was, his gaze on her, his expression unreadable.

She allowed herself a brief glance around. So this was Jack's getaway. The study had the same high turreted ceiling as the library. One corner was squared off by a huge fieldstone fireplace with a granite-slab mantel. The same irregular chunks of stone formed the walls on three sides, repeating the illusion of a north country hunting lodge. A bearskin draped the back of one of the chairs near the fire as if it had just been tossed there. The only sign that Jack Chaney wasn't some wealthy rancher retreating to tally his calf count was the massive gun cabinet on the far wall displaying everything from old-fashioned muzzle loaders to modern-day semiautomatics, and everything in between. And behind the glass of another case was every martial arts tool Bruce Lee could dream of. Jack was probably proficient in all of them. He seemed a hands-on type of collector.

The two men had been sitting at a gorgeous red-felt multisided poker table where Russell had two queens showing and Jack a possible flush.

She imagined a fire blazing with Tinker curled up on the skin rug while a blizzard wailed outside. A decanter of cognac and a game of Aces Wild. This was the kind of room she could retire to, where she could share conversations with the man she… But that wasn't about to happen.

Jack never took his intense stare from her face.

"Tessa D'Angelo, Zachary Russell."

"A pleasure, Ms. D'Angelo."

"I doubt that."

Russell's impassive facade creased with a smile she found annoyingly charming. Had the circumstances been different, she might have enjoyed his company.

"Forgive me for frightening you downstairs," came the soft purr of his voice.

"You didn't frighten me," she lied. "You woke me up." Woke her from the dream where Jack Chaney was coming to her rescue. Thank goodness she'd been roused from it in time. So why did her insides ache as if ravaged by a strong bout of the flu?

"Tessa."

The way Jack said her name brought a shiver along the surface of her skin. She ignored it and him.

"I'm sorry to have interrupted your discussion. I'll get out of the way."

"Tessa."

Dammit, she wouldn't cry. She squinted hard to defy the tears pooling along her lashes. She had no business expecting anything honorable from Jack. He'd said flat-out that he was no hero, that he was only interested in numero uno. Why hadn't she believed him?

"It shouldn't take me long to get my things together. I don't think there's anything else you can teach me that I need to know."

"I thought we agreed I would decide when you were ready to leave?" Jack challenged quietly.

"I'm sure you'll get over it."

"No, I won't."

She didn't know how to respond to that flat statement. She didn't know what he wanted from her. She had never known. He'd kept her off balance since the first time they'd met, telling her not to get involved in his life while pushing his way into hers. It wasn't fair. It wasn't what they'd bargained for.

"I'll need you to drive me into town."

Her cool command never rated so much as a blink.

"I don't think so."

Zach Russell expelled a breath. "I think I'm the one who should leave."

Jack looked between his oldest friend, his link to the life he'd led, and to the irate and weepy-eyed Tessa who represented the life he dreamed of but could never claim. Instinct told him to tell Russell to sit and Tessa to pack her bags. That he should run, not walk, to accept the job his friend offered.

That would be the smart thing, the cautious thing. Then life could get back to normal and he could be in control again.

But he heard himself saying, "I'll call you later, Russ."

Russell was too polite to grin at his predicament. But he was laughing on the inside. "I'll see what I can find out for you."

"Thanks."

"No problem. I always enjoy an excuse to come visit, especially now that the company has improved." He nodded to the stiff and stony-faced Tessa. A small smile crept out as he looked down at Jack. "I don't know if I envy you this evening or not, my friend."

"Goodbye, Russ."

Russell was definitely smirking when he walked past Tessa to jog down the steps. After the first couple of stairs, the sound of his footsteps disappeared and Jack was alone with a very big problem.

"You're angry."

"Your command of the obvious is overwhelming." She wasn't just angry—she was furious. And hurt. He could see the pain shimmering even though she tried to disguise it behind that magnificent temper.

"I wasn't planning to ditch you like a bad date."

"Really? That's not how it sounded to me."

"I made you a promise, Tess."

Her eyes glistened. "And that's supposed to mean something?"

"You mean, from a man like me?"

Her silence was his answer.

"I promised to help you."

"No, you didn't. You said you didn't want to get involved. Fine. I respect that."

"No, you don't."

"A lot more than you lying to me now."

"I haven't lied to you, Tess. I haven't said one thing to you that wasn't true."

He could see her indecision, her willingness to hope warring with her cold rationality. Her final summation devastated when he thought he was far beyond being wounded by mere words.

"I have work to do, Jack, and my business doesn't involve you."

"It does if you want to stay alive. I thought you wanted to see your father's killer brought to justice. The wheels are in motion, Tessa. If you get run over by them first, you'll never know the truth. Isn't that the important thing, that the truth come out?"

"No. The important thing is that I be the one to find it."

He could tell those words shocked her. She was silent for a moment as if she couldn't believe she'd said them out loud.

"Why, Tessa? Why is that so important?"

"Because I can't fail him now. It's my last chance to make him proud of me."

"To make him love you?" Jack added softly. Her reaction said more than she ever would. She jerked back as if from a slap, her lower lip trembling. Then her grit returned to steel her spine and frost her gaze.

"That's none of your business."

"It is if it makes you throw yourself into the path of danger. You'll die if you do and I won't have you scarring my soul, too."

She blinked at that "too" but before she could question it, he'd crossed to where she was standing. She stood her ground, not flinching when he gripped her upper arms.

"He's not worth it, Tessa. He's not worth your life."

"How dare you tell me what a man like my father was worth."

Because he didn't know how to argue that, the only way to shut her up was to kiss her.

When she got her breath back, she made a weak complaint. "You don't play fair."

His thumbs sketched the fragile line of her jaw as her eyes fluttered open to look up at him. He saw his every dangerous dream in those desire-drenched pools of blue. "I said I keep my promises. I didn't say I won't cheat to do it."

"Oh."

With that sighing word, she sank into him, her arms encircling his middle, her mouth lifting to meet his.

The taste of her was sweet heaven and hell.

"Am I forgiven?" he whispered against the moist part of her lips.

"No. Not yet. But close."

He nuzzled her satiny neck, breathing in that intoxicating fragrance that always made his senses spin. Her head fell back as he nipped at her collarbone. "I'm working on it."

"Work harder," she moaned.

Her hands found his head, fingers spearing into his hair to pull him up so she could kiss him again, this time with a greedy urgency that dropped his resolve around his ankles. Which was where his pants would soon be as she moved one hand to frantically tug at his belt and zipper.

"This isn't the best place for this."

Anyone could come up the stairs. Rose... Her tongue speared into his mouth and the power of coherent thought left him. Finally she gave him back a scrap of sanity by leaning slightly away.

"Jack, the only room in this house I haven't seen is yours. Please show me."

Chapter 12

Curtains were drawn across the windows, shutting out light to create a cavern of dark, inviting mystery, as inviting as the heat and enveloping power of Jack Chaney. He closed the door behind them then stepped in to pull her to him. His kiss was hot, openmouthed, without a trace of reserve or restraint. At that moment any thought that she might not be doing the right thing, the smart thing, melted before the scorch of his blowtorch intensity.

She wasn't sure what to expect from him. She liked that he didn't just toss her on the bed and have at her. Although, who was she kidding, that would have been just fine with her. Instead, while they stood toe-to-toe in the dark room, unable to see one another clearly, he took his time, learning her by touch like a blind man who needed to be sure of the way.

He started with her hair, slowly combing his fingers through it, then leaning to nudge his face into its softness. She tried to turn, to catch his mouth for another steamy kiss but he was already easing away.

"Like silk," he murmured. "Sweet-smelling silk."

A trembling started deep in her belly.

He charted her features with his fingertips, lightly following the smoothness of her brow, lingering where the stitching had left only a tiny scar on the outside but a tremendous tear to her psyche. His thumbs traced down the narrow bridge of her nose to its impertinent upturned tip before fanning across her cheekbones and circling to ride the contours of her mouth. Her breath brushed them in quick little puffs.

"From the first time I saw your police file, I thought you had the most kissable lips I'd ever seen."

"My police file?"

He leaned in close, his mouth sealing in her surprise. He took his time there, too, learning the shape, the taste, the feel of her lips, first with his own, then with the slow pull of his tongue. She groaned, parting the way to deeper exploration but again, he pulled back.

"I was right," came his husky whisper.

His fingers rested on the padded shoulders of her beige linen suit jacket while his thumbs rode the lapels down to their overlap, resting there where her breasts began a tempting swell. She managed to break from the sensual spell he was weaving long enough to undo the three buttons holding the jacket together. Her knees were shaking. She wasn't sure how much more of this tender assault on her senses she could withstand without them buckling.

He brushed the linen with its slick satin lining from her shoulders, letting it slide down her arms. Beneath it, she wore an ivory camisole with a stretchy bra built in. She took a tortured breath as his touch skimmed over the web of lace covering the upper curve of her breasts, ignoring the tingling tips that ached for his attention. Instead, his palms smoothed down the quiver of her sides to the waistband of her matching skirt. He charted the flare of her hips, following the trail downward to where fabric ended midthigh and her stockings began. His thumbs ran under the hem of her skirt, over the tops of her thighs, until they met in the middle. And then they moved upward.

"Jack."

His name escaped her with a fragile tremor as her skirt hiked up and his hands stroked higher.

"Who would have thought legs this luscious could put in five miles and still kick my butt?"

She started to laugh, relieved at the break in tension, but the sound strangled in her throat as he reached the very damp reinforced cotton crotch. Again, instead of lingering as she longed for him to do, his hands slid away to safely brush down her skirt. By then, her body was a quaking mass of need.

"I don't think this was part of our original agreement," he stated with a maddening calm. Surely he didn't mean to stop. She took a protesting breath, then he continued. "Perhaps we should amend it to cover any potential breaches of contract that might occur in the next few hours."

"I'll put together a waiver releasing the both of us from any claim that might be made at a later date or time based on what I hope to God happens very soon and continues for at least the next few hours."

"I love it when you get litigious."

He took her mouth for a rough savaging. All the restraint and leisurely movements were gone. He was now a man with a mission, with a definite goal in mind. A common goal they both pursued with vigor and determination.

She unfastened her skirt and let it shinny down her legs. Her panty hose were rolled down after it. As she straightened, he dipped his head, his lips scorching through the lace at her bosom to heat the skin beneath it. She clutched at his head, her back arching as he finally took a nipple between his teeth. A wavering moan escaped her. He shifted back long enough to pull the camisole over her head then went back to work, teasing, feasting, with lips and tongue and fingers until she was so alive with sensation, the briefest touch would have sent her flying.

That's when he scooped her up, with her wearing only a ridiculously tiny triangle of lace and silk, and carried her to his bed.

The blanket beneath her was woven, a scratchy wool, but the moment Jack plucked off her bikini panties and bent his head between her thighs, she could have been lying on broken glass and not have cared.

At the first hot touch of his mouth, she nearly lost her mind as quickly as she lost her self-control. Her body dissolved into a million fragments of feeling, each intense and sharp and amazing. Never had she let go so quickly, so completely, with such lack of inhibition. He was still fully dressed right down to his sport coat, shoes, socks and pistol! Even as the spasms worked their way outward from the volcanic core to her fingertips and toes, he was nibbling up the inside of her thighs, along the curve of her quivering belly, to suck at the tips of her breasts that were now so sensitive she writhed with pleasure. She'd known—hadn't she?—right from the start, that being with Jack Chaney would be like no other.

His weight was heavy between the loose sprawl of her legs. He rested on elbows that bracketed the wild tumble of her hair. And he grinned with such smug, wicked satisfaction that she couldn't let him get away with it. She hooked an arm around one of his, a leg around one of his, and neatly flipped him onto his back. As she rose up over him, his smile never faded.

"I am completely at your mercy," he told her. Such a total lie but she loved it.

"Yes, you are. And I mean to have my way with you."

"Be gentle."

She kissed the grin off his face, delving in deep to reach

for the hot, silky caverns of his mouth until he groaned in true surrender. Then she sat back upon his hips, now drastically altered in their contour, and began to unbutton his shirt. Pushing it open, she took her time, using her palms to acquaint herself with the sculpted terrain of his smooth chest and ridged abs. He had an amazing body and she wanted more of it. All of it. At her mercy now, and then inside her, soon.

She opened his belt and his trousers, surprised then intrigued to find he was a boxers rather than a briefs man. Neither could have restrained what pulsed to life at the slightest stroke of her fingertips.

"I see we can skip tomorrow's lesson on torture. You already seem quite accomplished in that area." His amused tone was roughened by strain and she delighted in the sense of power that gave her.

"Now who has whom begging uncle?" She released him from the taut hug of cotton to glove him, so hot and smooth and hard, with her hand. The pattern of his breathing hitched and quickened.

"My uncle always told me to be prepared, even when at the mercy of a naked woman." He gestured to the nightstand. "Top drawer," he instructed gruffly.

She reached over to retrieve a box of condoms, absurdly pleased to find it was unopened. As if he'd been waiting just for her. Not true, of course, but she liked thinking it anyway. She tore open the box and ripped into one of the packets. Jack grabbed for it.

"I can do that."

She held it away and purred with a rumble he found sexier than all get-out. "So can I."

So she did. And the act of unrolling latex went beyond one of necessity to a tempting bit of foreplay that had his fingers digging into the tops of her knees in an effort to maintain focus.

"There," she mused, admiring her work with the tease of her hand. "Snug as a bug in a rug."

"Not yet," he growled.

His hands cupped her saucy bottom, lifting, shifting, depositing her squarely atop his erection. She made a gulping sound and squeezed her eyes shut. She didn't look nearly so pleased with herself as the breath shuddered from her.

"Now I am," he corrected, angling his hips to adjust the fit to perfection. Then hoisting her up and lowering her by increments to prove it.

"Yes."

The sound hissed from her as her head fell back and her hands clasped over his to squeeze tight. He could just see the silhouette of her breasts, full, proud, beautiful. The rest he had to imagine or tried to until pure, frighteningly fierce sensation engulfed him. She encouraged it, demanded it, that almost out-of-body intensity. She was his only constant, his only reality in a world void of all but hot, spiking physicality.

Strong and bold, she rode them both to a shattering climax then sagged, spent and languid, upon his chest.

He thought he knew every defensive move but at the moment he couldn't seem to save himself from what he was beginning to feel for her. Protective and possessive, but he wouldn't call it committed.

He couldn't.

Just then, light pushed into the room from the hallway. The mattress gave slightly as Tinker jumped up, his purr revved and running. There was silence for a moment and he'd just started to think that maybe it was just the cat when a quiet voice intruded.

"Mr. Jack, there's a phone call for you."

"I'll be right there, Rose."

The door clicked shut.

"Do you think she saw anything?" came Tessa's agonized whisper.

He couldn't answer. He didn't want to even guess. What

had been one of the single most electrifying moments he could remember had shorted out into adult embarrassment. He lifted Tessa from him and rolled to his feet. After a quick jog to the bathroom, he had his clothing together in an instant and was raking his fingers through his hair.

"Get dressed," he told Tessa shortly. He regretted the tone but he was too stressed to be gentle with her feelings. "You can use my shower. I'll get the phone in my study."

Tessa said nothing. She snatched up her discarded belongings and shot into the bathroom with a flash of bare flanks before the door shut behind her.

Cursing softly at the unfortunate turn of events, Jack went down the short hall to his study. He listened to Stan's report without any real enthusiasm because he could see the top of Rose's dark head where she sat on the spiral stairs. He wasn't good at this sort of thing. He had no practice, nothing to go on when it came to children, or women for that matter. He was a straightforward, pull-no-punches kind of guy who never feared telling it like it was to any man. But the thought of explaining away a preteen's first exposure to sex scared the hell out of him. He could ask Constanza to step in, but that would be taking the coward's way out and, though appealing, it wasn't the way he did things. As soon as he hung up from Stan, he took a breath, straightened his jacket and went to take his medicine.

She wouldn't look at him when he sat beside her on the step. While he fumbled with what to say, Rose proved to be the more mature of the two of them, saying matter-of-factly, "Forgive me. I should have knocked first. I will knock first from now on. I did not know that was how it was between you and Miss Tessa."

"Knock first," he agreed, beginning to thank his lucky stars that he was going to get off this easy.

And then she looked at him and he saw the broken heart in that dark, glimmering gaze.

"Will you send me away now?"

He blinked, blindsided. "For what? Opening a door that should have been locked?"

She looked away. He could see from the tears on her cheeks that it was more than just shock or embarrassment that prompted her question. Then she stated plainly, "Because of how things are between you and Miss Tessa. I thought maybe now that she is here, you wouldn't want me to stay."

His jaw dropped at her practical logic. Floundering for the right thing to say, he came up immediately with the wrong thing. "You thought wrong. Miss Tessa is just a paycheck, just like the others. She isn't staying here and she isn't going to replace you."

Her gaze lifted, drenched with hope and gratitude. And something else that made him squirm inside. Love.

"Then you won't send me home?"

"This is your home, Rose. You and your aunt are my responsibility. That isn't going to change. Now, go on and do your schoolwork."

She leaned in to buss a salty kiss against his cheek while he sat frozen. As she scampered down the steps, he was just beginning to think, *That wasn't so bad,* when he heard a sound above him.

Oh, damn.

Tessa had passed on the shower. She'd dressed quickly and had come upon his little speech. He couldn't tell from the impassive face she presented if she'd heard every damning word he said. Until she walked right by him without so much as a thanks-for-the-memories.

He should have said something. He should have stopped her. But that fine-tuned instinct for self-preservation finally kicked in, saying, *Let it go. Let her go. You don't need this kind of trouble.* And while he was arguing with that cautious voice, she vanished below and with her, his apology window of opportunity.

* * *

Dinner was a late, silent and strained affair with the four of them picking at Constanza's flavorful empanadas. Tessa kept her stare on her plate, refusing to acknowledge Jack's covert glances while Rose and Constanza looked between them, seeing more than Jack should have allowed them to.

Let it go, his inner voice kept saying. She knew full well that sex between them was nothing but sex. Stunning, spectacular, mind-sapping sex. But it hadn't meant anything. No promises were made. No gooey words were exchanged that would imply anything except that they were two adults acting upon an attraction to one another. What was wrong with that? Nothing. Then why did he feel that apology bobbing up in his throat to choke him?

Because he knew she wasn't the kind of woman who indulged in casual sex. He knew it the first time he kissed her. He'd known it by the way she blushed when he'd grabbed a feel of her firmly toned thigh in her mother's car. And, dammit, he'd known it when she said his name in that smoky voice, all husky with desire and the unspoken plea of, *Don't touch unless you mean business.* He wasn't in the commitment business anymore. And if she knew why, she wouldn't have said his name like that. She would know why he couldn't act on the part of him that wanted to speak those promises. He'd allowed one of his feet to cross his permanently drawn line of uninvolvement when he started working her case. But that was still work, not personal. If he moved that other foot, everything would change, and he wasn't ready for that. He might never be ready for that.

Tessa excused herself from the table as soon as politely possible. Jack watched her go, even now mesmerized by the sophisticated swing of her hips and tormented by his memory of how they'd looked all sleek and buck naked. He put his palms to the table's edge, about to push off and go after her, when Rose spoke up from beside him.

"Mr. Jack, you need to go over my homework."

He looked from the inviting path to Tessa's bedroom to the expectant expression regarding him. Here was his obligation, right here at his table. This was all he had time for, all the room he had available in the jealousy guarded corridors leading to his heart. Rose had wiggled into a small nook that he refused to recognize. He couldn't afford to give Tessa the same opportunity. If he didn't admit to it, he didn't have to claim those emotions. Then they couldn't hurt him. That was his mantra. He'd been repeating it for years.

But tonight, it sucked.

He'd listened dutifully to a dissertation on global warming and softly spoken prayers, asking blessings upon him that he knew he didn't deserve. He tucked Rose in and whispered good-night and, as soon as he closed the door, he started looking for Tessa. The apology needed to be spoken, for the brusque words he'd spoken, for the feelings that had been hurt, to make clear the boundaries of their what could only be purely physical relationship.

But he couldn't find her.

Her room was empty. There was no sign of her outside or in any of the public rooms of the house. He checked the security monitors. No sign of an unwise exit. With concern edging toward panic, he was about to take another turn around the place to check out the trainee quarters, when he smelled smoke from a hopefully friendly fire. He followed it, surprised when it led to the stairs spiraling up to his rooms. Bracing for whatever lay in store for him, he began to climb.

A fire crackled invitingly in the stone hearth. It provided the only light in the vaulted room but he could see her clearly in the big leather chair, wrapped in the bearskin rug. A brief fantasy of her naked beneath it was quickly extinguished when she spoke in a cool, professional tone.

"I think it's best I leave before things get too complicated."

"I thought we went over this."

"That was…before."

Before they'd had stunning, spectacular, mind-sapping sex.

"Things don't have to change," was his rather lame argument coming from his typically male point of view.

"They already have, Jack. How much do I owe you?"

Guilt writhed. "If this is about what you heard me saying to Rose—"

Then she let him completely off the hook…for everything.

"It's not. I've decided not to pursue my father's case anymore."

He stood there, totally speechless. That was the one thing he'd never expected to hear her say. And instead of slipping the hook gratefully to swim frantically away from the dangers of the net, he grabbed on to the line, refusing to be shaken off.

"Tessa, we know your father didn't commit suicide."

"It doesn't matter."

Her spiritless tone alarmed him, made him push the issue. "Stan has the video from your building. Your mother is going over it. If she spots Allen, the first domino goes over. I think I know how he got into your father's office. Russell is checking it out for me tonight. If we can make the money trail between the payoff account set up in your father's name and O'Casey's kid's treatment fund and link them back to Martinez—"

She spoke again in the same flat voice. "It doesn't matter, Jack."

"Why doesn't it matter? You don't care that someone killed your father and the murderer just got away? What about your father's reputation?"

"I don't care. Not if bringing the killer to justice only damages it more."

She looked at him then. Firelight reflected brightly on the tears tracing down her cheeks. She said the final words as if they tore the heart and soul from her.

"Not if he was guilty."

Chapter 13

"Of what?" Jack demanded.

Tessa looked up miserably, his gorgeous, frowning face swimming in front of her eyes. "I don't know, Jack. And I don't want to find out."

Jack reached out to pull over one of the chairs, angling it so that when he sat, they were knee to knee. He leaned forward but stopped just short of touching her. His intense expression held no sympathy, no softness, as he said, "Yes, you do."

She started to shake her head.

"Yes, you do, Tessa," he argued firmly. "You can't stand not knowing. That's why you've been beating yourself up out here both mentally and physically, trying to prepare yourself for what you'll find out. Stan told me you were tougher than you looked. Hell, you're tougher than me. I would have backed down long ago."

A ghost of a smile moved her lips. "No, you wouldn't."

He smiled back, a warm, encouraging smile that gave off more heat than the fire. "No, I wouldn't. We're warriors, you and I. Lone wolves who get a scent then can't be shaken from it no matter where it leads. No matter how much it hurts you to follow."

"You mean, no matter who it hurts."

"Sometimes that happens."

Through her own pain and unhappiness, she caught a glimmer of something bleak and soul-crushing in his dark eyes, a brief hint of what worked deep inside Jack Chaney. Before she could pursue it, he placed his hands on her knees. Large, engulfing hands that could deal out death and desire with equal adeptness. And compassion, she was surprised to note.

He didn't have to be here like this, trying to help her through her pain. He could have agreed with her wish to back away if he truly was eager to return to his old hermit lifestyle. He would have if he was the man she'd believed him to be when she arrived. That man wouldn't have held her to still her nightmares as if she were Rose in need of his comfort. He wouldn't have circled his battered truck on the off-ramp to face down those who would harm her. He wouldn't have taken her problems to his family's door, invited her to his table…to his bed. A paycheck, he'd called her. But that wasn't how he was looking at her at this moment through dark, compelling eyes. He wouldn't have allowed himself to get this close, physically or emotionally, if she meant nothing to him at all. He'd once told her the money didn't matter and she knew now that that was true. What did? What did matter to him?

She knew why he'd told Rose what he had. To reassure her. To comfort her the only way he could. Some barrier prevented him from reaching out to her more personally, with love. Tessa understood that barrier. She'd lived behind it all her life. And finally, she couldn't stand crouching behind it anymore.

"He was a bad father," she admitted at last, the truth escaping not in an emotional rush but with a resigned sigh.

Jack said nothing, prompting her to continue with the light press of his fingertips.

"He didn't love me. I don't know why. That's the worst part. I never knew exactly what I did that made me so impossible to love. I thought maybe he only had so much to give and he poured it all on my mother. He adored her. Everything he did was for her and, for some reason, she never appreciated it. The more he did for her, the more she distanced herself. Then my brothers came along and he had no trouble caring about them."

She closed her eyes against the image of Robert D'Angelo bending to scoop up his boys, hugging them tight, pressing kisses atop their heads. Yet when she came close for the longed-for embrace, he pulled back, not slightly like Jack, but completely, moving himself both body and heart out of her reach. And for a little girl, who couldn't fathom the unfairness of it, that rejection scored upon her fragile sense of self, whittling it down to next to nothing. It hadn't made sense then, it didn't make sense now. But it still had the power to cut sharp teeth upon the ragged edges of her spirit.

"I stopped wondering why he didn't care and started concentrating on what I could do to earn his approval. I took up his profession, trying to make him proud. I gave up my own ambitions to help him achieve his, just to earn his respect. I worked so hard, Jack, but it was never enough, never enough for him to just hug me and say, 'Good job, Tessa.' He wasn't stingy with his praise until it came to me. He made me feel as if I'd never be quite up to the standard he used to measure the rest of the world."

Not up to the standard set by Barbara D'Angelo.

"He was a fool," Jack summed up flatly. "And he must have been blind not to see you for the jewel you are."

She shrugged, not really believing him, still unable to see

herself through Jack's eyes. Her injured pride, her hurt feelings weren't the important thing, not when faced with one more monumental conflict.

"He may have been a bad father but I always thought he was a good man. I believed in his work. I believed in his commitment to the truth, to justice, and I made those things my goals, too. What if I was wrong, Jack? His secrecy, the bank account, his relationship with Allen, his death. What if everything I believed about him was a lie?"

"What if he was just a man after all? Is that what you're afraid of finding out?"

She faced him and faced that question with a heartbreaking honesty. "Maybe it is."

She could devote herself wholeheartedly to the symbol of saintly goodness she'd held her father up to be. Had she been so disappointed in the real man, the man that hurt her continually with his rejection of her love, of her skills, of her worth, that she'd created one of untarnishable integrity so that she could adore and follow? One she could admire for his works because he was so lacking in true character?

"Tessa, you can't base your value according to his scales. They weren't fair. There's no way you could ever get them to balance out. Stop trying. You've given him your entire past. Don't give him your future, too. If you want to finish this, do it for the right reason. Because a crime's been committed. Because a wrong's been done. Not to prove something to a man you could never please. You don't owe him anything. He's not worth it, Tess. He's not worth your life."

"He was all I had, Jack."

"But he's not all that you are. He's not all that you can become. Don't you see that? How can you not see that?"

"Because no one's ever told me before."

He was silent for a moment. "I'm telling you now. And remember, you promised to listen to me."

His sudden grin cut through the block of anguish encasing her heart. In a single, gulping breath, it fell away, leaving an uncertain sense of freedom. She inhaled deeply, cautiously, testing the unrestrained boundaries. And it felt good.

He was watching her expression carefully, waiting for that moment of realization to come. And when it did, he smiled in satisfaction.

"Good girl."

She put her hands over his, not clutching, just layering gently over them. He went still.

"What am I going to do, Jack?" she asked quietly, not looking to him for an answer but for a direction.

"What do you want to do?"

"I want to do the right thing. I want to find out who killed my father and why. And then I want to walk away from it and not look back."

His hands turned, capturing hers in a firm crush. "You're a tough woman, Tessa D'Angelo. You'll do fine."

Yes, she would. The bud of encouragement took root deep and strong, promising a determined growth. All she needed was a little care. That's all she'd ever needed but she'd always been afraid to ask. Until now. Until she had so much to risk and so much to gain.

"Will you help me, Jack?"

There was a short pause, long enough for her to know that he'd considered the question carefully. Then his reply came sure and unwavering.

"Yes, I will."

Her breath expelled in a soul-cleansing rush and with it her weighty burden of guilt. If her father had done something wrong, she could face it. With Jack's support, she would face it and move on. What Jack hadn't said was that he'd be there for that next step, too.

Suddenly overwhelmed by weariness, she let her shoulders droop and her head hang low. She slipped her hands free of his to rub them over her face and through her hair. And when his palm cupped the back of her head, she didn't resist the pull that brought her to his shoulder. She rested there, safe enough to drop all defenses and linger.

"You're all right, Tess," he murmured against her hair. "You don't need anyone's approval but your own."

If that were true, why did it seem so vital to win his?

But then, she realized with some surprise, she already had it. Despite his gruffness, despite his cynicism, she'd always felt his admiration for who she was if not for what she was doing. She didn't need to do anything to earn it. It was just there. The concept humbled her—that something so frantically sought all her life like a personal Holy Grail was just there with no strings attached.

Who was this amazing man?

"Thank you, Jack."

She could feel his hesitation, then his slight smile. "Just part of the services I offer."

She smiled, too. "Somehow I doubt that."

She lifted her head and leaned back just far enough to see him. In the firelight, his gaze was dark liquid heat. As she held his stare and the complexities of their relationship resurfaced, she could see the protective shuttering begin behind his immobile expression.

Oh, no you don't, Jack Chaney. You're not going to wiggle out of this so easily.

She touched her fingertips to one taut, swarthy cheek, letting them stroke lightly along his fierce jaw. Muscles jumped beneath that slow caress but his gaze never flickered. It burned into hers, igniting her desire like raw oxygen touched by flame. It sucked the air from her lungs until she was starved for the taste of him as if it were her next breath. It made her light-headed. She went after what she needed to survive.

Slow and sweet, the kiss fueled her, feeding a flash fire of want and a deeper, smoldering sense of satisfaction.

Oh, but he could kiss. He teased her with a game of advance

and retreat, with the pressure of his mouth, with the part of his lips, with the touch of his tongue until she was mad for more.

"You promised me hours and hours," she whispered into their next shared breath.

"Yes, ma'am. I did." With her face bracketed between his big hands, he looked at her for a long moment. His stare devoured her. "That's a promise I'll enjoy keeping."

He unwrapped the bearskin rug from around her and, with a flip, cast it down on the hardwood floor in front of the hearth. He arched a black brow in question. Catching his meaning, she smiled.

The fur was softer than she'd expected and warmed quickly to the heat of the fire. She stretched out over it on her back while Jack spooned in next to her on his side. Before dinner she'd showered and changed from the rumpled suit into cozy knit pants and a plush chenille turtleneck the same color blue as her eyes. Jack's hand slipped under the hem of the sweater to rest hot and heavy on her midriff, letting it ride the rise and fall of her breathing as it increased with a roller-coaster intensity. He rolled toward her, claiming another will-warping kiss. He'd put on a navy-blue T-shirt that left his bronzed forearms bare. Her palm moved restlessly along the hard length of one of them. Such lethal power restrained into a tender touch. She sighed against his searching lips as he traced the lacy whorls on her bra with his thumb.

"Woman, you have the sexiest underwear," he murmured. "What color is it?"

"See for yourself."

He had the sweater over her head in a pulse beat. Her bra was powder blue, like the soft chenille, like the softer glow in her uplifted gaze. She trailed her forefinger down the warmed cotton of his T-shirt.

"And how about those boxers? That's a fashion statement I didn't expect from a guy like you."

"A man looks for all the freedom he can get."

"Then why don't you loosen up a little bit more."

She hadn't seen him naked yet and the suspense was killing her.

He sat up to strip off his shirt. His upper body was breathtakingly defined by browned skin over dangerous muscle. On his left shoulder was a small tattoo. A howling wolf's head framed by a full moon.

Lone Wolf.

Not tonight.

He got up onto his knees to undo his jeans and push them down, revealing those boxers she found so outrageously appealing, then sat to skin the denim from his long, athletic legs. He'd been barefoot already. He was so gorgeous, it hurt just looking at him. A dark pirate, a sleek, cunning warrior out to capture her body and to demand the surrender of her soul as his reward.

He had it. With one scorching look, he had all of her.

He sank back onto her lips, feasting there as if he'd hungered for a lifetime. Perhaps he had. She only knew that nothing had filled her so completely as the way he consumed her with a gaze and set her free to experience all he would give. If only for the night.

He lifted up and smiled slyly. Hooking a thumb beneath the elastic band of her pants, he pulled them away from her taut belly.

"Are the panties blue, too?"

She raised her hips. "Help yourself."

"Don't mind if I do."

He peeled down the snug knit and tugged off her bulky socks, leaving bare skin and nearly bare blue lace. As he traced the line of her scanty bottoms, her abdomen quivered.

"Now I know what they mean by less is more."

"And less than that is better still."

"No argument here."

He bent to press a hot kiss upon the small triangle of lace. Spontaneous combustion. She lifted her hips a second time, allowing him to remove the scrap of fabric. Then his mouth pressed upon the small triangle of curls. Tessa's hands fisted in the thick pelt. As he opened the way for a deeper, wildly intimate exploration, her legs began to tremble. That seismic quake centered beneath his attention, rippling along a fault line of intensity until a determined thrust of his tongue tore her asunder. Her body bucked with the tremendous rock and roll of sensation. A definite eight on the Richter scale because it had brought the walls of her inhibitions crashing down in one great earth-moving experience.

Before the last of the tremors eased away, Jack slid upward, tonguing her navel, up the center of her torso where he flicked open the center clip of her bra then pushed the cups aside. His mouth was molten passion atop the peak of one bared breast and then the other, streaking fire and the exquisite pain of delight straight to her very core.

She said his name, a low, lusty growl of want and desperate desire. Her hands gripped the sides of his face, dragging him up to meet her greedy kisses. She yanked his boxers down and let her palms roam over the hard contours of his butt, squeezing and kneading to appease the fascination she'd developed during those long runs. Staring him straight in the eye, she murmured, "The clock starts now, Jack."

"No time like the present."

He filled her with a strong, sure stroke, letting her know he belonged there with a hard, claiming kiss. And when he began to move, time stood still for Tessa. For hours.

And hours.

"Too. You said 'too.' What did you mean by that?"

Jack squinted one eye open. "What?"

"When you said you wouldn't have me scarring your soul, too. What did you mean?"

His eye closed and his expression closed up even tighter. She considered letting it go, letting him keep his secrets. But hadn't she just bared her soul to him…along with a lot more?

"It has something to do with Rose's mother."

It was just a guess but she could tell she'd hit pay dirt by the way he tensed by slow degrees. Either he would tell her or he wouldn't. This was a time for truth.

"What do you know about Esmerelda?" He asked without opening his eyes, without displaying any emotion in either voice or facial expression.

"Only that Rose said she'd died and that you brought her and her aunt to live with you afterward. Are you Rose's father?"

"No."

"But you and her mother were involved." Why else would he have brought the orphaned child back with him?

"Involved? I guess you could say that. I was in Colombia on a mission. Esmerelda was my contact. Her husband had been in their *policia nacional* and after his murder, she'd been instrumental in infiltrating a lot of places we couldn't get access to. I mean, who would suspect a widow and her young daughter of passing secrets to foreign government operatives?"

"Someone did," Tessa concluded softly.

A pause. "Yeah. Someone did." He stared up at the ceiling, his eyes a flat black, reflecting the firelight, but no sign of inner life. He looked a million miles away. Or at least a continent.

Hoping to encourage him to continue, Tessa laid her head upon his shoulder as her palm settled on the slow, steady rise and fall of his chest. Automatically his hand touched the back of her head, fingers kneading in a restless motion that told more of his mood than anything else had.

"She'd set herself up in a village we had under surveillance. It was dangerous but she insisted. She got a job in the local big cheese's house. His was the palm one had to grease to move anything from pot to pigs through the region. She kept track of who came to visit and of insurgent and paramilitary groups that were in the area so we wouldn't be surprised."

"What were you doing there?"

"Things you really don't want to know about. Tracking weapons mostly. She would hide me and Russell and a couple of other operatives, feed us food and information. We had a pretty sweet deal going for about five months."

"Were you in love with her?" Her throat tightened as she asked that. She didn't want to think about him in love with another woman after what they'd just shared even if she was no threat to Tessa because she was no longer a tangible flesh-and-blood rival.

Or perhaps she was more of one because of it.

"I should have been. If I had been, maybe she'd still be alive."

"She was in love with you."

He didn't deny it.

"All she could talk about was getting to America where fifty-five percent of the population didn't live below the poverty level, getting a house for Rose and getting her into a real school where she could grow up a happy, normal child and not as a potential casualty of some local or boundary war. She never came right out and asked me if I would take them, but I knew that's what she wanted. I knew that's why she was willing to take the risks she did. She was hoping that when our job was over and we moved on, I would take them with me."

"But you couldn't."

"I didn't want to." Jack could have made himself sound less the villain but he didn't. He summed up his own motives with a ruthless candor. "She was my source and it was my job to get information. It couldn't be any more than that, not in my line of work. I liked what I did. I believed in what I did. And I let her believe whatever she wanted."

He paused, waiting for Tessa to call him a cold, miserable bastard.

"Did you promise you would take her with you?"

"No. But I never told her I wouldn't, either. Don't ask, don't tell. It worked for me."

She was silent for a long time, letting him wonder what she was thinking. He plied her hair absently, winding it through his fingers while he marveled that something so fair, so soft, so fine could also have such tensile strength. But was Tessa strong enough to hear the rest of what burdened his soul?

"So what happened?" she finally prompted.

"We knew they suspected her but we kept letting her go back into the compound, to gather the intel we needed. Then one night she didn't come out. Connie, her sister, came instead with news that she'd been arrested and that they were torturing her to get her to tell them who she'd been giving the information to. We were gone, like ghosts, sure she would give us up to save herself."

"But she didn't."

He took a deep breath and shook his head, as if the magnitude of her courage, of her sacrifice, still perplexed him. "No, she didn't. After a week of doing what must have been unimaginable things to her, they marched her out into the square and shot her as an example to others who might think to collaborate with the enemy. They shot her like a dog in the street."

Tessa could see the horror of that moment replaying in his gaze, reflected by the dancing firelight.

"You couldn't have known that's what they'd do."

But he didn't take her easy way out to slip his yoke of guilt. "Of course I knew and we just let her make the sacrifice. They shot her while Rose and Constanza watched."

Tessa shut her eyes but, like Jack, couldn't shut out the image. It blended and blurred and became that of her father lying in a pool of his own blood.

"That night I went back," he continued in the same atonal voice. "I carried Rose and half dragged Constanza out to a landing strip in the jungle. In five minutes we were in the air on the way to the United States. Eight days earlier, Esmerelda could have been flying with us. I let her die, Tess. My mission was more important to me than her life."

Tessa jumped right by that to something that was more obvious in her eyes. "And your life was more important to her than her own."

He couldn't respond to that. He'd never known how to respond to that.

"Does Rose know?"

He shook his head. "She thinks I'm a hero. I've been too much of a coward to tell her otherwise. I resigned my commission the minute the plane touched down in the States. I called in every favor owed me to get myself declared her guardian. And I made it my mission to see her mother's last wish came true, that Rose would grow up in America, safe and happy."

"Doesn't that make you a hero?"

He glanced at her briefly, appearing almost angry that she wasn't holding him in contempt for what he viewed as an unforgivable crime. "Not when weighed against the rest. No job, no cause, was worth the life of that little girl's mother. It was a choice I didn't have the right to make but I made it anyway. And when Rose finds out, she's going to blame me as much as I blame myself."

Was that why he wouldn't let himself love the child? Was he holding her at arm's length to spare himself the future pain of her hate and scorn?

"Tell her, Jack. You might be surprised."

He glanced at her then, his stare stormy and dangerous.

"Would you forgive your father so easily if you found out he'd lied to you and paid for the clothes on your back and that enviable law degree with drug money?" He paused, studying Tessa's expression, as if waiting for the expected hurt, denial and finally anger, at him, to settle in. But her stare remained steady, her eyes filled with empathy, not blame. He shrugged. "Drug money, blood money, what's the difference? I can't bring her mother back and there's nothing I can do to give back to Rose what was taken from her."

"Nothing except to trust her and love her."

He jerked his head to the side to glare with a savage intensity into the flames. "Easy for you to say."

No, it wasn't. It wasn't easy for her to say or easy for her to conceive of. Could she forgive her father if she found out he was guilty? Could she absolve him of his sins after she'd spent her whole life struggling only to fall short of his impossibly high expectations?

"You have to do what's in your heart, Jack," she advised at last.

"There's nothing in my heart. Nothing but darkness. I don't have the luxury of feeling. That was taken from me in a jungle in South America when I let a woman endure unimaginable pain and then take a bullet that should have been meant for me. When she suffered so, I lost the right to feel alive."

She curved her hand to fit the side of his face, tugging gently to direct his attention back her way, so he could see the conviction in her own expression as she spoke.

"Jack, she died so you would live and she knew she'd be leaving her most precious gift with you, in your care. If she thought you were the kind of heartless monster you think you are, she never would have left Rose without knowing you'd do the right thing by her. She trusted you with all her heart, Jack, with the most important thing in her life. Don't you dare disappoint her."

"I've given Rose everything she needs." He argued in a fierce, flat tone that lacked the conviction it should have contained if what he said was true. Then Tessa exposed his charade with one simple fact.

"Except love. That's all she really needs. That's all she wants from you."

"Then she wants too much. And Esmerelda trusted the wrong man."

"I don't think so, Jack. I don't think you give yourself near enough credit. Your dad said you were one of the good guys. When are you going to start believing that again?"

"Are you going to make me a believer, Tess?" His tone was as cold as his mocking smile. But she refused to be discouraged. She could sense the fear behind his angry bravado. She recognized it from her own earlier behavior. Well, he hadn't let her hide behind bluff, either.

"Is that a dare? You know I can't back down from a challenge."

"Back down from this one, Tess," he warned somberly. "You can't win. You'll get hurt."

"Didn't you promise you'd never let anyone hurt me again? Was that a lie, Jack?"

Before he could answer, the shrill ring of his cell phone interrupted. He rolled up and over her to snag it off the belt of his discarded trousers.

"Chaney," he snapped. Then he was immediately all rigid angles. "When? Where? Son of a— On our way."

He closed the cell lid. The muscles in his arm were shaking as if he fought the desire to crush the phone into little micro receivers. His expression was one of stark fury and despair.

She was almost afraid to ask.

"What's happened?"

"That was your mom. Get dressed. Stan's in intensive care. They don't know if he's going to make it."

Chapter 14

Barbara D'Angelo huddled over a cold cup of vending machine coffee, looking small and tired in the empty waiting room. She lifted her head when she heard them approach. Her gaze swam with sorrow and relief. She looked to her daughter, awaiting a sign to go to her for shared comfort and grieving, but the sign didn't come. She slumped back into the seat cushions.

"He's in surgery," she said dully, her stare fixing on the contents of her cup. "A ruptured spleen and possible other internal injuries."

"What the hell happened?" Jack demanded. When he saw the fragile shake of Barbara's shoulders, his tone softened. "Barbara, what happened?" He assumed the chair next to the distraught woman while Tessa remained near the doorway, tense and silent.

Barbara clung gratefully to the hand Jack slipped over hers. "It all happened so fast. Stan went to check on a malfunction with the garage door. It kept going up and down and he thought something was stuck under the censor. He stepped out the door and told me to lock it behind him. The minute I did, they were on him, three of them with masked faces. They had Robert's golf clubs—" Her voice broke. Jack rubbed a comforting hand across her shoulders.

"And what were you doing while they were beating the hell out of him?" was Tessa's icy question.

"Stan led them out into the front yard, away from me. All I could think to do was to distract them. I turned on the lawn sprinklers and the floodlights we use for holidays and parties. That got them to stop. And when I activated the alarm system, they ran away. I told the police Stan had stopped a robbery attempt. I wanted to ride with him in the ambulance so they said they'd come down later to take a statement. What do I tell them? Was it a robbery?"

"That's how we'll play it." Jack gave her an encouraging hug. "You did the right thing. You kept them from killing him."

"Maybe not." She looked up, her eyes bruised by misery. "We won't know for another hour or so."

"What the hell happened?" came another intruding voice.

They turned to see Michael Chaney wheeling into the room. He looked as if he'd dressed in the middle of a hurricane but his eyes were rock steady.

"Pop, what are you doing here?"

"I heard the call on my scanner. I'd been listening, you know, just in case. How is he?"

"Not good. He's in surgery. Hello, Michael."

"Barb, I'd say it was great to see you under different circumstances."

She nodded.

Silence settled as they clustered together, restless and uncomfortable in their helplessness. A man they all loved and respected was beyond the double doors, beyond their reach, beyond all but their prayers. And it wasn't enough.

Jack came up out of his chair, the explosive movement catching Tessa's attention. His voice was deceptively calm. "Pop, can you stay here with the ladies for a while? I've got to check something. Are you packing?"

The elder Chaney patted the inside pocket in his chair. "Don't leave home without it."

Tessa stepped to intercept Jack. "Where are you going?"

His impassive features told her nothing but his gaze was hot with rage. "I'll only be gone for a little while. I'll be right back. There's nothing I can do here but maybe out there… You stay here where you'll be safe."

While he rushed headlong into who knew what.

Unwilling to be brushed off by that placating statement, she gripped his arm. "Betsy and I will go with you." She touched a hand to the small of her back where a holster held her Smith & Wesson. "It's part of my new ensemble," she said in response to his raised brow. "I don't leave home without it, either."

"I'd feel better if you stayed here and out of trouble."

Out of my way, was what he meant. Well, too bad.

"You won't know what to look for."

He thought a minute, studying her determined features, weighing the pros and cons of having her along. Apparently the pros won out. His nod was curt. "Do what I tell you."

"Don't I always?"

He quirked a wry smile. Then to the other two, he said, "We won't be long. Call if there are any changes."

The minute all the hoopla died down at the D'Angelo estate, Stan's attackers had obviously gone inside. They'd done a thorough, if hurried, job.

Tessa stood in the center of the destruction, surveying it with emotions quaking, afraid she was going to throw up. This was her home. She recognized the work. She was seeing her apartment all over again. The acid bite of fear burned in the back of her throat. Then Jack touched her elbow.

"You up to this, Annie O?"

She swallowed that bitter taste and nodded. "Just getting mad."

"Let's make it quick. You're not safe here. Look for anything they might have missed. Anything out of the ordinary that might give us a clue about what they were looking for."

Anything they might have missed. She noted the slashed couch cushions, the overturned curio cabinet. Even the rug had been torn up from around the baseboards. It didn't look as though they'd missed a trick. Angry tears smarted until she blinked them away.

"Divide and conquer?"

Jack's tone was level and sensible. "Stay in the room with me."

She didn't bother to chide him for his caution. She was seeing those creased trousers as she quickly began an up-close evaluation of the damage done. They went through the downstairs rooms, following the trail of savagery. Tessa fought against the hot emotion threatening to blur her vision. Crying over ruined memories wouldn't help them. These were just things. Her mind held the true remembrances of the past. Those wouldn't shatter or tear or topple.

The first floor was bad enough but the upstairs, where their more private lives were contained, became a more personal assault upon Tessa's vulnerable spirit. They started in neutral territory in her brothers' rooms where sports and music memorabilia cluttered the walls and desktops. Tessa could still hear the booming voices and feel the energy of the teen boys who had tormented her as older sister. Now those pesky boys were solid citizens, Todd, a computer whiz and Kyle, the security analyst. The ache of missing them rose sudden and strong. When had they all gotten so far apart that closing the gap seemed almost impossible?

Her parents' room was pure agony. Their scents mingled near the big four-poster where the fresh bedding had been stripped down and the mattress left askew. Near the walk-in closets, her father's suits had been yanked from their orderly row and his shirts torn from their tissued packaging. Her mother's designer dresses were scattered on the floor like exotic birds shot from the sky, and her jewelry glittered on the dresser top like the shards of Tiffany glass upon Tessa's apartment floor. No pretending this was a robbery. Her father's adoration added up to a fortune in those sparkly baubles.

In the bathroom, Barbara's row of specially mixed cosmetics were broken and spilled into the sink until it resembled an artist's pallet. Tessa picked up one of the few undamaged bottles of perfume. On her skin, the delicate floral tones woke to life, surrounding her with a field of hyacinths in spring. She glanced up at Jack's reflection in the mirror. His expression was carefully impassive.

"My father had this fragrance made especially for my mother at Bourbon French Parfums in New Orleans when they went there for their twenty-fifth anniversary. They have the formula on file. Forever Mine. He had it made up for her every year after that and sent to her with a bouquet of spring flowers. I thought it was so romantic."

Her hand began to shake. Gently, Jack took the fragile bottle from her and replaced it on the littered basin.

"Oh, God, Jack. If they'd gotten inside, they could have killed her. They could have…"

"They didn't, Tess."

His arms went easily around her, locking her tight to his chest where tremors ravaged her from head to toe. But she didn't cry. He pressed his mouth to her temple and told her with his own practical version of comforting, "It didn't happen, Tessa. She's safe. Don't dwell on the what-ifs. They'll tear you apart and spit you out."

"Like they did Stan? Jack, what are we going to do? You know the police won't do anything. They'll say it was a robbery, an unfortunate coincidence. They won't find anything that will lead to those men Martinez hired. Or to Martinez. There's got to be a way to get to her."

Because her tone had gone from fractured to furious, Jack squeezed her closer. "Then we'll find that way."

She nodded against the supple grain of his black leather jacket. How easy it would be to linger in his embrace, soaking up his strength and confidence. She sighed, breathing in the rich smell of leather and the swirl of fragrances they'd poured down the drain. Her mind began to click like a computer program processing new data.

Looking for what?

What could be hidden in a cosmetic jar?

"Let's finish up, Jack. There's got to be something here. Something they missed that we're not seeing. My father must have left a clue for us to find."

When she leaned back, in charge of her emotions once more, Jack scrambled them with a slow, plundering kiss. She remained, eyes closed, for a long moment, reveling in the taste of him on her lips, in the sturdy heat from the hands framing her uplifted face. When she looked up, it was into the dark promise of his gaze.

She'd been crazy to doubt this man's sincerity, his commitment to his word if not her cause.

He would keep her safe. He would stay with her to the finish. And then they could explore this crazy attraction between them. Once she'd put the past to rest.

"Only one more room to go," she stated with no trace of the clenching turmoil within her.

Her room.

Nothing had been changed. She hadn't lived here for almost ten years but, just like her brothers' rooms, time hadn't progressed from the last time she'd made her bed. The walls hosted several art prints, now hanging crooked on their hooks. Her closet held one bag of sentimental garments ranging from christening gown to prom dress and the various graduation robes. No knickknacks cluttered her desk or dresser. Viewing it from an adult standpoint—from what might have been Jack's viewpoint—her room reflected her personality. All business, no pleasure. Was she really that dull?

While Jack went through the clothing that had been pulled out of the cleaner's bag and strewn across the floor of the closet, Tessa went to regard the one item on her dresser. It lay facedown, glass broken. Her diploma from the University of Detroit School of Law. Her *Juris Doctor.* For that one moment, when she'd rejoined her family in cap and gown, she'd basked in the glow of her father's respect. He'd read the parchment she'd slaved for then straightened the tassel dangling from her mortarboard. He'd smiled and told her, "Education is the key, Tessa. It will unlock the law so justice can be served."

She brushed the fragmented glass out of the frame and set the document upright once more. Fingering the silky strands of the tassel that hung from the corner of the frame, she allowed the feel of accomplishment to warm her. Then she froze.

Education is the key, Tessa. It will unlock the law so justice can be served.

"Jack."

Alerted by her quiet voice, he was instantly at her side. "What is it?"

"The key to justice."

There, attached to the top of the tassel, dangling like the charm she'd once thought it was and hidden by the crest for her school and year of graduation, was a small key.

The clue her father had left for her to find.

Stan was in recovery by the time they returned to the hospital. The long surgery had gone well but the prognosis was still guarded.

"I'll stay awhile," Michael Chaney offered. "He didn't

leave me when I needed him, so it's right that I be here when
he wakes up." He tipped his head toward Barbara. She sat in
one of the unyielding chairs, crumpled physically and emotionally by the evening's events and the knowledge that her
home had been invaded. "Take her home with you, son. I'm
sure they didn't leave anything at her place that she'll want
to see. An officer already took her statement so there's no reason for her to hang around."

"I'll hang around if I like, Michael Chaney," came Barbara's surprisingly strong argument. "I have as much right to be
here as you do."

"Sure you do, Barb, but don't you think when he sees your
face it ought to be with you looking your best and not as
though you'd just spent the night in an alley somewhere?"

"You are such a flatterer," she muttered, reaching down to
pick up her purse. "Just a few hours' sleep and a shower and
I'll be back. I'll have to stop by the house and pick up a
change of clothes."

"You can borrow something of mine, Mom."

Barbara regarded her daughter's unexpected charity with
damp-eyed gratitude. "That's very nice of you to offer."

"It's just a sweater and a pair of pants, not a trip with a personal shopper through Nordstrom's."

Barbara shrugged off Tessa's judgmental comment with a
resigned sigh. "It'll be fine, Tess."

Tessa stopped the apology that sprang to her lips, surprised that she'd felt the need to speak it. Why had she always
made her mother the villain, the unprotesting target of her dis-
dain? And why hadn't Barbara told her to stop acting like such
a spoiled little snot years ago, instead enduring her meanness
as if she deserved it?

And an hour later, wrapped in Tessa's robe, curled up in
front of the living room fireplace watching the logs glow
with white-hot ash, Barbara did look fine. With her hair
scooped back and her face free of makeup, she, in fact, looked

younger, more vulnerable. She smiled wearily at her daughter as Tessa dropped into one of the suede-covered chairs.

"This is some house."

"Yes, it is. Mom, you should be in bed."

"I'm not quite tired enough to close my eyes yet."

Tessa knew exactly what she meant. So she thought to distract them both. "Mom, do you know of any place Dad might have kept a locker? We found a key but there are no markings on it."

"The club, maybe. He kept a change of clothes there in case he had time to sneak in a last-minute golf scramble."

That sounded too obvious. "Anyplace else? Someplace he might not have been to for a while. Someplace you might have forgotten about. Think, Mom."

Barbara pinched the bridge of her nose between thumb and forefinger, her brow furrowing with concentration. "I don't know of anyplace else. The office, the court, the club and home. That was pretty much it."

"That's okay, Mom. We'll try the club."

"What are you looking for?"

"Whatever they're looking for. Something Dad had to either convict…or blackmail Martinez and/or Chet Allen."

Barbara regarded her with a quiet intensity. "You think that's where the money came from?"

"I don't know," she admitted with a sad truthfulness.

"Tess, your father was not a criminal. He loved the law. Don't believe those things they said about him. That wasn't the kind of man he was."

"I don't know what kind of man he was, Mom. He never let me get close enough to find out."

Barbara was silent for a long moment, then she said with heavy regret, "I'm so sorry, Tess."

"All buttoned down tight." Jack walked in on their dialogue, then realizing he'd stepped into the middle of something serious, he searched for a way to retreat. "I've got to

make a few calls. I'll leave you two ladies to catch up on…
whatever."

"Thank you for you hospitality, Jack."

"No problem. You'll be safe here."

"Stan said you were teaching Tess to defend herself. Is
that true?"

"More like defend myself from her. Your daughter is quite
a scrapper. It's like going a couple of rounds with Sugar Ray
Leonard."

Barbara started to smile then her features stilled. "I'd almost forgotten."

"What, Mom?" Tessa leaned forward, encouraged by the
sudden heightened color in her mother's face.

"The gym. In Roseville. He and Chet and Tag used to spar
there when they were in high school. They used to bum cig-
arettes and beer from the regulars. When he came back from
Nam and started working in the prosecutor's office, he used
to go there sometimes to work out whatever he couldn't tell
me. He had a locker there."

Jack and Tessa exchanged optimistic stares.

"I'll check it out first thing tomorrow." He didn't betray any
outward excitement but Tessa could tell he was pumped. His
eyes glittered. "Ladies, it's late and you need your beauty sleep."

His tone brooked no argument so they gave none.

Beneath her covers, her mind and body limp with exhaustion, Tessa couldn't sleep. She lay tossing and twisting as the
minutes ticked by into an hour. Every time she closed her
eyes, she imagined her mother with those brutal thugs inside
her house. One of them wore knife creased trousers and had
a voice like sinister velvet.

The mattress behind her dipped with a weight more sig-
nificant than Tinker's. She smelled Jack's clean scent and
sighed as his arms wrapped around her, tugging her back into
the wall of comfort his body offered. He stayed on top of the
covers, layering his own heat through them.

"Thought the bedbugs might be biting," he whispered behind her ear where the caress of his breath quickened a shiver inside her.

"Not now, they're not."

"Then sleep tight, Tessa."

And on one long exhalation, she did just that. When she woke in the morning, he was gone.

Chapter 15

"I missed you this morning."

At Tessa's soft-spoken words, Jack looked up from his coffee. He offered a one-sided smile. "If I'd stayed, my intentions would have gone from humanitarian to purely self-indulgent."

"You say that like it's a bad thing."

And perhaps it was, was what his tight expression told her. They'd laid bare a lot of very personal baggage in front of the fireplace. Now, in the light of day, perhaps he was regretting that.

She had watched him for several minutes before deciding to make an overture. He had looked so isolated, so intense staring out over the creek but not really seeing it. The morning air was brisk with the harbinger of snow to come and full of the scent of musty downed leaves and pine. Dampness seeped in through the skin right to bone. Tessa had thought about the warmth she'd find tucked in against Jack's side but his mood seemed unpredictable and she wasn't sure the breach of his personal space would be welcome. So she'd lingered at a safe distance, wondering how to approach him until his body language advised that he was alerted to her presence.

Even as she approached him, his reception had been guarded. His posture was braced and withdrawn but his dark gaze smoldered as it did a quick once-over assessment of her choice of clothing.

"Thought I'd take in a quick five miles before breakfast," she said now as his silence continued. His fathomless gaze followed the movement of nylon over new muscle until she felt as though she was standing on display in her underwear. Or less. Jogging suddenly wasn't as appealing as the notion of dragging Jack back upstairs. But she stuck with the plan because he'd still made no attempt to act on what flared so hotly in his stare. She made her tone casual. "Funny how you start out hating every step then you find you can't start your day without that endorphin rush."

"You shouldn't go alone."

She refused to let his warning spoil the moment. Tessa patted the small of her back. "Betsy's keeping me company. I'll be careful. Yellow alert all the way." Then, she waited, hoping he'd volunteer to join her. She'd come to enjoy the way they tested their stamina in the woods. And in the bedroom. Her face heated, forcing her to look away, toward the barracks where not so long ago she'd been exiled. So why did the distance between them seem to yawn just as impossibly wide after the intimacies they'd shared?

"I'd join you but I'm waiting for a couple of return calls."

He didn't elaborate and the sense of secrecy left her feeling excluded and unfairly wounded. Back to the barracks on an emotional level. Used to coming up against that wall, she automatically backed down. "I'll hit the trail then and give you your privacy."

"It's just from my dad and Russell," he offered. The explanation, though vague and reluctantly tendered, soothed her ruffled feathers. A week ago he wouldn't have felt obligated to give her even that little tease of information. Not a great stride, but she'd known it was a long race.

"That's fine. Let me know what they had to say." *No secrets, Jack,* was what she didn't add, though it was subtly implied. He smiled thinly.

"Yes, ma'am. A full report when you get back." He nodded toward the wall of glass. "How's she doing this morning?"

Tessa followed his gaze through the window separating them from the living room. Barbara sat on the modern couch sharing juice with Rose. The two of them were huddled close over some glossy magazine that looked suspiciously like high fashion. Tessa experienced a sudden odd twinge. The intimate, companionable act was something a mother and daughter might share. Had she and her mother ever enjoyed such a relaxed and frivolous moment in the early morning hours? She couldn't remember one. She'd been in her father's study going over points of law and totally disinterested in discussing hem lengths or hair highlights with her glamorous mother.

Did Barbara regret that loss of simple girlfriend closeness from a daughter who thought her lifestyle trivial? Perhaps there were things her mother could have offered that weren't found between the leather-bound covers in her father's library but Tessa had never given her the chance to impart them.

Watching her with Rose, the way the young girl snuggled up under the inclusive drape of her arm and eagerly returned her smiles, Tessa mourned the loss of those moments.

"She's all right," she told Jack at last. "I don't think she got much sleep. She wasn't prepared to have all this dropped at her doorstep."

"Who is?"

She glanced up at him. *You are,* she wanted to reply but she held the words because she got the impression that he was talking about something else all together. Something more personal that had blindsided him when he wasn't looking. Something like a cause he couldn't ignore and a woman he couldn't resist. Or at least, that's what she was hoping.

She started her run, chasing the Zenlike calm she often found in the woods, but her mind refused to stop its own wild race.

Because of Jack and what remained unspoken between them.

She had his promise to help her but he'd given her no other assurances. Whatever flared and smoldered between them still burned like an uncontrolled fire. They had yet to establish perimeters that would reign it in and bank it more strongly for a longer lasting heat. Perhaps the brief yet all-consuming flare of the moment was all Jack was willing to offer a woman, especially one so obsessed with her own agenda.

While her feet hit the path in solid repetitions, echoing her heartbeat, her emotions rebelled against a similar flow of regulated logic. A mind trained to regimented facts was useless when it came to categorizing feelings. But still, she tried. It was the only way she knew how to approach the problem. Look at it from all angles.

Had she given him any indication that she was interested in more than just a physical romp and some professional support? Had she hinted that her emotions were engaged and that there was a whole area of her heart that lay unexplored and ripe for conquest? No. She was playing it as close to the cuff as he was. Because they were both afraid of what they were feeling. She was no more ready than he was and that truth surprised and saddened her.

How was she just going to let him go when this was over? What if he was willing to just walk away?

She pushed herself on the trail, racing after the exhaustion that would give her peace of mind. She couldn't find it. It was one step ahead, taunting, teasing, like the fluttering hem of Jack's jogging shorts.

What was she going to do about Jack Chaney?

He wasn't going to make the first move. If she wanted to know where he stood in regard to a potential relationship, she was going to have to back him into a corner. Not flattering but understandable now that she knew his story. It wasn't the commitment he feared, it was the risk of anticipated failure. How could she tell him his emotions would be safe with her when she wasn't sure how to handle her own?

She wasn't prepared to deal with a man like Jack. He defied definition with all his edgy contrasts. Moody and remote, dangerous yet curiously vulnerable, multifaceted and still direct. A constant puzzle she'd yet to solve even with the new pieces he'd revealed to her.

And then there was the way they were together. A spontaneous combustion of tempers, passions and ideals. She of the cool control, cut-and-dry, straight-and-narrow, and he of the brooding shadows, detached bemusement and bad-boy, curfew-breaking grin. But with all the clashing of strong wills, the underlying respect anchored them in what, frighteningly, could be something so good it scared her to consider it.

She paused to take a sip from her water bottle, continuing to move so her muscles wouldn't tighten up, the way her thoughts were bunching into hard, anxious knots.

Where would Jack fit into her future? Her apartment didn't allow domestic pets over twenty pounds. Where could she keep a wild and wary timber wolf that refused to be contained within the perimeters of her world?

She started off again, determined to reach her goal. To find an answer to the question Jack presented.

Breathing deep into the pain building in her calves and chest, she took a moment to appreciate the setting. Here, Jack had found a slice of heaven few in her office building would ever understand. They would be as fearful of the silence and the isolation as she'd been when she arrived. All those stars in the endless sky. All those hours with only one's thoughts to fill them.

Jack had invited her, albeit reluctantly, into his personal sanctuary and, over the past weeks, she'd made herself at home here. Could it be home? Her working in the city, the long commute…with Jack waiting as her reward.

She slowed as the house came into view. His fortress to protect him and his from her and those like her. Yet he'd opened the door to let her in. But that wasn't exactly like inviting her to stay.

And then there were the secrets. What he did, where he'd been, what he felt. He made no bones about what he thought, but that was just the surface of the intensely private man she found so compelling and yet, at the same time, frustrating. How could she blend the black and white of her existence with his murky half tones without compromising her beliefs? Could either of them bend without breaking? Would they want to try if it meant finding a way to meet in the middle?

She moved up the gravel drive, her steps weighted with more than just weariness. Two more stubborn, emotionally skittish and independent people she couldn't conceive of. There would never be harmony. Or boredom. Yet didn't they both thrive on high-stakes situations?

Jack was waiting for her on the porch. He came forward to meet her at the steps, his expression open and unguarded for once.

"My dad called. Stan is awake and real cranky. He wants you to stop by later to bring him his dirty magazine collection."

She took two steps up, locked her fingers behind the back of his head and pulled him down into a kiss so hard and hungry, it took him several startled heartbeats to respond.

It was more than happiness, more than simple desire and he knew it.

"What?"

She answered with another seeking lip-lock.

Searching for what? She could feel the question and his un-
easiness in the cautious placement of his hands upon her shoulders. Resting lightly, ready to crush her close or to lever her
away. Which would it be? she wondered as she tasted him more
deeply, more desperately, right out on his front porch for God
and everyone to see. His reaction was carefully measured and
oh, so wary. He didn't retreat but neither did he advance. He
met her overtures with an appreciative murmur and the light
stroke of his palms down her back. Neutral but not disinterested.

Finally he leaned back, his dark eyes probing for a reason.

"What's going on, Tess? Did I miss something?"

She looked up at him, seeing his heartbreakingly handsome face, his wry, clueless smile and the innate apprehen-
sion in his intent stare.

"I don't know, Chaney. You tell me."

And she slipped around him to go into the house, to an icy
shower designed to drive silly daydreams from her head.

Water didn't come that cold.

Jack and her mother were waiting in the living room, Jack
with a puzzled wariness and Barbara with hesitation.

"I'm going to check the key against the two possible
locks," Jack began. "Your mom wants to stop at her house and
pick up a few things first."

"I'll stay with her while you follow up on the locked box."

Jack quickly covered his surprise. He hadn't expected her
to choose Door Number One. "I don't like leaving the two of
you there alone."

"Come on, Chaney, what trouble can we get into?"

He scowled. "Do you expect an answer?"

She waved off his reluctance. "I'll make sure all the alarms
are activated. It's broad daylight. We'll be careful. And we
have to deal with the house sometime."

Still, he wasn't totally convinced that they could be trusted. "You'll wait there for me."

Both nodded.

"Let's go."

Rose met them at the door. She had an unabashed hug for Barbara and Tessa while Jack observed impassively. He rumpled the girl's hair. "You behave. Get your studies done. And stay in the house today."

Her brow puckered in curiosity but she didn't question him. "*Sí*, Mr. Jack. Will the misses be coming back with you?"

"Yes."

"*Bueno.*"

Rose was that quick to accept the situation. Jack wasn't sure to be grateful or alarmed by her easy embrace of the two women who changed the atmosphere of his house into a home with their mere presence. He didn't like change. But he didn't object to this one as strenuously as he once would have.

And that bothered him no little bit.

Barbara's reaction to the inside of her home was more restrained than her daughter's had been. She went methodically from room to room righting and straightening and tossing the irreparable. Tessa didn't know what to say so she stayed judiciously out of the way.

In the bedroom, Barbara pulled out a suitcase and began to fill it with her belongings. She handled each item gingerly as if it had been contaminated by those who had violated her private spaces. Her features were pale, her expression composed. Only her eyes held a haunted shadowing.

How well Tessa understood.

"I'm selling the house."

Tessa jolted in shock as her mother continued to neatly fold her blouses into the designer bag.

"It's too big for me now and quite frankly, I'll never feel

comfortable here again. Before I do, I'll give you kids a chance to take whatever you want and I'll get rid of the rest of it. A charity auction or something." She paused and took a breath. Her gaze moistened but she blinked away the sentiment and continued her task. "My needs will be simpler from now on."

"Mom, you don't have to rush into anything."

"I'm not rushing, Tess. I don't want to be here without Robert. This was his showplace. I always felt a bit lost in it."

Again her quiet words surprised her daughter. "I thought you wanted this house."

"Your father thought I wanted it. I'd never stepped foot inside it until he told me it was ours. I would have preferred something…homier. I feel more comfortable in your friend Jack's house than I've felt here in all the years we've been here. He's an interesting man, your Jack. Are you interested?"

Her mother was changing the subject and Tessa wasn't sure she should let it go. But she found herself answering, "He's a difficult man. A little too complex."

Barbara smiled wistfully. "There's nothing wrong with that. Sometimes it's the things you have to work at that you really appreciate."

What was she talking about? Tessa and Jack? Or herself and her husband?

"So what will you do?" Tessa never considered her mother's financial situation, assuming her father had had that taken care of. Her indifference to the situation now left a residue of guilt she wasn't sure how to handle.

"Get someplace small, maybe a loft condo in one of those reclaimed inner-city areas so I won't feel so alone."

Tessa could have told her that surrounding herself with noise and activity didn't equate to companionship. And maybe she would now that the tenuous barriers between them were beginning to come down.

"And I'm thinking of getting a job. Oh, don't look so startled. It's not like I've never done anything manual before. I worked in a restaurant while your father was going to night school. I clerked in a department store and did the books after hours for several businesses so we could make ends meet. This was before your father got his law degree. We didn't live out of your grandparents' checkbook. Those were tough times." But she smiled as she thought of them. "We were partners back then."

But Robert's success had changed that. Tessa could see it in her eyes.

Her mother working, living in an apartment, leaving the television on to provide a substitute for company. Tessa struggled with the image. Because she was looking at herself.

The phone rang and Barbara picked it up. She listened for a moment, her expression growing pinched and ever paler, then she thanked the caller and hung up. She didn't speak, so Tessa prompted her.

"Mom? Who was that?"

"Julianna Williamson. We've served together on several boards. I asked her to see what she could find out about that baby with AIDS and who was the main contributor to the fund that's paying for his treatment."

"And?"

"There's only one. It's called Save the Children. It's a foundation established by the former mayor, Paul Martinez. Rachel's late husband."

"Gotcha."

Before Tessa's elation had a chance to settle in, her mother hurried from the room and raced downstairs to the family room where the big-screen TV reigned in a recessed cabinet. By the time Tessa got there, Barbara had thrown open the doors and was searching around in the back for something.

She pulled out a video cassette and brandished it triumphantly. "They didn't get it."

"What?"

"The surveillance tape from your office. I'd only gotten halfway through it."

"Maybe it's time you saw the rest of it."

While Tessa cleaned up the mess in the kitchen, Barbara ran through the next few hours of comings and goings on the video tape, concentrating on the screen with a determined intensity. Tessa believed the key to wherever her father hid his secrets showed more promise but just after the two-and-a-half-hour mark, Barbara's call brought her running to see the picture her mother had frozen on the screen. It showed a rather blurry image of a man wearing a service uniform carrying a clipboard and a toolbox. The brim of his cap hid his face from view.

"That could be anyone," Tessa began.

"Watch."

And as Barbara started the tape again, the man was seen moving toward the elevator. Just as he pressed the button, he turned slightly in response to the guard—Maurice's—approach. And for an instant, immediately frozen by the remote control's pause, his features were apparent. Average-guy features. Pale, haunting eyes.

"Meet Chet Allen."

Chapter 16

The exclusive country club was a bust.

Robert D'Angelo did, indeed, have a locker there and after expending an annoying amount of greenbacks into the hand of the greedy young attendant, who would probably put it right up his nose behind the seventh green, he was allowed to try the key. It didn't fit. And neither did he in these posh digs where wealth and prestige created its own aura around the membership.

This was Tessa's world, one of privilege and pedigree, where money opened doors and power kept them that way. Its charter listed the crème de la crème of the city's social registry. Prospective joiners were screened and examined as if they were applying for jobs protecting national security. How would they view the son of a cop, a third-generation immigrant, with no Ivy League degree and a military service record even their prying eyes would be denied? They might hire him to do their dirty work but never would they invite him to sit down to share Heinekens and jokes in the elegant restaurant bar. They wouldn't want him dating their daughters.

What was he doing, thinking serious thoughts about Tessa D'Angelo? She was out of his league. Sure, they'd shared some great sex but when this case was solved, what were the odds she'd stick around to see what else he had to offer? She was cashmere to his cotton, Dom to his on tap.

But the way she'd kissed him that morning, nearly suffocating him on the sudden upward lunge of his heart. Good God, what had that been all about? He didn't want to guess. He didn't want to hope. He was paralyzed from doing either. Afraid to move or to speak lest he give her encouragement. The journey might be pleasantly distracting but it would be a short trip. He'd rather pass on the whole ride. And he had Rose to consider. Rose who clung to him as if he were her whole world, and he couldn't make himself return that trust by telling her the truth. What did that say about the kind of man he was? Tessa had summed him up completely. Coward. Damn right. Right down to his socks. Scared of living yet terrified of living alone.

And still there she was, pushing all his buttons, making him feel the rush of duty and pride, the thrill of conquest and desire. But he was what he was, not what she was trying to make him. He was not one of those good guys.

Damn her for scrambling his soul with that kiss. For coming into his life and turning it inside out. For making Rose smile and Russell smirk knowingly. And for making him wish he could be that better man she deserved.

He drove to Roseville under a dark cloud of emotion. The grittier streets and common surroundings suited him better than the civil clime he'd left in the rearview. The gym where Rob D'Angelo had sparred with his college buddies was still here, a dreary, uninviting building of chipped brick and boarded windows tagged colorfully by neighborhood artists. But once he opened the door to inhale the crisp, pungent scent of ambition and honest sweat, he felt himself relax. These were surroundings he fit into. Here, no one would ask to see his visitor's pass.

A gnomish character looking eerily like an African-American version of Burgess Meredith out of the *Rocky* movies was alternately coaching and cursing at two young Latino fighters. He saw Jack skirting the edges of the weight area and was quick to intercept him.

"Help you?"

"Looking for some information on someone who used to come here a long time ago."

"I been here forever. Ask away."

No hand outstretched for a little payola. Just an open curiosity.

"Do you remember a kid by the name of Robert D'Angelo? Used to come in to train before he was shipped off to Nam?"

He whistled. "That is going back a spell. Let me think. You mean, Robby? Didn't he get to be some kind of lawyer or something?"

"Yeah, something like that."

"Oh, sure, I remember him. Good-looking kid. Good right hook. Used to come in with his pals Allen and McGee. They were a rowdy bunch but never any trouble. All in love with the same pretty little girl. A cute little white-bread blonde from the other side of the tracks, if you know what I mean. Used to sit right over there and watch them work up a sweat. Wondered which one of them she would end up with."

"She was Mrs. D'Angelo."

"Huh. I would have guessed the other one." He shrugged. "You come here for something other than hashing up old times?"

"D'Angelo had a locker here."

"Sure does."

"Does? You mean he still does?"

"Pays monthly rent for it—'nough for me not to mind that he ain't sent a money order for a couple of months now. Not like I'd toss his stuff out or anything."

"Can you show me where it is?"

"Why not?"

The wizened old boxer led him back to the locker room where the smell of mold, ointment and stale body odor nearly knocked him back a step or two. A little pine cleaner and elbow grease would have done wonders.

"Right over there. Number 13. Lucky 13, he used to say."

Not so lucky, after all, Jack mused as he stood in front of the dented door. He took the key out of his coat pocket and slid it easily home. The door opened with a complaining click and rasp of hinges.

His cell phone rang. He reached for it instead of the neatly banded bundle of papers on the top shelf. They were all Robert D'Angelo had left behind.

"Chaney."

"Jack, I've got some intel for you. Meet me at Jo's?"

"Half hour."

The connection with Zach Russell terminated without pleasantries. He looked over his shoulder at the older man.

"Mind if I take these to Mrs. D'Angelo? She sent me down to get them if they were still here."

"Help yourself."

Yes, indeed, he would.

Barbara sat for a long while staring at the still shot of Chet Allen dressed in his service tech uniform. Finally she said in a cold, dead voice, "He killed your father. Rachel Martinez paid him to do it."

Tessa placed a comforting hand on her mother's shoulder. "We still have to prove it. And they're not going to make it easy for us."

"I can't believe it. Your father and I helped Paul Martinez

get elected to city office. He and Robert were always so close. That was before he married Rachel. She was the real power-house behind his campaigning for mayor. Smart, aggressive, with a background in humanitarian service that went all the way back to the sixties. She was a real asset to him. I never understood why Robert disliked her so intensely. He tried his best to talk Paul out of that marriage but it was true love. They say opposites attract and that was Paul and Rachel. He was upper crust and old money. She was inner city and ambition. They were so happy together until Paul had that massive stroke. She stuck right by him. Visits him every day in the rehabilitation center in St. Clair Shores even though they've told her he'll never regain any useful function. They say he doesn't even recognize her. So sad. I almost admire her. Except for the fact that she's a killer. Why, I wonder, when she had so much going for her."

"I don't know, Mom. Maybe the payments for her husband's care got to be too much. Maybe she just got in over her head."

"Maybe she's just a coldhearted bitch who got tired of a councilman's salary and decided to use those contacts from the Bureau of Substance Abuse to start her own Partnership for a Drug-Abusing Detroit consortium."

Tessa glanced at her mother, her eyebrows raised in surprise. "There's that possibility, too."

"Let's find out. I feel like going to a party. How about you, Tess?"

Tessa stared at her as if she'd gone mad. "A party? Now?"

"A good place to mix and mingle and have a casual conversation with the guest of honor."

"And that would be?"

"Councilwoman Martinez. She's being honored at a luncheon hosted by the Urban Improvement Council. They're making her Woman of the Year." Barbara turned in her seat to regard her daughter with a fierceness that surprised her.

"We can't let her get away with it. I won't let her get away with it. Obviously they don't know what we have. You were right before. Maybe we can shake her up a little and get her to give herself away."

Jack would strangle them both for even considering something so foolhardy. Rightly so. The smart thing would be to wait for him, to rely on his expertise.

"I need to call Jack first to see if he found anything at one of the lockers. If he has proof, we don't need to take the risk." But her pulse was pounding as she made the call. And got his voice mail. She hung up and regarded her mother thoughtfully. This wasn't the fluffy piece of decoration she'd always thought Barbara D'Angelo to be. This was a woman with a score to settle. And that made them two of a kind.

"I'll need something to wear."

The lunch crowd at Cuppa Jo's was bustling, with every booth and table filled. Squinting through the smoke, Jack still didn't see any sign of his friend.

"Hiya, Chaney," Jo called from behind the counter. "Come on back."

He skirted the counter and pushed through the bat-wing doors where the smells and sounds of the busy kitchen assaulted his senses. Zach Russell, glaringly out of place with an apron tied over his three-piece suit, was at one of the stoves leaning over a giggling young cook's shoulder. One hand rested on her tiny waist and the other held a ladle. He sipped from it carefully and nodded his head.

"You see, lovey, tarragon, just like I told you. Just a pinch to bring the stock to life. Jack, come over and take a taste."

Obligingly, Jack went to slurp up some of the chicken broth and his eyebrows shot up. "That's good. Compliments to the chef."

He inclined his head regally. "After growing up to bland English food, one appreciates a little stimulation to the palate."

Jack grinned. "I'm sure that's it. If your shift's over, think we can get down to some business."

Russell took off the apron and bussed a kiss against the young woman's temple. "Never be afraid to experiment, darling."

She looked up at him with a swooning devotion and at that, Jack had to walk away. Russell followed him back to a small metal table that served as the employee's break room.

"Moonlighting for tip money?"

Russell returned the wry smile. "Some tips are better than others, Jacky boy." He spun the chair and straddled it, getting right to business. "You have some very dangerous friends."

"How so?"

"Your three college chums weren't your average grunts. They went right into serious business behind sniper scopes."

"Are you sure?" Jack couldn't imagine the smoothly debonair D.A. taking out unfriendlies at one thousand yards.

"The government had it locked up behind some very heavy doors but I was able to peek around it for a wee minute."

"What else?"

"Allen went a bit mad out there and did some pretty nasty stuff to those who didn't deserve it. Doing a bit of business on the side for a private contractor, if you know what I mean. D'Angelo and McGee were bringing him in and somehow he managed to slip away on D'Angelo's watch. McGee went after him and then the trail grows ice-cold."

"What were they involved in, Russ?"

"Drugs, most likely."

"One or all?"

An elegant shrug. "Can't tell you that. D'Angelo was taken out a hero and given a medal. McGee went into Special Ops behind borders we weren't supposed to cross. And Allen, he just got more crazy and more dangerous until the government didn't know what to do with him."

"So the story about him getting killed?"

"Nice bit of fiction to protect his commanding officers from the whiplash of having one of their own run amuck. Swept him under the rug with the understanding that if he came up from underground again, they'd put him under it permanently."

"Wonderful."

This was the psycho stalking Tessa.

"The overseas telephone numbers you had me check connected to an Agency front in Southeast Asia. D'Angelo must have been tipping off his superiors on his pal Allen. Some pal. Want me to find him and take care of him for you?" Russell offered casually as if he were suggesting a favor akin to picking up his dry cleaning.

"No. I want him loose for a little while longer, until I find out who's holding his leash."

"A man like that doesn't take to a leash for long. You'd better keep your pistol close and your lady closer. Or I'd be happy to do that for you."

"What a pal. What you can do is lean on a suit by the name of Jeff Boetright at Engle, Steiger & Steiger. He had a date with Tessa on the night her father died."

"Checking out the former lovers?"

"Only if this one was encouraged to get her out of the office for the evening so she wouldn't get in the way. I suspect you'll find the ambitious Mr. Boetright got a nice little bonus for that piece of work. I'll bet some sweet thing in personnel could be convinced to provide you with the documentation."

"Could be. Kind of thin, though."

Jack brought out the bundle of papers. "Maybe our friend D'Angelo gave us something in here to beef up our firepower."

One by one, they went through the pieces of evidence Rachel Martinez had been willing to kill for. The materials were extensive—ledgers showing medical supplies that provided cover for the transportation of illegal drugs going in and out of Cambodia from 1968 to the present, pictures of the councilwoman meeting with unsavory characters on both sides of the ocean, receipts and records placing her at the helm of a long list of dummy organizations created to help her channel her product from point of purchase to point of sale, and a grainy photo of the lovely politician shaking hands with a supposedly dead Chet Allen. He pushed the evidence toward Russell. "Get these into the proper hands to have an arrest warrant issued."

His cell rang. "Chaney."

"Jack, I need you."

The fragile thread of fear pulling through Tessa's voice was all it took to transform Jack Chaney into the most deadly man alive.

The awards luncheon was in full swing when they arrived. Barbara D'Angelo's presence opened any door within the tight society circle so they were ushered in without question. Even with the cloud of scandal hanging over her husband's memory, none dared shun her outright. It was more a subtle shifting away before she could reach them.

Barbara seemed not to notice but Tessa fumed at their snobbery. After all her mother had done to chair their causes, to put a popular face on their needy ventures, to volunteer time and boundless energy, that they would shy away as if she were now some kind of pariah, it had to be a bitter pill to swallow. But Barbara put on her best serene smile and greeted everyone enthusiastically as if she didn't know they were whispering about her behind her back. Tessa saw her white-knuckled grip on her handbag. She knew and she pretended not to care. That was class. And Tessa felt a sudden surge of pride.

"There she is, sucking up to the Mendlesson money in the corner. Let's go say hello." And Barbara strode forward like a cutter under full sail, breaking through the crowded assembly with her bow high and parade of canvas snapping. "Rachel, dear. How wonderful to see you."

Rachel Martinez froze as Barbara leaned in for a pseudo-buss of either cheek. By the time she stepped back, the councilwoman had her political game face on. She was still a striking woman with jet-black hair styled high above her bronze multiethnic features. A trace of her rough background betrayed itself in her all too direct stare, like top dog willing the other to look away first to establish dominance.

"Barbara, what a surprise."

"I'm sure it is. I'll bet I'm about the last person you expected to see."

She smiled but Tessa could imagine the sound of her professionally whitened teeth gnashing. "Barb, you know I don't listen to any of those rumors. You have no reason not to go anywhere you please with your head held high."

"And why wouldn't I since the both of us know just how false those rumors are."

Martinez's features tightened, becoming harsh angles and gaunt valleys. "Nothing was ever proven and I refuse to think the worst about Rob."

"Why would you, knowing the truth as we both do now."

Martinez reached out to grip her forearm. Though she was still smiling and Barbara didn't wince, Tessa could see it was no gentle hold. "Maybe we should discuss this someplace a little more private."

Tessa laid her hand over the other woman's and squeezed tight. "Right here is fine. Right here in front of all our friends and witnesses. Let her go."

"Now, Tessa dear, that is hardly called for," she complained as if shocked. But she released Barbara.

"Oh, I think a lot of things are called for and your indignation is not one of them."

"I have no idea what you're talking about."

"Really? And if we were to go over to that very nice young

reporter over there and fill him in on your charitable support of the dying child of a man who smeared my father's name, you don't think he'd find a story if he dug deep enough?"

Martinez no longer bothered to pretend. Her expression was livid. "You don't have anything."

"No? Then why did you send Allen to kill my father? Why did you send him to intimidate me with his fists? Why tear up my mother's house? You know what we have and now we have you."

"What do you want?"

"I want my father's name cleared. And I want Allen."

Martinez's smile was thin and cruel. "In order to clear your father's name, he'd have to be innocent. And that, my dear, I'm afraid is not the case. Are you sure you want to pursue this?"

Tessa glanced at her mother, willing to follow her lead at last. Barbara's gaze was flint on steel.

"Very sure."

"That's unfortunate. I'd hoped we wouldn't have to take this any further."

"I told you she wouldn't go for it."

Tessa's insides turned to glass as she recognized the silky voice. Her pistol weighed down her handbag but she couldn't reach for it. Her best defense was a scream but suddenly her throat was parched and dry with fear. Something sharp pierced her skin beneath her rib cage. She couldn't move, could hardly breathe.

"Hello, Babs. Nice to see you."

Barbara's face turned the color of putty.

"Now, Barbara dear, you'll come with me without a fuss or my associate will carve your daughter up like those little strips of sushi over there. Do you understand?"

She gave a stiff nod, her glazed stare on the hand Allen had tucked in close against her daughter's side.

"You know I'm serious, don't you, Babs?"

Again the jerky nod.

"Ms. D'Angelo, we'll be in touch." Rachel Martinez turned and walked away with Barbara marching stiffly at her side. When they'd cleared the cluster of people in the room, Allen leaned in close so his breath brushed warm and soft against Tessa's cheek. She thought she was going to throw up.

"Now you be a good girl and nothing nasty will happen to that oh, so fine mother of yours. I want you to count to twenty before you even think of taking another breath."

Tessa stood still for ten seconds, twenty. And when she glanced around, she was alone.

Jack burst into the genteel party where fussy little watercress sandwiches were served up in lieu of real food. One of the servers dressed in white tie and tails thought to intercept him but after one quelling look, he thought better of it.

He saw her standing at the far end of the room. Her back was to him, the ivory skin of her neck and shoulders bared by the sophisticated unswept knot of her hair. She wore a gauzy, floaty dress that would have had him in a lather thinking of her wearing it with nothing underneath had the circumstances been different. He moved quickly, panic and fury powering his strides. As he got closer, he noticed an odd pattern dotting the side of her dress with crimson.

His heart bobbed up into his heart. He could scarcely say her name.

"Tessa."

She turned slowly. Her features were a stiff mask. Her eyes welled with terror.

"Jack, they have my mother."

And then he had her in his arms.

Once they started back to Jack's compound, he listened to her without expressing any judgment. None was needed. Tessa knew what they'd done was foolish and now her mother's life was in jeopardy. She'd felt so confident, so cocky, with the training Jack had given her, but as he'd said, she was far from ready to compete against someone like Chet Allen.

She'd heard his voice and it paralyzed her.

Councilwoman Martinez had waltzed away with her mother and she'd done nothing to intervene.

"Do you have the tape?" Jack asked when she'd finished.

"It's in my bag." Next to her useless pistol. The one she'd been afraid to draw. "I blew it, Jack."

"It doesn't matter, Tessa. We have them. Your father had all the evidence we need for a conviction tucked away in that old gym locker room. He'd sent it to your mother in that last letter from Nam without her knowing what it contained."

"They're going to want it, Jack. They're going to want it in exchange for my mother's release."

"Russell's already turned it over to the police. As soon as they can find a judge to sign it, there'll be a warrant out for Martinez and Allen."

Tessa turned to him, features stark with anguish. "But what about my mother? They'll kill her unless they think we have something to barter with."

"We don't need to tell them we don't, do we?"

"Jack, this isn't a game."

"It is to Allen. He's the one we've got to worry about, not Martinez. Martinez isn't a killer. She's a politician."

"But she had Allen kill my father."

"Maybe. Maybe Allen was just improvising."

"Jack, I'm scared."

"I won't tell you not to be. But we'll get through this. You have to trust me."

"I do."

They pulled into the driveway. Jack cut the engine and for a long moment they both sat there, staring straight ahead. Then Jack reached for her hand. She slipped hers inside and let his engulf it with warmth and strength.

The late afternoon was unseasonably warm. Rose sat out on the porch with one of her schoolbooks on her folded knees. Tinker lay stretched out beside her, soaking up the sunlight. They both looked up in welcome.

To Tessa, it was like coming home.

To Jack, it was like having a family waiting.

Dinner was quick and silent. Tessa sat tensely, watching the cell phone lying next to her plate, willing it to ring. Anticipation was eating her alive. Wondering what her mother was thinking, feeling, was an exquisite torture to endure while she sat here safe and secure in Jack's fortress.

What had they been thinking to attempt such a thing on their own?

She helped Constanza clear the table and sat with Rose to hear her read out loud. She moved on autopilot until Jack intercepted her in the hall and steered her to his upstairs room. There, he turned her toward the shower and wrenched on the faucet until steam hung in the air. He stripped her out of her frilly party dress and frillier underthings then directed her under the hot spray. After a few minutes he reached in to turn the water off and was ready with a fluffy towel to buff her dry and then to simply hold her.

He'd turned down the bed. She slipped under the covers, shivering until he joined her, bare skin to bare skin. He made love to her until passion thawed the panic, until her breathing raced and she cried out his name in wondrous release. And then she curled close in his embrace while he held her tight, his expression fierce and unreadable. His fingertips grazed the tiny nick in her side where he had pressed on a bandage. It was a small cut but the fear it inspired stabbed clear to the heart and soul of both of them.

They spoke for a short while of what tomorrow would bring and, too soon, Tessa was slumbering fitfully while Jack lay wide awake and worried.

How was he going to keep her safe?

* * *

Morning came with the vibration of Tessa's phone. She'd placed it under her pillow before closing her eyes. Carefully, so as not to wake Jack, she slid out of bed and padded into the bathroom before answering the call.

"Yes?"

"You know what we want."

"Yes, I do."

"Where was it?"

"In a locker at the gym you used to go to."

Allen's laugh was low and admiring. "Clever. Bring it if you want to see your mother alive again."

"To my father's office in an hour. Don't you hurt her."

But the line was already dead.

Cold with fear and tight with dread, she dressed, tucking Betsy into the waistband of her jeans. She scribbled a quick note and placed it on her pillow before slipping from the room. She didn't look at Jack. She couldn't and still have the courage to do what she had to do. He would understand why she didn't say goodbye.

A half hour later Jack opened his eyes to see Rose at his bedside.

"Hey, monkey, what are you doing in here?" Then the fogginess left him and he realized he was alone under his covers. Tinker was sleeping on the pillow Tessa had used. A slip of paper was wedged underneath him.

"Miss Tessa told me to come and wake you after she'd gone."

Jack sat up, remembering to clutch the covers to conceal his nakedness. "She's gone?"

"*Sí.*" The girl's features puckered with concern, sensing something was very wrong. "Is she coming back?"

"If I have anything to say about it."

"She took your truck."

"That's all right. I've got my bike. Scoot on out of here so I can get dressed."

As she turned, Jack caught her wrist. He wasn't sure he had the right words so he just spoke straight from the heart. "You know I love you, don't you, Rose?"

She stared at him, startled.

"You do know that, right?"

Slowly she nodded, tears bright in her eyes.

"When I get back, we need to sit down for a talk. I've got some things I have to tell you."

Again, the nod. She couldn't seem to speak through the emotion clogging her chest so she turned and raced out of the room.

After she'd gone, Jack reached for the piece of paper and read the short statement. He crumpled the paper and prayed for the first time in decades for the strength not to let her down. Her three words meant everything to him.

I trust you.

Chapter 17

The streets were empty. Even the most zealous workaholics took Sunday morning off.

Tessa used her key to enter the Parker-Thompkins Building from the parking garage. Normally she would have rejoiced to find a space right near the door. This morning it brought her one step closer to a trap about to be sprung.

The interior of the building was silent. Its floors gleamed, the cleaning crew having buffed them to a high shine the night before. Her reflections stretched out in front of her, a figure moving quickly, cautiously, on orange alert toward the main lobby and the elevators. She didn't draw her gun. There was no point until she got where she was going. No one was going to harm her until they had the evidence safe in hand. Then she knew what would happen.

Then they would kill both her and her mother. No witnesses. Dead men—or women—tell no tales.

The lobby yawned dark and cavernous with only the cursory lights burning and the sun not yet up to dazzle through the smoked front glass.

"Good morning, Ms. D'Angelo. You're in early."

A man in an office security uniform stepped out from behind the counter. It was neither Maurice nor Gary but some big hulk with a too wide smile.

"Good morning. Catching the worm, as it were. Where's Steve? I thought he usually worked the weekend shift."

"He's out of town. An aunt's funeral," he told her, managing to curb his grin long enough to appear sorrowful for the fictitious Steve. "My name's Bart. I just started a couple of weeks ago. I recognize you from the TV. It don't do you justice." Again, the huge grin, this time just a wolfish baring of teeth.

"Thank you," she murmured as if she really thought it was a compliment. "I need to go up to fourteen. There are some things I need in my father's office."

"No problem."

While the fake guard faced the elevator to unlock the panel, Tessa faced the lobby camera and held her fingers up. Nine then one then one. At least that would record she wasn't going of her own free will if they happened to leave the tape behind to document her voluntary ride upstairs.

"Have a nice day, Ms. D'Angelo," Bart said with a grin.

"I plan to, Bart."

The door swished closed between them.

The ride up seemed to take forever. It gave her too much time to consider what she was doing. This time, her father's honor wasn't the driving force but rather her mother's life.

He's not innocent, Martinez had said. Whatever his sins, she would face them. He'd planned to reveal them to her on the day he died. If he'd been ready to tell her then, he wouldn't mind her knowing now. She prepared herself mentally and emotionally for anything, for blackmail, for involvement in drug trafficking, for turning a blind eye to wrongdoing. Whatever it was, she would accept it and see Robert D'Angelo as no less a man because of it. Not because he would expect it of her and she didn't want to let him down, but because she was strong enough to handle the truth—that her father was just a man who maybe had feet of clay instead of flawless marble.

She wouldn't think of her mother, of what she'd been through, of the apologies she'd planned when they were reunited, of the future she anticipated getting to know the woman Barbara D'Angelo really was. She couldn't turn back the clock and become the innocent Rose beneath the drape of her mother's arm, but she could become a daughter, a contemporary, a friend. There would be time for those things. She had to believe it and not let her fears distract her.

Get ready. She braced herself as the doors opened on fourteen.

The hall was empty. By now, they knew she was on her way. Bart, or whatever his name was, would have signaled them from the lobby. No use trying to be discreet then. She strode toward the door to 1410 and swung it open.

Four men lounged in the outer office. She didn't think for a minute that they were temps from the secretarial pool. They looked mean and lean, and the business they were in didn't involve knowing how to type. Or to fix the heating and air-conditioning as their faux uniforms would suggest.

"Where's Martinez?" she asked the closest lump of hired muscle.

"She's not here for this meeting. Mr. Allen's inside, waiting." His beefy hand gestured toward the closed door of her father's office.

So Martinez didn't think them important enough to waste her Sunday morning. She'd be busy appearing humble and repentant at Mass, someplace highly visible so she couldn't be linked to the ugliness Allen had planned for them.

Tessa crossed the office without giving the men a second

look. They weren't the ones who worried her. Allen was. She opened the door and stepped inside. At first it appeared as if the room was empty. Then slowly her father's big leather chair revolved.

"Good morning, Ms. D'Angelo. Nice to see you again."

From the stories she'd heard, Tessa expected to find a cross between Hannibal Lecter and the reptilian villain from *Platoon*. Chet Allen was surprisingly nonthreatening with his pleasant angular features and welcoming smile. Until she looked into his eyes. They were pale and empty windows to a contrastingly black soul.

"Where's my mother?" she demanded without preamble.

"All in due time. We have some business to discuss first."

"We don't discuss anything until I know she's all right."

"She's fine. Babs isn't as delicate as she looks."

Tougher than she looks. Like mother, like daughter.

"And I'm supposed to take your word for it?"

He shrugged. "Bart has her down in the lobby. He'll bring her up when I call."

"Call him now or this conversation is over."

"You're a real bulldog. Just like Robby." He punched a few numbers on the intercom. He was wearing thin surgical gloves. A careful man. "Bart, bring Mrs. D'Angelo up, would you please?"

Tessa stood just inside the door, her heart pounding, her hands damp. The proximity to this monster made her nauseous. But she'd remain alert. Their lives depended on it.

"Where's your friend, the intrepid Mr. Chaney?"

She was careful not to betray her surprise that he knew Jack's name. He obviously didn't know much more than that or they would have been paid a visit at Jack's residence.

"When I left him this morning, he was still sleeping."

"Am I to expect him at any minute then?"

"He doesn't know I'm here. If he did, he'd want to do something about it and I'm not willing to risk my mother's life."

"How practical of you. And smart. Mr. Chaney has a bit of a hero complex. I must admit, he has given us a run for our money. He certainly knows how to cover his tracks. Martinez actually considered going after his father but I convinced her that Babs was the easier target. Chaney had too many unknown variables, but you, Ms. D'Angelo, are a predictable quantity, just like Robby. Besides, I'd rather deal with you for old times' sake. Call me a sentimental fool."

He was nobody's fool. Tessa stood, teeth clenched to keep them from chattering while she stared directly into the face of her father's killer.

"Have a seat, Tessa. We might as well get acquainted while we wait for good old Babs."

"I know enough about you already. A little polite conversation isn't likely to change my opinion."

He laughed out loud, a pleasant sound belied by the flat quality of his stare.

"Isn't there anything you want to ask me, little Tessa? Anything at all?"

He was taunting her. She knew better than to take the bait but the need to know, the need to expunge the demons of doubt, had her plunging ahead, feeding the killer's thirst for entertainment at her family's expense.

"How was my father involved with Martinez?"

"You go right for the big one, don't you? Right for the throat. Good for you. If you actually have the evidence you say you do, you should know all that. You do have it, don't you? I'd hate for this reunion to be an exercise in futility."

"I know you were running drugs through Martinez's humanitarian front in Asia. My father had pictures of you meeting with her and transferring product into the trucks that supposedly were carrying medical supplies. My guess is that's the over-the-counter pain reliever that made Martinez her first fortune."

"You'd be right. A sweet, sweet deal until Saint Robert stumbled onto it."

"Then he wasn't your partner?"

Another jovial laugh. "Not hardly. It didn't fit in with his prospectus for the future. He had it all planned out even then, returning home to his beautiful, now pregnant wife, finishing a law degree on his GI bill. Using his military records as a stepping stone to politics. Only I managed to muck that up for him a bit. He didn't come back to the States to the hero's welcome he'd expected. He had a blotch on his record that made using it for promotional gain a gamble instead of a shoe-in."

"You."

"It was my pleasure. He got in the middle of my plans and it was only fair that I did likewise. But enough about ancient history. We'll get back to it shortly, after your mother arrives. Let's fast forward to present day. Imagine your father's dismay to find me back in the picture on the eve of his first political campaign. It was naive of him to think I'd be gone forever. Martinez figured I could use our past ties to convince Robby to back off from declaring his intention to run and from his snooping around in the councilwoman's business. I could have told her what Robby's reaction would be."

"He told you to take a hike." An acquitting sense of satisfaction gripped Tessa. Her father hadn't faltered after all. He'd been one of the good guys.

"In so many words. So we had to manufacture some manure for your father to step in. The money in the bank, O'Casey's testimony. Nothing fancy but effective enough to create that shadow of a doubt over Robby's good name. But it wasn't the smear to his professional name that the D.A. feared the most. It was the past rising up in all its ugly glory that had him quaking in his loafers. Your daddy was a man of secrets, Tessa. Want me to tell you the big one? The one that made him risk his military career and Goody Two-Shoes reputation? Can you guess what it was? No?"

"Shut up, Chet."

Both of them turned at the sharp cut of Barbara's voice.

Tessa's relief at seeing her mother, tired, worn and slightly worse for wear, took the venom and confusion from Allen's mocking game.

"Babs, come join the party. Tessa and I were about to start without you."

"She doesn't want to party with the likes of you, Chet. Leave her alone. You have no idea what you're talking about."

"Don't I? Could be I do, Barbie. Could be I know I lot more than you think. Family skeletons are rattling, just dying to get out."

"Why did you kill Robert? I can't believe Rachel Martinez ordered you to do it."

Chet smiled, a slow, spreading gesture like an oil spill contaminating a placid surface. "No. That was my idea. Rachel was pretty peeved about it. Just about canceled my contract, if you know what I mean."

"Why, Chet? He was your friend."

"Friend? Rob didn't have any friends. He had people he could manipulate to get what he wanted. The ultimate political machine even back then. And you know what he wanted, Babs? He wanted you. And he was willing to do anything to get you and then to keep you. Anything." Allen's gaze narrowed into hard, angry slits. His breath seethed with the remembrance of past perceived wrongs. "Too good for everyone else, he was. The perfect athlete, the perfect scholar, the perfect soldier and he planned to be the perfect husband. Not so perfect there, was he, Barbie doll? And we know why, don't we?"

"Why did you have to kill him? I'd think ruining him would have served your purpose far better," Tessa interjected to give her mother time to regroup. Something in the direction of the conversation was getting deeply, dangerously personal and Barbara wasn't ready to face it yet. Tessa stalled for time.

"That was the plan and it was too good to be true. The perfect Robert D'Angelo knocked from his soapbox of justice by his own character flaws. How perfect is that? But the bastard wouldn't play the game like he did in Nam. I tried the same old tricks and he wouldn't jump through the hoops. Told me to go to hell, that the past couldn't hurt him anymore. He was wrong." Allen's palms slapped down on the desktop, startling both women. He leaned forward, oozing menace. "He was wrong."

After a moment he dropped back in Robert's chair, tenting his fingers in front of him. His gaze grew speculative as it touched on Tessa. "Let me tell you a story of three buddies about to go off to Vietnam."

He laid it out in a cheerful recollection, Robert, Tag and Chet, idealistic kids on the cusp of manhood, each driven by different dreams. Tag's number came up in the draft. He was the most unlikely of the trio to go off to war but made no attempt to shirk his duty to his country. Robert saw the military as a way to get ahead, the means to pay for his schooling and a backdrop to build his image as a supporter of what was right and good about the American system. And Chet was eager to escape what he saw as a dead end of mediocrity. The chance to excel at something he'd prove to be very, very good at. Killing.

The three finished basic training. Chet and Tag stayed at the base getting ready to deploy. Robert made a quick trip home to marry the woman who would make all his future dreams come true. And then they were shipped out.

"It was a different world over there. You could do anything, be anything, with nothing to hold you back. We'd go out on three, four missions a week, hunkering down in the mud and bugs and rot to wait for our chance to pop one for our country. Only on one of my trips out, way out, I ran across Rachel Martinez, it was Drury back then, with one of the province warlords. They made it worth my while not to pull the trigger. And then they were paying me well to run interference for their transactions. Until Robert got wise and took some pictures. He was going to have me brought up on charges, Mr. Holier-Than-Thou D'Angelo. He was going to ruin everything we'd set up out there in the jungles to come out of the war rich men…and women. Couldn't let that happen. So I took my buddy Robert aside and we had a little meeting, a kind of lay-it-all-out-and-weigh-the-options. And Robby boy decided it would be in his best interest to turn his back and let me get on with what I was doing."

"I don't believe you."

Allen laughed at Tessa's outrage. Then he looked to a very silent and pale Barbara. "But Babs does, don't you, Babs? Because you know what I was holding over good old Robby's head. You know the one threat I could make that would have him turning his back on the red, white and blue and truth, honor and the American way. You know, don't you, Barbie?"

"Oh, my God. This is all my fault," she moaned softly.

"I don't blame you, Barbara. You saw a way out and you took it. A nice girl like you from a fine, upstanding, church going family, the pillars of the community. How would it look if we'd left you behind, pregnant and unmarried?"

Tessa gasped but Barbara and Chet didn't notice. Their stares were locked, Allen's as mesmerizing as a snake paralyzing its prey.

"Things like that just weren't done back then. The scandal, the whispers. So good old Robert saw his opportunity to lock on to the woman who never returned all his passions, who never shared his dreams or ambitions. He came back and made her his wife. His every wish fulfilled, the son of a bitch. Only tell her the kicker, Babs. You tell her or I will."

Tessa looked between them, panic and foreboding massing inside her to an unbearable degree.

"Tell me what, Mom?" she demanded at last.

Barbara looked to her, her eyes welling up with misery and

regret and an empathy for the pain to come. She did the merciful thing and cut right to the heart.

"Robert wasn't your father, Tessa."

There it was, the secret her father kept, the reason he would never hug her close or tell her that he loved her. She wasn't his child, in body or in heart.

Tessa's senses reeled but her mind remained amazingly clear, the eye of the emotional storm. That was the truth Robert D'Angelo had wanted to share with her that day, not some confession to criminal activity or theft but that he was guilty of stealing almost thirty-four years of devotion and love without the slightest intention of returning it. She stared at Barbara, seeing her anguish, her pleading for an ounce of understanding and all she could think to say was, "Why didn't you tell me?"

"I wanted to. So many times." Barbara's voice broke and Allen's taunt filled the strained silence.

"He didn't want you to ever know. That's the man you've been fighting to avenge," Allen sneered. "A man who spent his whole life pretending to be what he wasn't. He bargained for my silence all those years ago so he could hold on to a dream family built on a lie. We traded, Robby and I, my sin for his, but when I came back to hold him to it, to keep his mouth shut about what he knew, he said he couldn't do it anymore. He couldn't let Martinez win even if it meant he'd lose. Stupid. Stupid. I went to him that night to try one last time to persuade him to be reasonable. All he had to do was to step back and say nothing. Martinez would get her spot as congresswoman and Rob could run for something else. He could even have walked away richer for it. The money was real. He could have had it all. The bank account, the all-American family, his reputation. His secret safe forever. No one else would have ever known."

"But he knew," Barbara said at last, her tone strengthening, her gaze becoming defiant. "He knew and he couldn't let it happen. He couldn't let a cheap drug dealer like Martinez prosper because of what he'd done in a moment of weakness thirty-some years ago. He knew if he went along with what you offered, he'd be just like you. And he couldn't live with that."

"And he didn't." Allen smiled narrowly. His eyes glittered like a bared knife blade. "And neither will you if you don't give me Robert's little insurance policy right now. You can walk away from this. I don't have any reason to harm you if you cooperate."

It was Tessa's turn to laugh. The sound was as sharp and fractured as those pieces of glass on her apartment floor. Allen regarded her narrowly, his smile frozen, his brow beginning to furrow in aggravation.

"You're not going to let us go. Don't be stupid."

He flinched at that, his jaw clenching in a tight spasm.

Tessa continued, her words hard, fierce and fearless. What did she have to lose at this particular point?

"There's no way Martinez would trade one albatross around her neck for another. No. She'd want the vicious little secret to end here. That's why she didn't meet us herself. No ties while you clean up the mess. Right?"

A reluctant smile quirked at the corner of his mouth. "Cut right to the chase and damn the cost. Just like your daddy. He wouldn't compromise no matter what was in the balance. Good old Tag saw a wrong and he had to right it. He was a sanctimonious bastard but I had a lot more respect for him than Robby. Rob wasn't afraid to go after what he wanted by bending a rule or two. He let ambition become his god. You know why he wouldn't trade on his war record? The real reason? That nice little wound in the line-of-duty scratch he got, that wasn't enemy fire. I gave it to him. I pulled that trigger. It was the only way they'd believe him, he told me. The only way they'd swallow the story and let it go to save a potential scandal. They'd have Robby as a hero and I'd no longer be an embarrassment. Good press and problem solved. Everybody wins. It's the American way.

"He never expected me to show up on his doorstep thirty odd years later to call him on that little arrangement. I almost thought we had him but then he had to go and get all honorable and throw the past in my face. He let his pride push him into taking integrity over his family's good name. A little late, I told him, but he wouldn't bend. The rest of the story you already know. Now give me the clippings or I will shoot your pretty little mother right in the head."

His gun was out and leveled before Tessa could blink. Barbara didn't move, her gaze drawn down that deadly barrel as it yawned wide and deadly in front of her face.

"I can't," Tessa told him flatly. "I don't have them to give. They were turned over to the police last night." She glanced at her watch and said with some satisfaction, "They're probably picking your boss up out of her pew about now. So I guess I have to ask you, what's the smart thing? Complicate your options with two more killings or get the hell out of Dodge before they come after you?"

"That would be the sensible thing, wouldn't it? I mean what loyalty do I have to Martinez? Yep, running away would be the smart thing to do but then, the smarter thing would be to leave no witnesses. That's kinda been my policy all along." A cold glaze settled over his stare. "Sorry, Babs. Nothing personal."

Tessa's mind scrambled. *Do something,* it screamed. The muscles in her calves bunched. Her body became coiled-spring taut. And just as she readied to throw herself across the table at a man she had no chance of defeating, she caught a glimmer of movement behind him.

And then everything exploded.

Chapter 18

Glass fell inward and shattered across Allen's back and the desktop. Jack swung through the opening but already Allen was recovering, remembering his purpose. Bleeding from countless lacerations, he lifted the gun once more as Jack rolled to hands and knees.

Using one hand to push her mother from the chair, Tessa lunged for Allen's wrist with the other. She wrenched it upward, away from the target Barbara made sprawled upon the floor, and stepped in closer for more leverage. The discharge was deafening. She felt something tug at the loose spill of her hair but had no time to process the fact that a bullet had just missed her head. A man like Allen couldn't be allowed to remain armed.

With her hand clamped down on his wrist, Tessa wrapped her other arm around his, locking that hand over the one holding his wrist. Turning slightly, she managed to torque his arm up at just the right angle to force his grip to lessen. The gun hit the desk and bounced harmlessly to the floor. But unfortunately, that left her within his reach.

His hand went to her neck, fingers pressing, forcing hot dots of color to swirl through her vision. Before they could form a solid curtain of blackness, she exaggerated the natural movement of a sneeze, whipping her head back then forward. Right into his nose. His hold opened so she could stagger back a safe distance and then Jack had him.

She would have liked to have stepped back to watch the two professionals engage in deadly hand-to-hand but the sound of the shot drew the four from the other room. Knowing Jack was fully involved with the dangerous Allen, she brazenly rushed the others as they pushed through the door. They weren't prepared for her aggressive, hands-on assault and she used that surprise as her weapon of opportunity.

She grabbed the first man's gun, letting his arm pass beneath hers, then locking down tight to hold him immobile. Her knee found his kidney and he dropped. She went over him to confront the second man who had yet to recover from his astonishment. Keeping his body between her and the others, she dealt him a hard jab/cross/hook/cross combination that had him shaking his huge head like a stunned ox. Not giving him a chance to gather his senses, because if he hit her, he was going to hurt her and most likely stop her cold, she threw all her energy into a left jab and right cross followed by an uppercut with the left elbow and a horizontal right elbow strike. Then she shoved him back into the other two. Before they could regroup, Tessa had snatched Betsy from her waistband.

"Stop! Everybody freeze."

They stared at her, at the gun, weighing her capability. She worked the slide with an I-mean-business rifling.

"Don't even think that I'm not ready, willing and able to take out your kneecaps if you so much as scratch your noses. Mom, are you all right?" She risked a quick glance.

"I'm fine," Barbara announced as she got carefully off the

floor. But her eyes were on Tessa and that look was filled with concern. Tessa looked away. She couldn't afford to let her attentiveness slip even a notch. Not now. Not yet.

Jack had Allen's pulped nose buried in her father's expensive carpet, a knee in his back and the killer's arm twisted up at a stay-put angle. The start of a spectacular shiner attested to the ferocity of their struggle.

"I must be getting old," Allen panted. "You're still alive."

"Me, too," Jack replied. "Because you can still talk."

"And I'm going to have plenty to say, right, ladies?"

If he thought to intimidate them, he was wrong. Tessa glared at him. "Say whatever you like, Allen. And keep saying it for the rest of your miserable life behind bars."

"What about your career, missy? Won't the scandal put a black mark on your perfect record?"

"I can take it," she promised him with a fierce smile. "I'm tougher than you think."

Allen chuckled. "Just like her old man, eh, Babs?"

"Anyone in here need some members of the law enforcement community?" Zach Russell peered in and assessed the situation. "Looks like my timing is a little off. It would seem that the two of you handled things quite nicely." Behind him the four goons were being cuffed.

"All but the reading of the rights." Jack dragged Allen to his feet. "You have the right to remain silent, scumbag. You might consider using it."

Allen smirked at him. "Glass houses, Mr. Chaney. We're the same, you and I. The only difference is this time you get to walk away."

"If you believe that, you are a fool. I'm nothing like you. I never was. There were lines I wouldn't cross and you never recognized any lines at all." He pushed Allen toward one of the officers Russell brought with him to the scene. "Mirandize him and make sure you enunciate every word. No glitches to keep him from going down for the murder of Ro-

bert D'Angelo and attempted murder of these two very-will-
ing-to-testify ladies."

"It's hard to keep a truly bad man down, Chaney. Remember that," Allen vowed as he was being handcuffed. "And,
Barbie, I'll see you again so we can go over old times."

Barbara said nothing as she moved back to give the police
officers plenty of room to escort her husband's killer away.
Then she looked to her daughter. "Tess, we need to talk."

"Not right now. I have to have time to think…to think
about what all this means." She turned to Russell to escape
the tension of issues she wasn't ready to deal with. "Mr. Russell, thank you for coming to the rescue."

"My pleasure, although I regret missing my friend's rather
grand Errol Flynn entrance."

Tessa looked toward the window, her brow furrowing in
confusion.

"That's how he got in and out, Tessa," Jack explained.
"When Allen came in dressed as a repairman, he took out the
glass and replaced the seal with a temporary adhesive. When
the office closed down for the night and your father went to
answer nature's call, he rappelled down from sixteen the same
way I did. There's a conference room up there. He used suc-
tion cups to hold the glass while he pushed it inside so he
didn't make the same kind of mess I did. I'm afraid I was in
a bit of a hurry and, well, I wanted to make a dramatic entrance." He grinned and Tessa returned the gesture faintly.
Then he was all sober business once more. "He was here
waiting for your dad. He offered him a bribe and when that
didn't work, he went straight for blackmail but D'Angelo
wasn't having any of that, either."

"So Allen killed him and set up the frame," Tessa concluded wearily.

"And while you were trying to get into the room through
the door Allen locked, he went back out the way he came,
pulling the window back in behind him. I'm sure he planned

to return to fix the seals before someone with an intuitive insight happened to notice. Russ stopped by the other night to confirm my theory. It's a good thing Allen didn't have time to clean up after himself or we might never have figured it out. He was too busy chasing a very stubborn young woman who refused to believe the neat little scenario he arranged for her to find. Must have really ticked him off."

Tessa made no comment. She was busy trying to process all she'd just learned. Allen's plan was brilliant. He never would have been discovered had it not been for Jack. And she never would have uncovered the truth about the lies surrounding her life.

"Martinez was picked up a half hour ago. She's lawyered up and promising to sue everyone. Looks like business will be good for your constituents." He stopped brushing the bits of glass from his hair when he noticed the silence was thickening. He'd missed something. Something that had to do with a letter he'd locked away in his safe at home. Something to do with secrets kept too long and consequences that got too big. He glanced meaningfully at his friend.

"Mrs. D'Angelo, may I take you home?" Russell offered. "You look as though you could use some good strong tea."

"Thank you…Mr. Russell, is it?"

Jack quickly made the introductions.

"I think I'd like to go to the hospital first," Barbara stated. "I'd like to see Stan."

There was silence. Tessa still wouldn't meet her imploring gaze.

"Tessa, we'll talk later?"

"Jack, I'm ready to go," was all she'd say before walking away from her mother's emotional entreaty.

In the noisy Dodge Ram with Jack's motorcycle loaded into the back, they left the city for the woods. Word had already leaked to the press and Jack had to do some fancy driving to avoid flattening several persistent reporters. They lost interest in following him after his first few hairpin turns. By then, Jack had lost interest in them, too. He was covertly studying his passenger.

He'd been so damn proud of her. She hadn't lost her cool. She'd reacted with an instant, gut-level aggressiveness that had probably saved her mother's life. He couldn't have gotten to Allen in time. His heart had stopped when he'd seen her wrestle the gun away from its intended target, becoming one instead. He'd known right then.

Some said life flashed before one's eyes when confronted with death. The future had panned in glorious full color through Jack's mind in that single second. A future with Tessa sharing his days, his nights, his dreams and disappointments. At his side, to watch Rose grow up and, God forbid, to begin to date boys. There to make him laugh with her acid tongue and to think with her intuitive reflections. There to force him to face the turmoil of his past and to look to the promise of the days to come with something closer to optimism than resignation.

When had he fallen so heart over head in love with her? And how was he going to tell her now that her world was falling apart?

"I've decided to make a career change," he mentioned casually, then waited for her to come back at him. She didn't let him down, even though her response was lower key than usual.

"You've decided to become a priest."

His laugh boomed in the truck's cab. "Not hardly. That's where I've been, not where I'm going." When he didn't elaborate, she couldn't stand it, and was coaxed from her own miseries to consider the tease of his statement.

"What, then?"

"There's not much satisfaction in training a bunch of gung-hos to travel to foreign countries to handle causes you'll never even hear about on the news."

"I could have told you that."

"Mmm. I believe you did. Repeatedly. Anyway, I've decided to walk away from that particularly lucrative venture to try something a bit more rewarding. I got the idea from you. And your mom."

Now he had her hooked. Her curiosity had gotten the best of her self-pity and that's exactly what he'd planned. So far, so good.

"I've got the tools and I've got the talent," he allowed with a smug smile.

"To do what? Come on, Chaney. The suspense is killing me."

Good.

"I'm afraid your do-goodership has infected me and since I can't seem to find a cure, I guess I'll just have to find a way to live with it. When I saw you at Jo's that first time, and your beautiful baby blues were so filled with helplessness and fear because your life was out of control, I started to feel something I hadn't felt in a long time. Outrage. No one should ever be that alone and that afraid with nowhere to turn and no one to help."

"So who you gonna call, Jack?" She'd turned toward him on the seat, her expression engrossed, and that had his emotions engaged.

Damn, he loved her. But he was getting ahead of himself.

"Sometimes people need a guardian angel to watch over them, to keep them safe, to keep trouble from finding them and maybe to get involved, just a little, in making things right again. All legally, of course."

She smiled. "Of course. But you're forgetting one thing."

"What's that?"

"You're no angel, Jack. You're a warrior and a lone wolf at that."

He grinned at her wry observation. "Well, even wolves can run in packs. Or lead them. There are a lot of out-of-work and war-weary wolves out there who might welcome the opportunity to undo some of the things they've done in the past, to rectify some of the choices they've made."

"So you're going to lead a pack of warrior wolves to do what, exactly? Protect mankind against the evils of the world?"

"No. That's your job. Nothing quite so grand as that. Just to protect the innocent from becoming victims until your justice has a chance to work in their favor."

"Bodyguards?"

"Personal protection has a better ring to it. A bit more marketable, too, don't you think?"

"Lone Wolf's Warriors, personal protection professionals." She smiled again. "I like it."

He allowed himself a moment to wallow in her appreciation before continuing. "I figure I've got the setup already to train and hone skills and you've got a network of those in need. Together, we can make that difference you're always going on and on about."

Smooth. He was beginning to pride himself on how slickly he'd slid in that togetherness bit when she finally caught on. Her eyes narrowed slightly. Her gaze grew suspicious.

"We?"

He rushed on, thinking to lessen the impact of that one little word. "I figure I can get things started while you're busy setting up your practice. I can interview and Stan and my dad can do some discreet background checks. By the time we have enough wolves in our pack, you'll be in place to send the worthy and wealthy our way."

"Sounds like you've done a lot of figuring. When were you planning to include my input in this scheme?"

"That's what I'm doing now." He turned his best bad-boy-begging-for-forgiveness look her way. She might pretend to be immune but he could see his killer charm seeping in to coax a reluctant consideration through her initial irritation.

"You'd need office help," she suggested. "Someone to run the phones and do the paperwork."

"I've got some ideas."

"Yeah, you're just full of them, aren't you, Chaney?"

She settled back in her seat, her expression growing contemplative. That was good, wasn't it? She hadn't said no. She hadn't exactly turned handsprings, either.

"You can stay at my place, if you like. Rose loves having you there and she and your lazy cat have become annoyingly inseparable. It's not like you have other places you have to be."

That was stupid. Rub it in her face that she had no place to go, no home to return to. But she didn't attack that blundering statement. She appeared to mull it over. And he'd just have to be patient while she did.

Patience was his new middle name.

Like coming home.

That's how it felt to Tessa as she climbed out of the truck. She studied the soaring walls of glass that reflected the two of them approaching. She and Jack, together. In a partnership? In more than that? What exactly did "stay here" entail? Office space or that "more" that she had begun to desire? Had he offered out of pity or was he, in some clumsy, commitment-phobic way, trying to tell her he wanted her here for other reasons? And if he did, would she stay?

It wasn't as if her world was overflowing with options at the moment.

She could never go back to her apartment. That broken glass would haunt her forever.

Return to her family home now that she knew her life had been a lie? Pain echoed dully within her chest. Even more unlikely. Her mother was moving on to make her own future. Whether Tessa wanted to be a part of it, to build on the relationship that had begun between them, would depend on whether forgiveness could overcome a lifetime of necessity-driven deception. As an adult, she could empathize with Barbara D'Angelo's decisions. But as a daughter, she felt bruised by the lack of trust and the missed chances to enjoy a mother's love. That ache was going to take a lot of time and tenderness to heal. Time she had. Was Jack going to provide her with the other?

She didn't even have office space. She was technically unemployed. Tomorrow was Monday and she had no place to be. No place to belong.

Except here.

And she wanted to belong here more than anything else. But Jack had to ask her with a bit more clarity before she could say yes to whatever he might propose. She was too beat up inside to settle for second best or charity. She'd spent a lifetime doing that. Time to demand what she wanted from life then be brave enough to take it.

She wanted Jack Chaney on almost whatever terms she could get him. Almost. But she had just enough pride left to insist on hearing words spoken.

And then she would have to say them back.

If he could, she could.

Rose came out to greet them on the porch. Her round face was wreathed in a smile. "*Hola,* Miss Tessa. I brushed Señor Tinker and fed him his dinner already."

"And he sat still and let you brush him?"

"He was not happy about it at first but when I told him how handsome he was with his fur all shiny and soft, he began to like the idea."

How to handle the difficult male, as taught by an all-too-wise twelve-year-old. Tessa smiled and shook her head. "He must trust you an awful lot. He hid under the bed every time I tried to groom him for the first six months."

For Rose, it was simple logic. "He knows I love him and would never hurt him."

"Cats can sense that," Tessa told her, very aware of how close Jack was standing beside her.

"So can wolves, or so I've heard," he murmured against her ear, leaving her all shivery and hot as he went to scoop Rose up in his arms.

"I saw Mrs. Barbara on the news," Rose chattered away. "She was there with your friend Mr. Russell. He said some bad words and pushed the camera man down."

"Good for him."

"Is Mrs. Barbara coming back here?" She looked to Tessa hopefully and an uncomfortable Tessa didn't know how to answer.

"Not right away," Jack told her. "She's got some things she's got to take care of first." And one of those things had to do with mending a family breach into a fabric of trust. And he meant to do what he could to help that happen. When Tessa was ready. "It's been a long day, little monkey. Have you got a hug for me?"

Her arms whipped tight around his neck for a monumental squeeze. The same squeeze Tessa was feeling around her heart as the girl proclaimed, "I love you, Mr. Jack."

"And I love you, too, Rosebud." He pressed a loud smacking kiss to her temple and set her down. "Now, get your schoolwork all ready for tomorrow because after dinner, we need to sit down together and have that talk I promised you."

"I will," she vowed then bounded away, all high-octane energy.

Jack sighed, his shoulders taking a heavy rise and fall. "It's killing me knowing how much this is going to hurt her."

"You're going to tell her about her mother?"

"I have to."

"It won't be as bad as you think. I promise."

"I'd like to hold you to that. I want to move on, Tess, and I can't do that until I put the past away."

She stepped up beside him and slipped her arm around his

waist. His settled in a comfortable drape around her shoulders. She snuggled in close and said, "I will if you will. I love you, too, Mr. Jack."

She hadn't meant to just say it out loud like that. The words hung like a plume of frosty breath on a winter morning. And just as quickly, they dissolved in the heat of his embrace.

"Yeah? Seems like an awful lot of that going around all of a sudden. What goes around, comes around."

"Which means exactly what?" She had to hear the words.

"You are the most aggravating woman I've ever known."

"Is that supposed to be a compliment?"

"Yes, it is. You won't be ignored, you won't be dismissed, you won't settle for anything except one hundred and ten percent. And you don't hit like a girl."

"Wow, Mr. Chaney, your smooth talking is overwhelming me."

"I'm just getting started."

She could feel his smile against her hair and her emotions started doing a tango.

"Since you came barging into my world, uninvited I might add, you have frustrated me, fought with me, challenged me and never backed down from what you believed in for a minute. I love that in a woman. And dammit, you made me love that about you. You've made me want to protect you, strangle you and bed you since that first day. You're that song that gets stuck in my head and I can't get it out even though it's driving me crazy. You drive me crazy, Tessa. You push me into being the man I need to be and I want to be that man for you."

His cell phone started to ring.

"Hold on to that thought a minute." He moved back and pulled out his phone. "Chaney."

Tessa had to hold on to something. Her knees were wobbling like a baby about to take its first steps. Her hands fluttered as nervelessly as her heartbeats. She took a deep breath, willing the shaking to stop but, at the same time, wanting it never to end.

"Hey, Barbara. Yes, she's here and she's fine. We were just having a discussion about the rest of our lives. That's okay. You're not interrupting. I'd just gotten to the good part but a little suspense will make her appreciate me all the more."

He grinned at Tessa, that killer flash of predatory teeth that in tandem with dark bedroom eyes was a one-two punch she couldn't evade. She went down for the emotional count, her senses reeling. He went back to his conversation to give her time to shake it off. As if she could.

"I heard you were on the news. How'd that go? Good girl. Don't let them push you around. Keep your head up but don't drop your guard, either. Barbara, do you know how to type? Never mind. We'll talk about it later. Right now I'm planning to do the decent thing by your daughter so we can indulge in indecent things for the rest of the evening." Jack winked at Tessa.

"Thank you, ma'am. I appreciate the vote of confidence. I'm a man of my word. I told you I would take care of her and I plan to, for as long as she'll let me. Patience is my middle name. I'll tell her to expect your call. Late tomorrow would probably be better." His expression went suddenly serious and his reply echoed that sincerity. "Thank you, Mrs. D'Angelo. I'll make sure you don't regret it." He flipped the phone shut and paused a moment before meeting her curious gaze.

"What was that about? The 'no regrets' part."

"She was welcoming me to the family. That's a bit premature though. I think you have to do that first to make it official."

His prompting gaze had her at an abrupt loss for words. Then when she started to talk, she knew she was babbling, her words a froth of bubbles after the pop of a champagne cork.

"You won't be getting the Cosby family, you know. We're not all that functional. We've got this nasty scandal to deal with, some mother-daughter issues to resolve, two brothers who will probably want to beat you up."

"Those are just the perks. What about what's really important?" His thumb traced down the side of her cheek and he waited.

She realized then that Jack Chaney was the man she'd wanted Robert D'Angelo to be, a man of honor, of conviction and of limitless acceptance. With Jack, she didn't have to be perfect to be loved. She could fail and falter and never lose his respect because he understood what it meant to make and forgive mistakes, with others and now himself. And he trusted her to do the same. If only her father had learned that lesson sooner. If only he hadn't taken for granted what Jack prized the most. Her value, her worth, her love.

"I think you and Rose and Constanza would make everything complete. You make me complete."

"We're going to be good together." And he kissed her thoroughly as a down payment on that promise. When he leaned back, deviltry danced in his black eyes. "Now that we've got the respectable stuff out of the way, what say we go upstairs and get to the indecent things?"

"Jack, it's not even noon." But it was a weak protest belied by the way her hands molded to his backside.

"That's why I've got locks on the doors and bulletproof glass. To protect what's mine by keeping the world out and you inside."

"That's where I want you, Jack Chaney."

"I love pushy women."

And? Say it, Jack.

"And I love you, Tessa D'Angelo."

Enough said. Now, it was time for action.

"Show me."

"Yes, ma'am. For the rest of my life. You'll find I'm a man of my word."

She was counting on it.

* * * * *

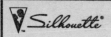
Silhouette®

INTIMATE MOMENTS™

presents a provocative new miniseries by
award-winning author

INGRID WEAVER

PAYBACK

Three rebels were brought back from the brink and
recruited into the shadowy Payback Organization. In
return for this extraordinary second chance, they
must each repay one favor in the future. But if they
renege on their promise, everything that matters
will be ripped away…including love!

Available in March 2005:

The Angel and the Outlaw
(IM #1352)

Hayley Tavistock will do anything to avenge the
murder of her brother—including forming an
uneasy alliance with gruff ex-con Cooper Webb.
With the walls closing in around them, can love
defy the odds?

Watch for Book #2 in June 2005…

Loving the Lone Wolf
(IM #1370)

Available at your favorite retail outlet.

If you enjoyed what you just read,
then we've got an offer you can't resist!

Take 2 bestselling
love stories FREE!

Plus get a FREE surprise gift!

Clip this page and mail it to Silhouette Reader Service™

IN U.S.A.	IN CANADA
3010 Walden Ave.	P.O. Box 609
P.O. Box 1867	Fort Erie, Ontario
Buffalo, N.Y. 14240-1867	L2A 5X3

YES! Please send me 2 free Silhouette Intimate Moments® novels and my free surprise gift. After receiving them, if I don't wish to receive anymore, I can return the shipping statement marked cancel. If I don't cancel, I will receive 6 brand-new novels every month, before they're available in stores! In the U.S.A., bill me at the bargain price of $4.24 plus 25¢ shipping and handling per book and applicable sales tax, if any*. In Canada, bill me at the bargain price of $4.99 plus 25¢ shipping and handling per book and applicable taxes**. That's the complete price and a savings of at least 10% off the cover prices—what a great deal! I understand that accepting the 2 free books and gift places me under no obligation ever to buy any books. I can always return a shipment and cancel at any time. Even if I never buy another book from Silhouette, the 2 free books and gift are mine to keep forever.

245 SDN DZ9A
345 SDN DZ9C

Name	(PLEASE PRINT)	
Address	Apt.#	
City	State/Prov.	Zip/Postal Code

Not valid to current Silhouette Intimate Moments® subscribers.

Want to try two free books from another series?
Call 1-800-873-8635 or visit www.morefreebooks.com.

 * Terms and prices subject to change without notice. Sales tax applicable in N.Y.
** Canadian residents will be charged applicable provincial taxes and GST.
   All orders subject to approval. Offer limited to one per household].
   ® are registered trademarks owned and used by the trademark owner and or its licensee.

INMOM04R   ©2004 Harlequin Enterprises Limited

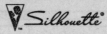

SPECIAL EDITION™

Introducing a brand-new miniseries by
Silhouette Special Edition favorite author
Marie Ferrarella

The Cameo

One special necklace,
three charm-filled romances!

BECAUSE A HUSBAND IS FOREVER

by Marie Ferrarella

Available March 2005
Silhouette Special Edition #1671

Dakota Delany had always wanted a marriage like
the one her parents had, but after she found her
fiancé cheating, she gave up on love. When her
radio talk show came up with the idea of having her
spend two weeks with hunky bodyguard Ian Russell,
she protested—until she discovered she wanted Ian
to continue guarding her body forever!

Available at your favorite retail outlet.

Where love comes alive™

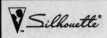

INTIMATE MOMENTS™

Don't miss the eerie
Intimate Moments debut
by

MARGARET CARTER

Embracing Darkness

Linnet Carroll's life was perfectly ordinary
and admittedly rather boring—until
she crossed paths with Max Tremayne.
The seductive and mysterious Max
claimed to be a 500-year-old vampire…
and Linnet believed him. Romance ignited
as they joined together to hunt down
the renegade vampire responsible for
the deaths of Max's brother and Linnet's
niece. But even if they succeeded, would
fate ever give this mismatched couple a
future together?

***Available March 2005
at your favorite retail outlet.***

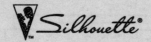